# The Bicycle Book Club

## ROMANTIC WOMEN'S FRIENDSHIP FICTION

### FIVE ISLAND COVE
### BOOK TEN

JESSIE NEWTON

ISBN-13: 978-1-63876-330-7

# Chapter One

Tessa Simmons wished she could smile as the express ferry from Nantucket pulled up to the northwest dock on Diamond Island. She lived on Sanctuary, so she'd still have another boat ride to make before she could return home.

But the express ferry only went to Diamond Island, and Tessa had to work today anyway. She'd grab lunch somewhere—alone—and then walk herself over to the library.

She finally turned her face toward the early summer sunshine, a tickle of a smile touching her lips. She loved the island life far more than living in New Jersey, but she didn't want to stay on Nantucket.

Rather, she couldn't.

The brief life she'd led there had been borne in hope, but quickly marred by mystery and death. Memories of the horrors she'd lived through—waking up from a drugged state, the sound of gunshots, the red-blue of police lights...

She suddenly felt cold despite the warm temperatures and the frilly sunshine.

Just as quickly as she remembered, the images, the sights, the sounds, they all faded. Tessa contained them behind a wall in her mind, the way her therapist had been teaching her.

A sigh filled her lungs and leaked out of her mouth as the ferry docked and people moved toward the steps that would lead them to dry land. As if on auto-pilot, Tessa's legs moved too, and she joined the small swell of people who'd come to Five Island Cove from Nantucket today.

Tessa didn't think many of them were tourists. Most likely, they were like her. They had business on Nantucket, but they'd come home. Or, they had business here, and would return to Nantucket and their homes later that day.

A particular weariness accompanied her as she disembarked and faced the row of shops that lined the street opposite the ferry station. She could get something to eat there, as she had many times before. She adored seafood, and the cove had no shortage of it.

Sometimes, Tessa just wanted a burger, or maybe a salad, but today, she honestly didn't know what she wanted to eat. Her stomach felt hollow, and she knew she had to have a little something before she started her shift at the library.

She only worked a few days a week, but that meant the shifts were longer, and she'd be closing tonight.

Her fingers tightened around the strap of her purse, which she wore across her body, as she thought about getting out her phone and texting someone to ask if they wanted to eat lunch with her.

She hadn't quite integrated herself into the friendships here in the cove the way Maddy had, but everyone still welcomed Tessa with open arms. To anything she could get to, that was.

"You need to get to more," she muttered to herself, bypassing the taco truck and deciding then and there to get a ride downtown. She'd be closer to the library, and she could spend the next couple of hours in the sunshine, sipping tea and enjoying a slow, carefree meal at her favorite bistro here in the cove.

As she backtracked to join the RideShare line, which only had a couple of people waiting, Tessa did text Maddy. *I'm on Diamond for the next few days. Lunch?*

The power blonde she'd met in Nantucket had gotten married about a month ago, and Tessa had been there in her flowing lavender gown, which now hung in her boyfriend's closet in Nantucket.

The closet Abraham Sanders was nowhere near cleaning out, packing up, and moving here. He'd claimed to be passing his deli in Nantucket to his son once fall came, then the New Year, but that had been almost six months ago, and Abe still went into his meat shop every day.

Tessa had been splitting her time between working at the library here in the cove, riding the ferry back to Nantucket, and walking the beaches there while she waited for Abe to finish up working.

She had a house there, but Tessa couldn't stay in it. Her

sister lived in Nantucket too, but Tessa had a love-hate relationship with her. She loved her, because they had the same blood flowing in their veins. But Tessa didn't particularly love spending time with Janey.

As she sank into the back seat of the sedan which had just pulled up to the curb, Tessa said, "The Harbor Bistro, please."

"You got it." The man smiled at her in the rear-view mirror, and Tessa guessed his age to be close to hers. She leaned back and closed her eyes, wondering what to do about Abe.

They'd been dating for almost two years now. Two years, and while she loved him, and he'd said he loved her, actions always spoke louder than words.

He had not moved here, despite claiming to want to be here with her full-time. She'd started going to Nantucket more and more, and he hadn't been to the cove in a couple of months now.

*Maybe it's over*, she thought. At the very least, they were horribly stalled, and one of them would have to say or do something to get things moving again. Tessa wasn't sure if she wanted to be that person or not.

Thoughts of AvaJane Hymas ran through her mind. She didn't know the woman all that well, but what she did know was almost enough. She'd waited and waited for men who never truly wanted her.

Was Tessa doing the same thing?

"Ma'am," the man said, and she jerked her eyes open.

"Sorry," she said a bit groggily. "I think I fell asleep." A hint of embarrassment tugged through her, and Tessa hastened to get her purse and get out of the car.

"Are you okay?" the man asked, and Tessa paused at the question. He twisted and looked at her, concern in his blue eyes.

"Do I not look okay?"

"I don't know," he said. "It's just a...feeling I have. I see a lot of people with the driving." A smile flickered across his face, there for a moment, and then gone.

Tessa wished she knew what her face looked like or what vibe she gave off to alert someone like him that she wasn't okay. "I'm okay," she said as firmly as she could, and she tapped her card to the RideShare pad to pay for her ride. "Thank you."

"Sure thing," he said. "Enjoy your lunch." He re-positioned his ball cap on his head as the pad beeped. Tessa got out of the car and slammed the door, then stood on the sidewalk and watched the car drive away.

Seconds seemed to slow, and she wasn't even sure why. Her phone beeped and buzzed, and she startled back to the present. Back to reality. She looked at her phone and found Maddy had returned her text.

*Lunch sounds amazing! Tomorrow? Should I invite Julia?*

*If you can tear her away from Liam,* Tessa said, smiling to her screen. She lifted her face, feeling better with plans with her friends. That alone gave her enough courage and stamina to face the bistro, knowing she'd be dining alone for today.

"TESSA?"

She turned away from the shelf where she'd just inserted a hardcover book to find her boss, Bonnie, standing there. "Hey, Bonnie."

"Do you have a minute?" She nodded back toward the offices and check-out desk in the small library. Bonnie was at least fifteen years younger than Tessa, and she'd been hired as the new library director only two months ago.

Tessa liked her a lot, because she had good ideas for the small island community library, and she was willing to work to get the programs, the funding, and the concepts in her head out into the public.

"Sure." Tessa took the few books she had in her arms with her as she walked down the aisle between bookshelves behind Bonnie. She'd worked or volunteered in a library for many years, and there was nowhere she'd rather be than around books, books, and more books—except maybe flowers, as Tessa adored gardening too.

Bonnie led her into her office, which was lined with books, and held carts of books, and had stacks of books on her desk. "Close the door, would you?"

Tessa did, and she balanced her few books on her lap as she took the only chair across from Bonnie. The room smelled like oranges, and Tessa wasn't at all surprised to watch a gray cat leap lightly onto the librarian's desk and meow.

"Not now, Dusky," Bonnie said briskly. She'd inherited

the cat with the library, as it lived here. The first librarian who showed up in the morning fed her, and there were no less than three beds for the feline around the library, all of them on top of bookshelves, so the cat could look down condescendingly on all the patrons who dared to look for something to read.

Dusky meowed again, then sat down and looked at Tessa. She smiled at the cat, as she owned two of her own. She'd adopted them from the local shelter here, and her neighbor took care of them while she went to Nantucket.

"All right." Bonnie sighed like an older woman and folded her arms in front of her. She looked past the cat and all the books and beamed at Tessa. "We need an assistant library director to help run all the programs starting up this summer."

Tessa's heart began to pound. An assistant library director was a full-time position. She wouldn't be reshelving books from the return cart, and she'd be expected to work every day.

"I want to offer it to you," Bonnie said, her smile growing. "I think you're perfect for it, because we have programs I want to get off the ground for men and women your age. It's not just summer reading for kids and teens anymore."

"I know." The words scratched on the way out of Tessa's mouth. She attended all staff meetings, and she'd heard and seen all of Bonnie's ideas. She'd voted on some of them, and she liked how the director didn't take offense when her ideas got shot down.

She simply moved onto the next one, or she went back to

the drawing board to refine the idea before she brought it up again.

"The book club," Tessa said, her voice only slightly stronger.

"For young moms, moms of teens, and those beyond."

Tessa smiled, because she knew she was in the "those beyond" category, and no one wanted to label people her age as *old*. Bonnie had never used the word, and she gently corrected anyone who said anything like, "older generation."

The truth was, Tessa *was* part of the older generation who didn't think of the library when it came to their hobbies or how to spend their afternoons. Tessa worked here, so it was completely different for her.

"It's a full-time position," Bonnie said, plucking a yellow file folder from somewhere on the other side of the stack of books. "Monday through Friday, with some Saturday work. I want you to work on all of our adult programming, including the book clubs, because you're perfect for it. Everyone here respects you, and—"

She stopped when Tessa held up her hand. "You don't have to flatter me." She smiled at Bonnie. "I'm honored that you thought of me."

Bonnie's eyebrows went up, and she casually pushed her strawberry blonde hair over her shoulder. "But?"

Tessa paused, because she didn't know what came behind that word. If she lived here full-time, she could go to lunch with her friends any time she wanted. She could become better friends with Robin, Alice, and Eloise. Heck, she might even learn the whole story behind AJ, Kelli, Jean, and Clara's lives.

She wanted relationships with those women, but she'd been choosing Abe over and over...when he hadn't been choosing her.

Her throat narrowed, the walls of it nearly sticking together as she weighed her options in mere nanoseconds. The human mind was so amazing, and Tessa blinked, the answer to this job offer right in front of her.

"I'd be honored," she said, her own smile finally reaching way down deep inside her and touching a hidden spot of happiness.

Bonnie squealed and clapped her hands together. "Perfect. I still want you to take this." She got to her feet and rounded the desk. "It goes over your salary and your benefits. Ask me or the city lawyer any questions. I had to work hard to get this position."

She grinned and ran the last few steps to Tessa. "I'm so happy you said yes."

Tessa hugged Bonnie back, a bit awkwardly because she still sat and Bonnie stood. She even managed to laugh a little. She stood and took the yellow folder from her boss, looking at it with eyes that felt like they could see for the first time.

"Thank you," she said again.

"If you accept everything," Bonnie said. "You could start as early as June first."

"June first," Tessa echoed. "That's next week."

"Yes," Bonnie said. "And I'd love to sit down with you as soon as possible to talk about a focus group for your age group, to find out what would get them to utilize the library more."

"My age," Tessa said, her mind starting to work again. "I know just the women."

Bonnie hadn't stopped grinning, but her smile sure seemed to somehow get brighter and bigger. "I knew you would."

Tessa looked up from the folder, so much to suddenly do before then.

And the top item on her list: Talk to Abe and find out if he was ever going to leave Nantucket...or if things between them should just be done.

# Chapter Two

R obin Grover took the box Arthur handed her and turned. Mandie stood there, still talking, and Robin waited for her daughter.

"I need more than just a few hours in the soda shop," Mandie said. "Have you heard of any other part-time jobs?" She'd been home from college for about a month now, and the job hunt had not been going well. "Or do you have anything for me to do?"

Mandie took her box from Arthur and joined Robin on the sidewalk. Clara and Scott had found a house they could afford to buy, and they'd moved on it quickly. Thus, they were moving again today. Thankfully, they'd already made the big move from Vermont to the cove last year, and Clara had really pared down the things they owned.

"I'm sure I could have you do a few things," Robin mused, though she didn't want to employ her daughter.

Mandie thrived when on her own, and Robin liked being home alone in her office.

Of course, school would be out for the summer in a couple of weeks, and then her youngest daughter would be home too. Jamie was fifteen this year, and Robin thought a job would be beneficial for her too.

"I can help you look," Robin said.

"Look for what?" Alice asked as she passed them going the opposite way. Her face held a flush from the exertion of carrying boxes up and down steps, as Scott and Clara's new house had ten of them just going up to the porch.

Robin could admit she'd been trying to take boxes and items that would then go on the main level, so she didn't have to climb another flight of stairs to the second floor. Right now, her box had been labeled *kitchen*, and a few items clanged around in there to suggest as much.

"A job," Mandie said. "Charlie got so lucky at Cutter's."

Robin only caught the whiff of Alice's smile as they passed. Her twins had split themselves in half for the first time in their lives, with Charlie returning to the cove to work for an outdoor adventure company for the summer, and Ginny staying in New York City.

She was living with her father, something that Robin knew troubled Alice greatly. They'd talked about it a couple of times, but Robin always let her best friend bring it up.

She suspected that Charlie's decision to come back to the cove had a lot to do with her daughter, though Mandie had not indicated that they were any more serious in their relationship now than they'd been during the school year.

"I've got to find something soon," Mandie said, her breathing turning to panting as they ascended the steps. "I hate looking for a job."

"You need a job?" Tessa Simmons asked from the top of the steps.

Robin took the last two and paused on the porch, mostly to hear what Tessa had to say but also to catch her breath. Moving really was the worst activity on the planet— maybe right behind looking for a job.

"I'm working at Soda Spectacular," Mandie said, moving further onto the porch and out of the way of others entering and leaving the house. "But it's only about twenty hours per week—and that's with the extra shifts I pick up."

Tessa had the luxury of standing in the shade without a heavy, bulky box in her arms, and she smiled prettily. "I wanted to ask you about doing a focus group at the library, Robin," she said. "Maybe you should come too, Mandie. I have a few things I need to work out, but I'm anticipating needing to hire more people."

"Full-time?" Mandie asked.

Matt came out onto the porch too, and Robin slid her box into his arms, relief filling her tired limbs. The first pod had gone quickly, but she felt like the things in this second packing pod would never end.

"No," Tessa said, shaking her head. "It would be part-time."

"That's perfect," Robin said. "You don't need full-time."

"Two part-time jobs is what I want." Mandie wore such

hope in her eyes. "I'll only be here through the end of summer."

"This is for our Summer Reading programs," Tessa said, her face brightening with every word. Her dark eyes sparkled, and Robin had seen a look like this before. Maybe not on Tessa's face, as she was still very new to their friend group.

Robin watched her for a moment, sensing something. "You have news," she said slowly.

"Yes," Tessa said. "I was going to wait until the pods were empty, because Maddy said she had an announcement to make then too."

Robin looked down the steps to the stream of people still coming into the house with boxes and then going back for more. Mandie passed her box to Shad as Kelli joined them, her baby in her arms.

Robin smiled at her and Daphne, wanting to reach for the infant. She didn't, because she'd come to work, and Kelli shouldn't be lugging heavy items up and down steps.

Maddy and Julia came outside, chatting back and forth, but they quieted as they joined the group. "What's happening over here?"

"Nothing," Robin said quickly, exchanging a glance with Tessa.

"I just have some news too," Tessa said, her voice much quieter than Robin's. "I thought, when the doughnuts come, and the moving-in is finished, I'd tell everyone." She nodded at Maddy. "Like you will."

"Am I missing something?" Alice asked as she reached

the porch, two plastic bins stacked on top of one another in her arms.

"No," Robin said, taking Mandie by the elbow. "We'll wait until announcements." She steered her daughter toward the steps. "Go on. There's more to bring in."

Mandie glared at her, but Robin was used to that look on her face. She complied and went back to the pod, where Arthur handed them each another box to carry in. Robin went back and forth three more times before she ran out of things to carry.

Reuben, Shad, and Aaron wrestled with an enormous dresser, finally getting it to submit and enter the house. They still had tons of work to do to get unpacked enough to live in the house—get beds set up, put dishes in cupboards, and fill the fridge with something to eat—but Robin stood in the shade and accepted the water bottle Eloise handed to her.

"Doughnuts are here," Clara called from the street, and that caused a commotion. She carried a long, wide white box that probably had fifty doughnuts in it, and Aaron's girls cheered as she neared.

"Let's go inside," she said. "The AC works, and we can get the doors closed and see if we can't cool off."

"Let me take that," Matt said, relieving Clara of the pastry box.

One more trip up the steps, and then Robin entered the house and let someone else close the door behind them. Scott and Clara had bought an older home in the southern corner of Diamond Island. It was two levels, with a bedroom and a bathroom on each one.

The kitchen sat straight back through a living room that held a side-den off to the right. Robin would use it for an office, as she ran her wedding planning business from home, but she had no idea what Clara and Scott would do with it.

Boxes had been piled there. And in the living room. And in the kitchen.

Still, Matt found enough space for the doughnuts, and the kids weren't the only ones to descend on the box and get a treat. They'd all come to help with the move this morning, and Robin smiled at Jamie as she came to her side.

"Were you helping out in here?"

"We got Lena's bed set up," she said as she gathered her hair off her neck and held it in a ponytail. She let it drop, her smile finally appearing.

Others had started to chat as they ate, but Robin really wanted to know what the news was. She'd kissed her husband good-bye for the summer fishing season in Alaska only two days ago, and she wanted a weekend at home to normalize herself back to being a single mom—at least for a few months until Duke returned.

"All right," Eloise said, which sent a bolt of surprise through Robin. El wasn't usually the one to quiet everyone and start spilling secrets. Today, however, she beamed at Aaron and the girls and lifted one hand until the conversations waned.

"We want to invite everyone to a beach bonfire at our place," El said. "Next Sunday."

"Tomorrow?" AJ asked from somewhere in the recesses

of the room. A small dining room added to the kitchen, with another pass-through to a sunroom at the back of the house.

"No," El said. "Next Sunday."

"Tomorrow *is* the next Sunday," AJ said.

"Then the next one," El said, and she turned to look at Robin, her expression conveying all of her annoyance. Robin wanted to burst out laughing, but she thankfully controlled herself.

Alice twittered a little and then said, "We'll be there. Well, maybe not Charlie. I'll check with him." He worked full-time doing canoeing and kayaking tours around Diamond Island, and that included weekends.

"We are having a tasting menu at The Glass Dolphin," Maddy said next. "It's a private event, and we're asking those who come to provide feedback for a possible new menu item."

"I want to come," Robin said immediately. Her mouth watered right now over the food at The Glass Dolphin, and lately, it had become *the* place they met for lunch.

"Me too," Julia said, as did a few others.

Maddy beamed at them. "I knew you would. I'll text out the time and date, and you can let me know if it works for you."

"That kind of goes with my news," Tessa said, and all eyes shifted to her, Robin's included. The room seemed to grow even quieter simply to match the demeanor of the person speaking.

Tessa reminded Robin of a mix between Kelli and Eloise. She had dark hair and eyes, and she thought before she spoke. But she also possessed a fierce strength swimming just below the surface.

"I took a promotion at work," she said. "You're looking at the new assistant library director."

"Oh, that's wonderful," Kristen said, her delight genuine as it slid across her face.

"I'm going to be in charge of the adult programming," Tessa said as Julia reached over and squeezed her hand. "I want to do a focus group in the next week or so, and then I'll be able to put a few things together, and...get started."

"What does 'adult programming' mean?" Alice asked. She glanced around the group like it might be something nefarious. "Like...?"

"Programs for adults," Tessa said.

"Duh," Clara added, and the two of them laughed lightly together. They'd also worked on a dilapidated inn together for a few months last year, and their smiles made Robin happy.

"Our new library director wants more adult programming," Clara said. "For those in their twenties, thirties, and beyond."

"Like...knitting classes?" Kelli asked.

"Sure," Tessa said. "I was thinking of crafting as something we could do. We already have the Cove Crocheters use our multi-purpose room on Thursdays. It's kind of that idea, but it's more like an eight-week program that focuses on something. It starts and stops. Then we have something else come up."

"So like, similar to the rec center," El said.

"Yeah," Tessa said. "But specific to books. To reading. To reading more books." She smiled, and her eyes landed on Robin. "I have some ideas I'd love to run by specific groups of people. So Bonnie—she's the director—and I have been setting up focus groups to come into the library next week and provide some feedback."

"I'd love to do that too," Robin said, knowing that sometimes people wanted someone else to speak up before they would. Not everyone wanted to be first, or out in the spotlight.

"I'd love that too," AJ said as she came forward. "I'd especially love to see something for moms."

"We have programming for children," Tessa said. "That's what you'd bring Asher to." She glanced over to Robin and Jamie, and then El and her girls. "And lots of stuff for teens."

"But that's a day for *Asher*," AJ said. "I'm talking something for moms—like how to choose books for your kids, or what kinds of books to read to them."

Tessa focused on her again. "I'd love it if you came to the focus group for that." She pulled out her phone. "Bonnie is running the one for parents of teens and children. I think that would be the best one for you."

AJ said nothing, but her jaw jumped a little.

"You can come to any of the adult ones too." Tessa flashed her a smile. "I'm running three next week. One for men and women in their twenties."

"I'm out," Aaron said, and a few people chuckled or laughed.

21

"Thirty to forty-five," Tessa said next. "And then anyone older than that."

As Robin looked around the room, the only people who wouldn't be in the "anyone older than that" category would be Laurel and Paul. Maybe Jean, though Reuben had definitely turned forty-five already.

Tessa looked at Mandie. "And I'd love it if you'd come to the single young adult one. Bonnie and I are running it together."

"If I can, I will," Mandie said.

"What are you thinking?" Robin asked, still watching Tessa. The woman had secrets, and she kept them *close.*

"I'm in charge of all the book clubs," Tessa said. "And I'd love to see our younger population working with our older one."

"You know what we need?" El asked. "A small library branch on all the islands."

Tessa swung her attention to her. "That's one of our ideas." She swallowed as she took in the tall, dark, Chief of Police next to Eloise—her husband. "It might require some additional funding and permits, though, so Bonnie hasn't done much with it...yet."

"Programs for dads might be good," Paul said, to which Aaron nodded.

Tessa started thumbing into her phone, her face turning more and more crimson by the moment.

"Research skills," Alice said. "You would not believe what people can't do."

Robin's stomach growled, and she decided that was the

perfect impetus to get Tessa out of this situation she'd somehow fallen into. "All right," she said as she stepped in front of the poor woman. "She's having focus group meetings, you guys. This isn't the time to fire all of your suggestions at her."

She gave Alice a pointed look, but her friend only smiled. She surveyed the small area where they'd all crammed. "Okay, let's get this house livable."

"Be sure to RSVP to our beach bonfire," El called. "You can just do it on the group text, with how many to expect."

"We can all bring something," Jean said, but El shook her head.

"This one is on us. Our start-to-the-summer beach day." She looked so pleased about it, and Robin would gladly show up with her favorite drinks, sunscreen, and a chair to sit in and let someone else do all the work. She had no problem with that.

"Let me know about the tasting," Maddy said. "Group text is fine too."

"And I'll text out the dates for the focus groups," Tessa said, her eyes still glued to her phone.

"Perfect," Robin said. "Now, Clara. Scott." She looked at both of them." Boss us around and put us to work."

# Chapter Three

AvaJane Hymas groaned as she lifted her almost two-year-old son out of his car seat. "Come on, baby," she said to him as she set him on his feet and tried to steady him. "You walk with Momma."

He gripped her finger with his chubby hand and toddled along, babbling about something only he understood. He could say a few words—like Mama and Dad and a few other simple words—but otherwise, Asher spoke his own language.

They moved into the library at the speed of a sloth, and AJ took the moments to enjoy the island breeze on her neck, the way the trees had started to leaf up nicely here in the center of Diamond Island. The post office, courthouse, and City Hall sat along this block, and the town of Five Island Cove kept the grass immaculate, the sidewalks swept clean, and this area of town gloriously beautiful.

All five islands that made up Five Island Cove had gotten

a sprucing up in anticipation of tourist season, but AJ and Asher had come to the library today as locals. Tessa had invited her for a study group, and AJ felt like she'd been misunderstood when they'd been moving Clara and Reuben into their new house over the weekend.

She didn't want more library programming for Asher. The children's programs were already robust, and they ran year-round. She'd been bringing him to story time and arts and crafts mornings for a few months now. She also didn't want a Mommy book club, where women who didn't have jobs other than raising their children gathered to read the latest bestsellers or books about parenting.

She wanted a real, adult program for someone about to lose their mind *because* they didn't have a job other than caring for their kids. She wanted self-help books on remaining a real person, or balancing a work-from-home-job and a toddler, or a class about real-world Mom-things, like putting fruit in a glass Mason jar immediately upon getting it home from the grocery store. Then, it didn't rot in less than forty-eight hours, and she could enjoy a few raspberries here and there with her cereal instead of binge-eating them the very day she brought them home.

Or a photography class, or how to pack lunches that everyone loved on beach day. She wanted practical skills that she felt like she lacked, and she wanted to meet other moms in the cove while coming to the library to learn such things.

Inside the library, AJ started looking for the sign that would take her to the study group. She should've known she wouldn't need it, because she'd only looked left before she saw Laurel poke her head out of a room down the hall in that direction.

She grinned and gestured for AJ to come her way. Laurel was at least a decade younger than AJ and a lot of the other women in their friend group, but she seemed to have a soul of the same maturity. She wasn't the loudest voice in the room, and she had a good mind that thought about things in a way others didn't. She'd been an excellent cop because of that, and she raised her son with a calm, steadiness that AJ envied.

"Look at him walking." Laurel came toward them, and Asher squealed. AJ smiled as she tucked her hair behind her ear and Laurel arrived in front of them. She scooped the little boy into her arms and said, "Look at you walking, buddy. You're so good at it."

He toddled, which was why he was a toddler, but he smiled and laughed as Laurel showered him with kisses along his cheek and neck. They both giggled, and then Laurel looked at AJ. "There's not very many people here," she said. "Tessa will be so happy to see you."

AJ swallowed, not wanting to cause a problem. "Okay, let's do this." They started toward the room Laurel had come out of.

"Do you think Eloise is really okay with moving her beach bonfire to our regular beach day?" Laurel asked.

AJ hadn't meant to antagonize El over the date, and she cut a look over to Laurel. "I think so, yeah. She said Aaron had to work unexpectedly."

"Yeah," Laurel said. "That happens a lot. I just know El wants to be important too, and things like beach day..."

"Fall to Robin and Alice," AJ said when Laurel wouldn't say it. She took a breath and focused on the library hallway in front of them. "You're still okay to go to lunch after this?"

"Yep," Laurel said. "Paul has James today, and they're going to see his sister." She flashed a smile at AJ and added, "I love your tank top. You always have the cutest stuff."

AJ looked down at her feather-covered tank. "Thanks. Matt's daughter actually gave this to me for Christmas. I wasn't sure about it at first." She pinched the silk away from her body. "I mean, it's a little...pheasant-y, you know?"

"It goes with your hair," Laurel said. "And if anyone can wear pheasant feathers, it's you." She grinned as AJ opened the door, and then she slipped in, Asher perfectly happy in her arms.

Inside, AJ found four other women, and she knew none of them. Her anxiety and insecurities rose up the way the tide did every day. Twice a day. AJ swallowed and put a smile on her face, reminding herself that she'd come here voluntarily. This wasn't a firing squad. She wanted to be part of this community.

"This is Marta," Laurel said as she sat down in front of an open notebook. "And this is Asher." She waved his hands, as he'd wrapped his fingers around hers. She smiled over to AJ as she pulled out the chair next to hers. "And AJ."

"Hello," AJ said, wishing she did more interviews than she did. She hadn't traveled for work for a while, and everything she did happened over chats, phone calls, or video conferencing. She didn't interview high-profile athletes anymore either, and AJ only picked up public interest pieces in the sports world now. Things like a retired baseball pitcher donating his time to a Special Olympics team, or what a popular basketball player's new fish tank looked like.

She didn't need to work, as her husband managed the only golf course in the cove. They'd expanded to two locations and facilities now, and with tourist season upon them, AJ would need to rely heavily on her friends to stay sane. Matt worked a *lot* in the summer, and AJ couldn't complain. She and Asher sometimes stopped by the course to take him lunch, and she filled her mornings with walking—sometimes with Kristen, Jean, and Laurel, and sometimes alone—reading and working with Asher on his development, and getting lunch out.

Her afternoons turned hazy, as Asher napped, and AJ often felt a bit bedraggled herself. She often felt like she should be able to do more than she could, and the guilt of that could cripple a person and make it even harder to get out of bed each morning.

Tessa came rushing into the room, a few manila folders in her arms. "Hello, everyone." She smoothed her hands down the front of her jacket, and AJ wondered how she wore that. The true summer heat hadn't arrived in Five Island Cove yet, but it wasn't exactly cool either.

She sighed as she looked up and ran her hands through her hair. Her smile followed, but she was clearly rushed and nervous and unsure. "Welcome," she said in a strong yet quiet voice. "I'm so glad you could all come today." She surveyed the six of them and then seemed to remember she'd brought folders with her.

She hurried to flip the top one open. "I'm required to have you sign in as a participant of this study group. We'll be doing some online surveys as well, and then we'll have the data we need." She started passing out papers, and that helped to loosen her up. "So just fill this out quickly. It's just for demographics."

AJ took a pen out of the can and started to fill out the paper. Tessa kept talking, and again, she outlined all the things AJ didn't want as a mother of a toddler. So, before the meeting could get too much further, she raised her hand.

She'd muscled her way to the front of plenty of mobs before. She'd entered the opposite gender's locker rooms and done interviews with athletes as they showered and dressed. She'd met confidential sources in sketchy locations. She could ask a few questions in a small town library study group.

"Tessa?" she asked.

"Yes, go ahead, AJ." Tessa kept rifling through her folder.

AJ took a breath and flicked a glance over to Laurel. "I'm just wondering if you're going to consider anything like, uh, this is a group for moms, right? Like, things that moms need help with. Time for themselves. Skills classes for raising kids of all ages, that kind of thing."

Tessa blinked at her. "Skills classes?"

"Yes." AJ held her head high. "You do skills classes for kids. The teen program has a 'prepare for a first date' class. I think moms would love a class on preparing healthy lunches for their kids or a time management class for working moms, or a co-parenting class that couples could take together."

To Tessa's credit, she furiously scribbled down what AJ had said. "I'm not sure these are within the scope of the library," she said. "Perhaps the community center?" She raised her eyebrows at AJ, and AJ simply nodded.

She wasn't going to get what she wanted here, and she suddenly wanted to leave. But she did like Tessa, and she didn't want to add to her stress. Asher played happily on the floor nearby, and AJ fought the urge to get out her phone and scroll through her email or social media.

She stayed for the duration of the meeting, which didn't last longer than the forty-five minutes Tessa had promised, and she even hugged the other woman on the way out the door. Her frustration accompanied her, and after she buckled Asher in the car and started it so the air conditioning would start to blow, she turned back to Laurel.

"I think I'm just going to head to Bell," she said. "See my sister and get my dad. He's coming to dinner tonight anyway, and I don't know." She sighed as she looked up into the blue sky. She hated feeling lost like this, but she didn't know how to ground herself very well. That was something she still needed to work on, and she'd been making slow, baby steps in being able to find her own inner peace, her own inner self, who and what made AvaJane into AvaJane.

"Hey." Laurel moved in front of her and grabbed onto her shoulders. "You can do all of that after lunch. Put Asher down for a nap at Amy's." Laurel's eyebrows went up. "Okay?"

"I feel like not coming back to the library," she said. "I like Tessa and all that, but it seems like she's not even on the same planet as me." So much of AJ's life felt like scrambling, and when she remembered how old she was, only shame filled her.

Shouldn't she have her life more put together than she did? She should know about lunches, and fruits, and what to do when she got frustrated. But she didn't, and she hated that her natural and first instinct was to run the way her mother had.

So standing in front of Laurel, AJ made a conscious choice. "Let's go to lunch," she said.

"Yes," Laurel said. "Because Jean is already at the restaurant, and your BFF is almost off the ferry."

AJ smiled thinking of Kelli coming to Diamond Island with her new baby, a little girl named Daphne. She'd been a complete surprise, but everyone loved her. Kelli had come alive since returning to the cove a few years ago, and AJ could admit that she had too. At the very least, her life wasn't anything like what it had been before she'd faced the demons in her past and come back to these five islands, the most eastern spot of land in the United States.

"Let's go, then," AJ said, turning back to her car. "Do you want to come with me, and I'll bring you back here?"

"Yes," Laurel said. "Because the parking down on the boardwalk is going to be murder."

"And summer hasn't even really started yet." AJ smiled over the top of her SUV to Laurel, and then they both ducked into the car.

"I think Tessa's trying hard," Laurel said. "She probably feels like she's drowning."

"Probably," AJ said. "And she has an idea for what to do already, and it's okay that she's not interested in deviating from that." Those words sounded mature to her, and they rang true to AJ. She took a deep breath, feeling the enormity of the oxygen in the air as it entered her lungs.

Breathing could do so much to help, and AJ appreciated something so simple could do so much. Here in her car, she felt safe, and she breathed again a little lighter so Laurel wouldn't notice.

She was safe at lunch with her friends. She'd be safe with her sister, and back at her own home tonight, where she'd order dinner and have Matt pick it up on his way home. Being safe was incredibly important to AJ, and she managed to get herself back into her safety zone before she even got to the restaurant.

"Let's see if heaven will shine down on us for a spot," Laurel said as she leaned forward. After a couple of times back and forth in front of their chosen lunch spot, heaven's beam had not manifested itself, and they had not found a place to park.

"Let's just park in the overflow lot," she said. "I have Asher's stroller." She made the turn and went down a block to the overflow lot. It too held a lot of cars, but AJ found a spot, and she and Laurel set about getting everything it required to take a two-year-old to lunch in a beachfront restaurant.

AJ loved The Blue Lobster, but by the time she stepped

inside the door, she was semi-ready to be done dealing with people that day. But Jean rose from the bench, her smile bright. She stood a good foot shorter than AJ, so she couldn't hide her mother-in-law, who held baby Heidi on her lap.

"Hey." Jean moved into AJ and hugged her. "The parking is terrible, right?"

"Just awful," AJ said, but she didn't want to talk about it. She wanted the growth on Five Island Cove, and their friend group had been splintered, along with the rest of the town, over whether the City Council should fund the growth in the cove—which included roads, walkways, recreation, housing, and yes, parking—or slow it intentionally.

Because she and Matt depended on tourist season to pay their bills all year long, they'd voted to accelerate and fund the growth. So she didn't want to talk about the parking situation along the boardwalk here, on one of Diamond Island's busiest beaches.

"Kristen," she said smoothly. "I didn't know you were coming." She didn't mind, but it just meant more talking, and AJ wanted to sit back and let the others speak around her.

*Then do that*, she told herself, and she did have to go against her natural inclination to stand out in a crowd. She'd once been a star athlete here in Five Island Cove, and she'd gone to college in the spotlight. She'd never shied away from that, but perhaps in her advancing age, she now realized she didn't have to step into the spotlight, even when it came shining her way.

Behind her, Kelli walked in, and AJ's smile appeared in a genuine way for the first time that day. "Kel." She hugged her best friend for life, wrapping her and her two-month-old baby in a quick embrace. "Can I have her?"

"Yes, you can," she said. "She's teething already, and she's a slobbery beast." She relinquished the darling, redheaded girl to AJ, who couldn't stop herself from leaning in to kiss her. Sure enough, her lips got wetter than they should've, but AJ only laughed as she wiped the baby slobber from her face.

Daphne screeched, and AJ couldn't decide if it was a happy sound or an upset sound. Then, it didn't matter, as the hostess said, "We're ready for you," and the five of them and their three little children started through the restaurant to a table.

Everyone settled down, and AJ had just figured out how to hold the wiggly Daphne and look at her menu at the same time when someone said, "Well, look who's out to lunch together."

Her pulse leapt straight up into her brain, because she knew that voice well. She looked up and into Alice's face, and standing right next to her was Maddy, and then Robin.

AJ's mind whirred, because the three of them were obviously out to lunch together and hadn't invited anyone else, but it sure felt like those of them sitting at the table had been caught doing something they shouldn't.

# Chapter Four

A lice Rice wasn't sure why her pulse had leapt over itself when she'd seen the group of women in front of her. Since she ran a law office out of an office at her house, she couldn't always make it to every social event in the cove.

She knew some of the women walked together in the morning. She knew AJ and Kelli had a closer relationship than she had with either one of them. One glance over to Robin reminded her that she and Robin were extremely close. Out of all of them, Alice would tell Robin things she wouldn't even consider bringing up some of the others.

And yet, something pinched in her gut and she wished she'd known they were coming to lunch today.

"We had that focus group this morning," Tessa said, and Alice switched her gaze to the brunette across the table. She glanced over to Kristen and then Kelli. "Would you guys like to sit down? Have you eaten?" She stood up and started to flag down a waiter.

"We were just picking up," Robin said, and Alice pressed her eyes closed. "We were going to have a working lunch at..." She trailed off finally, and Alice opened her eyes, and everything seemed too bright.

"My daughter is about to get engaged," Maddy said. "So I wanted to talk to Robin about planning something." She looked at Robin and Alice. "And Alice happened to be there when I called Robin."

"Things happen," AJ said. "Tessa, I think they're going."

A waitress arrived and surveyed the group. "You guys need more seats?"

"No," Alice, Robin, and AJ said together, and another woman approached them.

"Your order is ready."

"Thank you," Robin said crisply, and she took the large bag of food they'd ordered twenty minutes ago. "Beach day this weekend." She smiled around at everyone, and how she did that in such an awkward situation, Alice couldn't even fathom. "El said she'd text out the details, okay?"

"Sounds good," Laurel said. "The weather is supposed to be amazing this weekend."

Now that they were talking about the weather, Alice turned toward the exit. "You girls enjoy your lunch." Thankfully, Maddy and then Robin started to walk, and Alice smiled and waved until she had to face forward to walk without tripping.

Outside, she drew in a long breath and pressed one hand to her heartbeat. "How awkward."

"Why does it annoy me they're together?" Robin asked. "It makes no sense."

"Because we got together and didn't tell them." Alice reached into her purse and pulled out her sunglasses.

"But ours felt like business." Robin shot her a look that said there wouldn't be anything to change her mind, and Alice shouldn't try.

"We're just in different phases of our lives," Maddy said easily. She was new to the cove and their friend group, but that didn't mean she was wrong. "They have little children. We don't. Can you even imagine?" She pealed out a round of laughter into the sky. "I envy some women some things, but having a baby when I'm almost fifty is not one of them."

Alice could smile at that. "I agree," she said. "They are somewhere different than us."

"They're still our friends," Robin said. "We've known AJ and Kelli our whole lives."

"Of course they're still our friends," Alice said. "Them going to lunch without us doesn't change that."

"Maybe it'll make the times when we do all get together that much better," Maddy said, looking past Robin to Alice. "I mean, I don't know. I'm new here, but I know Tessa doesn't have a mean bone in her body, and she isn't trying to cause a problem."

"She doesn't have little children either," Robin said.

"She was running the focus group." Alice shook her head, done with this conversation. "Let's leave it. It's not that big of a deal." Her car sat up ahead, and she fished through her purse to find her keys. "Let's just get back to Robin's and eat and talk about Chelsea's wedding."

Maddy pulled out her phone and checked it. "No text about her engagement yet." She sighed as she repocketed her device. "She's sure Rob's going to propose soon."

"Why does she think that?" Robin asked.

"They bought a diamond a couple of weeks ago," Maddy said. "Like, together. He bought it right in front of her."

"Sounds like a proposal is coming then," Alice said, her thoughts quickly shooting to her son. To her knowledge, Charlie had not been ring shopping with his girlfriend, Mandie. They'd both gone to the city for college, and they'd both come back to the cove to work this summer. The only peace of mind Alice truly had about their relationship was the fact that Robin monitored it more closely than she did, because Mandie was her oldest daughter.

Alice's nerves still twittered at her, because relationships only ended in one of two ways: happily-ever-after or utter heartbreak. There wasn't much in-between that she knew of, and Mandie and Charlie were far too young to get married.

Not only that, but she really wanted her kids to have more and different experiences than the ones they'd had here in the cove for the past few years. She wanted them to spread their wings and fly, fall down, crash to the ground, and get up again. She wanted Charlie to date different women, from different places. She wanted the same for her daughter, Ginny, who at least had ended things with her high school flame.

She hadn't come home for the summer, and that only tripled Alice's worry. She lived in a downtown apartment with her father, and she'd started a job in Central Park a couple of weeks ago. She seemed happy every time Alice spoke to her, which happened almost every day. She hadn't started dating anyone else, and she never said anything bad about Frank.

So maybe she really was okay. Alice would never stop worrying about her, though, and as she unlocked the car, she told herself it was okay to fret over her children. She only had the twins, and she'd worked hard every day of their lives to protect them, help them, support them, and love them.

"What's Arthur up to today?" Robin asked once they'd all transitioned to the car. Alice pressed the ignition button and glanced over to her friend in the passenger seat.

"Uh, he went running this morning," Alice said. "I'm not sure what he was going to do after that. Maybe something in the garage." Her husband worked as a school counselor, but classes had ended a week ago. "He's got it in his head to go through all the closets this summer too, and hey, I'm not going to argue with him on that one."

She grinned in the rearview mirror and backed out of the parking spot they'd managed to find. Someone honked, and she jammed on the brake, looking for the danger. "Is that... car in front of me honking?"

Behind her, more honking sounded, and Alice's gaze flew back to the rearview mirror.

"And the one behind you," Robin said.

"They want your parking space," Maddy said.

The woman in front of her laid on her horn and gestured for Alice to move, and the noise only caused the car behind her to honk back. Her pulse hammered through her veins, and Alice suddenly knew what a deer in the headlights must feel like. She couldn't move, and her mind overflowed with thoughts, none of which stuck or computed.

"My word," Robin yelled above the honk-fest. "Go, Alice. Let them fight it out."

Alice realized she'd stopped halfway out of the spot, her car curved and blocking both lanes of traffic along the board-walk. Coming to her senses, she continued backing out and into her lane, which blocked the car behind her.

Before she could flip the car into drive, the woman in front of her swung into the now-empty parking spot. That seemed to enrage the driver behind her, and Alice pressed on the gas pedal to get away from the situation before she got rammed.

Her adrenaline flowed through her body like hot lava, first from seeing and confronting part of her friend group, and then from all that honking. She gripped the wheel with both hands, and no one spoke.

Finally, several blocks away, she came to a red light and stopped. She breathed, so grateful for the calming effect of air in her lungs. "What about Duke?" she asked Robin. "How's he settling in up in Alaska?"

"He loves it there," she said miserably. "The only thing keeping us here at this point is Jamie."

Her almost sixteen-year-old daughter.

"She's got two years of high school left." Alice looked

over to Robin, who'd turned to stare out the passenger window.

"Yeah," she said. "I honestly think Duke might push for us to move to Alaska full-time after that." She finally swung her attention to Alice. "And then what will I do?"

"Plan weddings in Alaska," Alice said without missing a beat. Robin wore a terribly unhappy expression, but Alice didn't know how to help her with this. She'd been married to a very rigid man in the past, and she knew marriage and relationships required a great deal of sacrifice. She also knew Robin loved Duke with her whole heart, and Duke worshipped the ground Robin walked on. So if Robin didn't want to move, they wouldn't move. Period. The end.

But she wanted Duke to be happy...

"It's a couple of years away," Alice said quietly. "Maybe try not to worry about it until you have to."

"Have you met me?" Robin muttered as she went back to staring out the side window.

Alice grinned, because yes, she'd met Robin, and no, she wouldn't stop worrying about things. All things, this included. She loved having a plan, and she didn't like it when those plans didn't turn out the way she'd, well, planned.

"All right," Alice said. "Another hard topic, and then we can enjoy lunch and talk weddings."

"I know what it is," Robin said. "And no, she hasn't said anything about Charlie."

"They're still together."

"I'm aware."

Alice wanted more information. "Surely she tells you something. Charlie's a boy. A vault. He says nothing."

Robin sighed mightily, like talking about their dating mini-adults sapped the very life out of her. Maybe it did. "I asked her point-blank if they'd been sleeping together when she first got home."

Alice waited, her pulse doing weird cartwheels through the veins in her neck. "And?" she snapped when Robin didn't finish the story.

"You won't like this answer."

"I won't?"

"She said, 'not yet'."

Alice exhaled, all the oxygen that had been so good for her previously now gone. "You're right," she choked out. "I don't like that answer." She repositioned her grip on the steering wheel. "I'll talk to Charlie about it."

"Honestly," Robin said. "I'm getting tired of thinking about them. She's chosen him; he's chosen her. They really seem to like each other. They get along. What exactly don't we like about this?"

"He's nineteen," Alice said, pure disbelief running through her. "You're not worried about them anymore?" She blinked and wished she wasn't driving so she could look right at Robin for longer than two seconds. "I can't lose my ally in this. Come on."

A shriek from the backseat interrupted their conversation, and Alice's heart once again leapt to the back of her throat. Her first instinct was to stop the car, look for the danger she'd obviously missed. She did, not quite jamming her foot on the brake this time.

She checked her mirrors. Nothing.

In front of her. Nothing.

Behind her. Nothing.

"What?" she griped at Maddy, who'd done the shrieking.

She held up her phone, her face positively beaming with joy. "He proposed! She's sending pictures right now."

"That's great," Robin said with a smile, turning to look at Maddy in the back. "Tell her congratulations from us." She met Alice's eyes as she faced the front again.

Alice glared at her. "Are you telling me that'll be your reaction if my son proposes to your daughter?"

Robin stared right back. "They're doing this," she said evenly. "I would like to support my daughter, not drive her further from me."

Another car came up behind them, and Alice got moving again, Robin's words swirling through her mind. Perhaps she was on to something here, and Alice suddenly couldn't wait for Charlie to get home so she could take him into her arms and let him know that she loved him and would support him in anything he chose—even if that meant he and Mandie got married at a young age.

# Chapter Five

Tessa bustled from task to task, finally taking her lunch at her desk she'd been given in the shared office space on the lower level of the library. The turkey and cheese she'd packed for herself that morning tasted so good, and she pushed her shoes off to give her feet some relief from all the back and forth she'd been doing.

They hosted events down here on the lower level of the library, but it didn't get used as much as the upper two levels. There were no bookcases down here, for one, and their children's rooms got used far more than these basement spaces.

Tessa planned to change all of that, and she pulled the map she'd drawn for the big room where she planned to start holding some of her adult classes. "If only you knew what those were actually going to be," she muttered to herself.

Then she put another bite of sandwich in her mouth, determined not to talk to herself more than necessary. It was an old habit, and one she didn't normally mind about herself. But two other desks sat in the room, and their owners could show up at any time. Tessa didn't want to be caught mid-sentence, because she was already new here, and plenty of people kept giving her side-eyed looks, like maybe she wouldn't be able to do what she'd been tasked with.

Truth be told, Tessa wasn't sure she could. She'd not been given much time, and she sighed as she finished her sandwich and sat back from the map she'd spent evenings developing.

She needed a beach day, but it wasn't until tomorrow. Tessa wasn't sure she'd go for long, but she wanted to bask in the golden heat of summer and laugh with her friends, maybe hold a baby or two. She liked doing that, because she could give them back to their mothers when they started to fuss.

She didn't need to know how to soothe them, or what to do to keep them happy. She simply kissed them and passed them back to those who did.

"Tessa?"

She turned at the sound of her name and found Mandie Grover standing there. "Hey, Mandie," she said, pushing her chair back and planting her palms against the desk to get up. Her feet protested, but Tessa ignored them. "You found the dungeon."

Sweeping her trash off the desk and into the tiny can beside it, she then turned to face Mandie fully. "You look cute."

Mandie looked down at her light blue dress. It fell to her

knees and had full sleeves that went to her elbow. As she neared, Tessa saw the pattern of tiny white sailboats, and while she never would've worn those shoes—a pure white pair of Converse—Mandie looked amazing.

"You said to dress nicely. That people would see us." She glanced around as if they'd have an audience now.

"Yes," Tessa said with a smile. "Maybe not today, but yes." She cleared her throat and twisted back to get her rudimentary map. "Okay, we're going to start by cleaning out some parts of this big room behind me. Did you come down the main staircase?"

She stepped back into her shoes, moved past Mandie, and out of the long room filled with desks.

"Yes," Mandie said.

"Then you crossed through it." Tessa glanced over her shoulder. "It hasn't been used for much in the past couple of years, but we're going to change that." She entered the room and stopped only a few steps inside.

Small toys and child-sized chairs took up the corner immediately to her left, with a big open space in front of her and to the right. A long table stood there, but Tessa wasn't sure why or what it was used for.

One of those retractable dividers had been pulled open to reveal another space as large as the one where they stood, and it looked like the stuff of old seventies homes and buildings. Tessa hated it on sight, but she couldn't rip it out of the walls and ceiling and replace it with something more modern.

Just like she couldn't rip out the beige carpet with flecks

of darker brown and make it something more inviting. She couldn't put together bookcases and fill them with adult favorites. She couldn't fix this library and the reading community—or lack thereof—in Five Island Cove in a single summer.

In fact, she'd only been at this job full-time for a week, and her official hire date wasn't until Tuesday.

"So." She pushed her frenzied thoughts out of her mind. "I've gotten approval to clean the whole thing out."

"Even back there where they have the used book sale?" Mandie nodded to the far dark corner, where several tables did hold piles of books.

"Is that what that is?" Tessa had seen that area, obviously, as she'd measured this entire space as she planned where she could have reading nooks, open book club discussions, and more.

"Yeah," Mandie said. "My mom used to bring us when we were younger and make us pick five books to buy and read every summer."

Tessa looked at her, learning a bit more about Robin with that information. "What did you pick out?"

Mandie grinned and shook her head. "The thinnest things we could, and I don't think I ever read one all the way through."

Tessa smiled too. "Your mom let you get away with that?"

"Oh, she'd forget about her reading requirements about halfway through June." Mandie waved her hand in a casual way that Tessa felt sure she wouldn't be doing if Robin stood there with them.

They laughed together, and Tessa liked how it calmed her thoughts and narrowed her focus. "Okay," she said. "Let's start over there in the used book area."

She crossed the room, flipping on a light just past the pulled-back curtain that could separate the space into two rooms. Part of her felt like she was marching to a death sentence, and another part of her vibrated with excitement to be doing something to make a difference. No, it might not happen in a single summer, but Tessa wanted to be part of this community for a while to come.

They arrived in front of an old armoire, and Tessa reached to open the double doors. "What ideas do you have for this summer?"

"I—what do you mean?" Mandie asked as she stepped to Tessa's side.

"If you were in my place," Tessa said, staring at the mess of papers and books on the bottom of the armoire. "What program would you put in place this summer?"

"I have no idea," Mandie said. "Five Island Cove is this weird beast of a place. I couldn't go over to one of my best friend's houses after school until I was thirteen, because that was my parents' rule for when I could ride the ferry by myself."

She gave a light laugh, but Tessa had never thought about such things before. "It wasn't like I could just ride my bike over there, you know?"

"I can see that." Tessa reached for a pile of papers and

pulled them all together into a neat stack. A spiral notebook came with them, and Tessa turned to make a stack on the table behind her. As her eyes glanced over the stuff, she thought she saw a recipe for meatloaf.

"So most of my friends lived on Diamond Island," Mandie said. "Every island sort of has its own community. I mean, every city has neighborhoods—you know like the different sections of New York City or Boston or London."

"Sure." Tessa turned back and accepted a couple of volumes from Mandie, then twisted back to the table. She had no idea why these books had been discarded in the bottom of the armoire instead of set out on the table to be sold for a dollar. They didn't look any different than the books in the used book sale.

"But the cove is different. You can't just cross a street and be in the Theater District, you know? The ferry system is vital for us. If it goes down, you suddenly have five separate communities that need to be able to sustain themselves."

"Sure."

"We saw that when we had a tsunami a few years ago," Mandie said. "Since then, every island has built a grocery store. We have small stations with emergency services on every island now, and we didn't before."

"Really?"

"Really." Mandie handed her another stack of stuff. "That's all of it."

Tessa set the last pile of dirty pages and dusty volumes on the table. The scent of old paper that might have been wet at some point met her nose, and she turned away from the pages. This whole corner of the library needed to be burned to the ground, in her opinion. She kept that to herself for now, though, because she didn't need to gripe to a woman half her age.

As she faced the armoire again, she asked, "Does the library have branches on all the islands?"

"No," Mandie said slowly.

Tessa turned toward her, a spark of excitement igniting inside her. "No?"

"You know what you should do? Put little libraries— you know what a little library is, right?—on every island." Her eyes shone with that same excitement flowing through Tessa too. "Then there would be books on every island."

"I can't believe people on the outer islands have to come here to get books."

"It would take a lot more people to have a mini-branch on every island," Mandie said.

"No," Tessa said. "We don't even need people to check us out at the grocery store anymore. You're telling me people can't scan a book?"

"Who would check it back in?"

"The person who checked it out," Tessa said easily. "All we'd need is a scanner or a check-out kiosk like what we've got upstairs. We have the system with barcodes and library cards already." Not the scanners, and Tessa could admit she didn't know how much four scanners or check-out kiosks would cost. "They could even be housed in the buildings where the cops and other emergency services are." She glanced over to Mandie. "Do they have physical buildings?"

"I believe so, yes."

Tessa knelt down to open the bottom drawer of the armoire, but she didn't find anything inside. Thankfully. It smelled musty, and despite the bright fluorescent light, Tessa felt like she was looking into a black hole.

She physically recoiled from the depths of the drawer, and she moved to push it back in when she caught sight of a corner of a piece of paper. "There's something in there," she said.

"Are we throwing this away?" Mandie asked. "It's a great piece of furniture."

"I'd like to keep it," Tessa said. "It is a great piece, and we can build a homey atmosphere around it." She reached for the papers, way back in the far left corner. "Can you see those?"

Mandie got down on the ground too, and the papers were on her side of the armoire. "Yeah," she said, straining. "I've got them." She pulled, and the tell-tale sound of ripping paper met Tessa's ears. "Oops." Her hand came back, and she only held a few half-sheets of paper. "There's more back there."

"I'll try," Tessa said, and she leaned into her palm inside the drawer as she reached for the larger flaps of paper now showing. She'd just pinched them when the bottom of the drawer collapsed away.

She grunted in surprise, and then a shot of pain moved through her palm. She yanked it back to find she'd been scraped by the broken wood, and disappointment filled her at the sight of the broken drawer. "I think I got a splinter."

"Whoa, look at that," Mandie said.

Tessa's attention returned to the drawer as Mandie removed half of the now-broken false bottom of the drawer.

"This—there's stuff hidden in here." She set the bottom of the drawer aside and looked at Tessa with wide, almost afraid eyes.

Tessa stared at her for a beat, and then looked in the drawer, almost afraid of what she'd find. "My mother had a diary," she whispered, not really sure where the words had come from.

"These look like recipes," Mandie said in a reverent voice.

Tessa remembered the one for meatloaf she'd pulled out from above, but she had no idea why someone would be hiding recipes in an old piece of furniture meant to store clothing. "Maybe they have a family name on them."

She reached back into the drawer, but paused. "Maybe I should be wearing gloves."

"Why?" Mandie asked.

"Old documents," Tessa said. "I don't know." She picked up a small portion of the papers in the bottom of the drawer and brought them closer to her. The paper had yellowed, but it didn't turn to dust at Tessa's touch.

The handwriting was in loopy, slanted cursive, in an ink that was a deep, dark black.

"Lobster bisque," she read from the top of the paper. She scanned the ingredients, and there at the bottom of the page, she found a circle with words in the same shape along the edge of it.

"Tessa," someone said, and she startled toward her boss. Bonnie walked toward her in her pencil skirt and professional heels. "Mandie found you, good." She smiled at the pair of them. "How's it going?"

"Great." Tessa wanted to hide the recipes behind her back for some reason. "We just got started." She handed Mandie the pages and got to her feet as Bonnie arrived. "Do you know where this armoire came from?"

Bonnie surveyed it for a few moments, then shook her head. "No." She looked back to Tessa. "We used to take donations from anyone," she said. "Most items were logged, so we could look back through the donation records to find out. Why?"

"No reason," Tessa said. "Other than it's so beautiful, and I want to know if it's an antique."

Bonnie smiled. "I can see you're going to build a reading area around it."

Tessa grinned back. "I told you that yesterday."

Bonnie laughed and said, "Oh, right." She didn't seem uncomfortable or like she cared about the contents of this armoire. "Well, come see me later, and I'll get you the donation logs."

"Great," Tessa said. "Thanks, Bonnie."

"Good to have you on, Mandie."

"Yes, thank you, ma'am."

Tessa waited while Bonnie left the room, and then she dropped to the floor again. "Can you see what's in that circle at the bottom?"

Mandie didn't answer, but her eyes had stuck on the

THE BICYCLE BOOK CLUB

papers in her hand. She started to nod, and Tessa's old eyes just wanted her to tell her what it said. "And?"

Mandie looked up, and a mixture of shock and fear lived in her expression. "It says 'From the Kitchen of Anna Elmer.'"

That name meant nothing to Tessa, and she gently took the pages from Mandie. "Who's that?" she asked.

"I'm not a hundred percent sure." Mandie swallowed. "But I think it's my great-great grandmother."

# Chapter Six

E loise Sherman pulled up to the stoplight just as Billie gasped. She'd had her head bent over her phone since they'd left for today's beach day, and Eloise first checked in the backseat to make sure Grace was okay.

"What?" she asked her sixteen-year-old step-daughter.

Billie scoffed and looked up. "Claire is doing the black-sand beach party on the same night as Addie's birthday party."

Eloise couldn't remember her teenage life being quite so dramatic, but she reminded herself she didn't have technology practically hardwired to her bloodstream. If something happened on Rocky Ridge, Eloise wouldn't know about it until the next day at school, if at all.

She hadn't had to see the perfect meals her friends ate, or who they spent time with after school, or any of it. She was glad of that, but it made navigating today's teenage problems difficult and confusing for Eloise.

"What are you going to do?" she asked.

"I'm not taking a ferry to Rocky Ridge, I can tell you that." Billie gave Eloise a cross look. "But Claire's really popular, and she'll invite everyone, and that means Addie's party won't be what she wants it to be." She sighed and ran her hand through her hair. "I need to think of something to make it amazing for her."

"You're really popular too," Grace said.

Eloise allowed a small smile to touch her face. The light turned green, and El went through it while Billie talked about how Addie's invites had already gone out, and Claire should be embarrassed she was trying to take the date as her own.

They arrived at the beach, and it was still early enough in the day that Eloise didn't have too much trouble finding a place to park. "Everyone has to carry their own chair and towel," she said before either of the girls could get out. "I have the big beach bag. Grace." She met the younger girl's eyes in the mirror. "You've got your backpack?"

"Got it," Grace said as she opened the door. She bellowed as she got out, ever the most enthusiastic person in the family. She made Eloise's heart take flight and soar above the sea the way birds do as they ride the wind, and she got out as Grace yelled, "I—love—beach—day!"

"Grace, knock it off," Billie griped as she came around the front of the car. "If you want Coby to ask you to the summer dance, you're not going to do it by screaming into the sky."

Eloise kept her mouth shut as she walked past Grace, her

eyes stuck on the younger girl. She was thirteen now though, and by the bright redness spreading through her cheeks, she clearly liked boys.

Apparently one named Coby.

Eloise opened the back of the SUV. "When is the summer dance?" she asked as casually as she could. She pulled the giant canvas bag she'd filled with sunscreen, extra cover-ups, snacks, their lunches—which she'd put in Robin's cooler as soon as she found where Robin had set up.

Not that it would be hard. Robin had a trio of bright red umbrellas she put up to mark their spot, and pilots could probably see her from the sky as they flew over.

Neither girl answered her, and instead, Grace started whispering furiously at Billie as they started across the sidewalk to the sand. Eloise trailed along like a lost puppy who wasn't sure she should be following the two blondes in front of her.

"Red umbrellas to your right," Eloise called to the girls, and she couldn't wait until Aaron arrived with their dog, Prince. He'd only gone into the station today to catch up on paperwork, and he'd promised he'd be at the beach before lunchtime.

"Hey, girls," Robin said, and she came out from behind the far left umbrella. "Wow, Grace, that swimming suit is so stinking cute."

"Thank you, Robin," Grace said, and that made Eloise smile too. Grace had grown up into a polite young lady, and most of that had to do with her father.

Robin's gaze moved past the girls to Eloise, and she

smiled and waved. Eloise grinned and crossed the last few yards of sand. "You have a new swimming suit."

In her brand new, bright teal, single-shoulder strap suit, Robin put one hand on her hip and cocked it out. "Isn't it great?"

Eloise wished she had the confidence of her friend. Maybe if she ran on the beach every morning the way Robin did, she'd have a better beach body. Then she nearly laughed out loud at herself.

Eloise was nearing fifty, and she ran a very busy business. She had a hot husband and two teenage girls to take care of, and she had never enjoyed wearing a swimming suit. The fact that she came to beach days in her perfectly normal swimming suit—all black, with a skirt—was more than she'd have done a decade ago.

Around the umbrella, she dropped her bag on the sand and started setting up her chair next to Robin. Only Kristen had already arrived, and she was currently talking to Jamie and Mandie about something.

"Hey," a man said, and Eloise turned toward Charlie. He wasn't a man, but his voice certainly held a bass timbre, and he seemed far more mature than last time Eloise had seen him. "My mother is on a rampage."

He dropped the cooler in his hands and turned to duck back around the umbrella. "Don't tell her I said that," Charlie called over his shoulder, and Eloise looked at Robin. She looked back. Then they both started to laugh.

"Wonder what Alice is on a rampage about," Eloise said through her giggles.

"I'm sure we'll find out." Robin moved to pick up the cooler Charlie had deposited, and Eloise pulled the sandwiches and fruit out of her bag and put them in Robin's cooler. She'd made a fortress of them, and as she set Alice's down, she said, "I think AJ is bringing one too."

"So we'll have four," Eloise said. "I think that's plenty." Probably two more than necessary. She didn't say anything, and as more people started to arrive, Eloise was able to relieve Jean of baby Heidi, and she did what she did best: she found a seat out of the way and let the crowd and noise swell around her.

She hugged the baby close and greeted everyone, enjoying the sunshine, the smiles, and the way she fit here, with all of these people, even if her life wasn't the same shape as any of theirs.

Alice wore enormous sunglasses, and she'd barely said two words to anyone but Arthur, and Eloise still wasn't sure what she was upset about.

"Can I sit here?" Tessa asked as she arrived with her bag slung over her forearm and a beach chair gripped in her hand.

"Absolutely," Eloise said with a smile. "How did your meetings go this week?"

Tessa sighed as she sank into her chair. "Good enough," she said. "But it's been a long week." She pushed her hair off her forehead and looked out to the waves. "Have you ever felt like your mind has too many thoughts? I'm not even sure which way to turn. It's like I can't' think. Like, it's just this constant deluge of ideas."

Eloise smiled at her. "I can relate to this completely," she said. "Cliffside consumed me for a long time." She let out a long sigh. "Sometimes it still does, but I've been putting up sandbags to keep the deluge back, and they work. Mostly."

Tessa nodded and stretched her legs out in front of her. "I just don't even know what to do."

"Tell me some of the ideas," Eloise said.

"I said she could put a little library at the lighthouse," Jean said as she pulled her chair up. "Tons of people walk or ride their bikes by."

"That was an idea," Tessa said, and Eloise could tell she didn't like it. "But the little libraries don't need to be on Diamond Island. The main library is here. That idea was more for the other islands, so they'd have access to books."

Jean smiled and handed Heidi a slice of apple. "Yeah, I get that now."

"And anyway, Bonnie says they don't have funding for little libraries on the other islands. Not for scanners or personnel or kiosks." She let out a breath. "Did you know those kiosks are seven thousand dollars?" Tessa shook her head. "Unbelievable."

Eloise's mind overflowed with thoughts now. "I know Aaron's got micro-stations on all the islands," she said. "Maybe the little libraries could be there."

"I thought of that," Tessa said. "It's still a lot of logistics to get books in and out. Little libraries are like, not the same as a library system. We don't want people to take the books forever. It's a check-out, check-in system."

AJ spread her blanket half in the shade and half in the

sun and set Asher on the shady part. "So how are you thinking of getting books on every island?"

Tessa shook her head. "I don't know. But Mandie and I got that bottom floor cleaned up pretty good yesterday. I'm meeting with Bonnie on Monday, and we're going to put together our adult programming." Her phone chimed, and she pulled it out from under her leg to check it.

"You know what I was thinking?" Mandie asked as she wandered closer. She'd been bent over the cooler, getting out a can of soda pop. She snapped it open, the *crack-fizz* so classic of cola.

Eloise found herself in the middle of a group suddenly, and she definitely felt others watching them. Alice and Robin from where they sat on the other side of the cooler bank. Kristen and Maddy from further down.

Laurel and Paul had also just arrived, and as Paul ran off toward the waves with James on his shoulders, Laurel turned back to the ladies under the umbrellas.

In that moment, as Mandie drank her cola, and the conversation had paused, Eloise realized there were two groups sitting under the umbrellas. And Laurel came over to hers, where she sat with Jean, AJ, Tessa, and Mandie.

"Hey, guys," Kelli said. "Parker, the bigger kids are over there." She nodded to where Billie, Grace, and Charlie were, and her son went that way without hesitation.

"I want her," AJ said, reaching for Kelli's baby. Daphne was like a bag of flour, and she got passed from woman to woman easily. She did gurgle a bit, and Eloise pushed against the blip of jealousy when it came.

Thankfully, it left quickly, and she looked over to Mandie. "What were you thinking about the library?"

"Oh, right." Mandie shook her head slightly. "Tessa wants to get more books out to the other islands, so they don't have to come to Diamond to participate in library events." She looked around at everyone, and Eloise realized then that she hadn't seen Julia or Clara yet. Perhaps Lena, Clara's daughter, had to work this morning.

"Right," Tessa said. "That's the goal."

"But the kiosks are too expensive," Mandie mused. "And the cops don't want to play librarian in the outlying stations." She smiled around at everyone. "You know what this town needs? A book club."

Eloise's gaze shot over to Tessa, who frowned. "We have a library-sponsored book club already."

"Right," Mandie said. "Here on Diamond Island. But what about for those on Rocky Ridge? Sanctuary? Bell? Pearl?"

"We could host a book club at the yoga studio," Kelli said. "Something like that, you mean?"

"No," Mandie said. "With so many people doing things from home now—like meetings and even classes. Did you know I have the option of doing online classes or in-person now? Video technology is amazing. We can choose a book and have a real book club, and people on the outer islands wouldn't have to come in."

"So they'd read eBooks?" Tessa asked. "We wouldn't have enough books for everyone."

"They could buy their own," she said. "Or yes, they

could do eBooks. Or the library could sponsor a certain number of them, and they could be delivered."

"Mailing books is expensive," Tessa said.

"So then, you'd just need a delivery person," Mandie said, grinning. "And you know what I saw a whole bunch of just down the boardwalk?" She got up and marched past all of them to the edge of the umbrella. With dramatic flair, she pushed the flaps hanging down out of the way and said, "Electric bikes."

Everyone in the vicinity, even Robin, Alice, Maddy, and Kristen, hung on those two words. Finally, Eloise said, "Like a..."

"Bicycle book club," Mandie said. "And you don't have to be in shape to get around the islands, because it's an electric bike. We could put a basket on it, and someone could deliver the books. Deliver questions to people who sign up. And then, they could have the option of coming in to the library for book club night, but they could just as easily dial in and participate via video."

Another round of silence waved through the group. It was Shad, Kelli's husband, who said, "I bet the city could find the library a few good E-bikes." All eyes flew to him. "Bonnie would just need to fill out the request form. We bought hundreds of them this year. What's two or three for city business?"

He looked at Kelli, who beamed at him.

"A bicycle book club," Tessa mused. "It has a nice ring to it."

"Hey, everyone," Julia trilled out as she came around the

umbrella. She'd brought her boyfriend, Liam Coldwater, with her, and he had his son with him. Eloise immediately looked over to where Billie lay on her back, baking in the sun.

She didn't so much as move a muscle, because she obviously didn't know Ian had arrived. Eloise wondered if she'd known he'd be here today. The young man looked over to the teens and said, "Dad, can I?"

"Yep, go ahead," Liam said easily.

"What did I interrupt?" Julia asked.

"Doughnuts!" Lena yelled as she arrived down by Kristen and Maddy. "Look, Grandma, we got so many doughnuts!" She carried three boxes of them, and Clara and Scott arrived with more.

Immediately, the teens were up, including Billie, and headed for the pastries. Eloise once again faded into the background, her eyes on Billie and Ian as they talked and laughed and ate fried dough. And then to her great surprise, a couple of boys approached the teen area.

"That's Sawyer," Robin said, and Eloise looked over to her. "He's Jamie's...I don't know what. She likes him. He came to the beach with us last year, remember?"

"Sure," Eloise said, though she saw a lot of people and couldn't remember one teenage boy from a beach day a year ago. "Who's that with him?"

The other boy couldn't be that much older than Grace, and he was definitely younger than Billie. Eloise didn't know everyone in Five Island Cove the way Robin and Aaron did, so she wasn't surprised when Robin said, "That's the Hatch boy. Alice, what's his name?"

But it was Frank who said, "Eli. That's Eli Hatch." He looked over to Eloise, but she only saw him out of her peripheral vision, because Eli Hatch had started flirting with Grace hard enough for Eloise to see it from where she sat, a good twenty yards away.

"He's a good kid."

"Is he now?" Eloise murmured, and Mandie got to her feet.

"I'll go see what I can find out." She went to join the others more her age, and she squealed as Charlie grabbed onto her and pulled her onto the blanket with him. They laughed and laughed, and normally, Eloise would've liked to have seen Robin's reaction to that. Alice's too.

But she couldn't look away from Grace and how brightly she glowed with a little male attention.

"Hey, baby," Aaron said, and Eloise dang near dropped Heidi she was so startled.

"Hey," she said, wanting to jump to her feet and block Aaron's view of the beach. "You're still in your uniform."

"Yeah, I'm gonna go change right now." He leaned down and kissed her quickly. "Then, do you want to float?"

"Sure," she said. Out on the water, she could tell him about Grace's crushes, and he wouldn't be able to jump right down the girl's throat. Of course, Aaron had learned a lot with Billie, and he'd always been fair, if not a bit barky, when he asked questions.

"Where are the girls?"

"Over there," she said with a pounding heart. Aaron looked over to the teens, and perhaps he was going blind, because he said, "Great. Be right back." He then left to go change out of his police uniform, and Eloise finally released her breath.

"Ah, beach day," Laurel said with a huge smile on her face. "Gotta love it."

Robin started to chortle, and then Alice joined in. Laurel giggled too, and Eloise found herself joining them. Before she knew it, everyone under the umbrellas had started to laugh, even baby Heidi, and whatever divide or tension that had accompanied them to the beach today completely disappeared.

# Chapter Seven

**M**andie Grover put a bite of cold cereal in her mouth as her mother came in through the back door, huffing and puffing. She twisted to look over her shoulder, and she raised her spoon in a breakfasty hello.

"Hey, sweetheart." Her mom looked like she'd dipped her face in hot water, as it held patches of red from forehead to chin. That was why Mandie didn't understand running. But her mom seemed to love it, and Mandie appreciated how her mom worked out her problems while she ran instead of working them out on her.

"Good run?" she asked after she swallowed. "I have a shift at the soda shack in a bit, and then I'm going to go look at the E-bikes with Tessa."

Her mom finished splashing cold water on her face at the sink and turned to face Mandie. She spooned in another bite of cereal, and her mom said, "I don't think you should," as she reached for a hand towel.

Mandie gaped at her. When she could, she asked, "You don't think I should help the library?"

Her mom shook her head and rehung the towel over the handle of the oven. "No, I don't. It's not your job to get Tessa's programs off the ground."

"I do work at the library," Mandie said. "Specifically as her assistant, so...I think that's exactly what my job is." She picked up her bowl, which held only milk now, and moved over to the sink. Her mom edged out of the way, and while Mandie liked this house—it was far bigger and nicer than the one where she'd grown up on the east side of Diamond Island—it still didn't feel like home to her.

She still had to open at least three drawers before she found the utensils or tools she needed, and she wasn't used to having a disposal at all. Now, she poured her milk and the last few bites of her cereal down the drain and flipped the switch to make it all go away.

Sometimes Mandie wished she had a disposal for her thoughts. Something to chew them up and grind them to dust so they wouldn't bother her anymore. So she wouldn't have to take a sleeping pill once a week just to rest for longer than two hours. She hadn't told either of her parents about that. In fact, the only person who knew was Charlie, and he'd worn enough concern in the lines between his eyes for Mandie to know not to tell anyone else.

She suffered from insomnia, and she always had. A single sleeping pill at a well-timed place where she could sleep as late as she wanted to wasn't a problem.

Dealing with everyone's expectations definitely was.

THE BICYCLE BOOK CLUB

Shouldering the way her mother looked at her, trying to see inside her head, added a lot of weight to Mandie's mental load. Still, she loved her mother; she respected her; but she didn't always agree with her.

"Was Grandma an Elmer?" Mandie asked as she rinsed out her bowl and opened the dishwasher.

"My mother?" her mom asked, her tone of surprise echoing off the walls in the kitchen.

"Yes." Mandie faced her. "Before she got married. Remember when we were looking through that photo album, oh, I don't know. Ages ago. There were all those typed stories, and I swear I saw the name Elmer."

Her mom was one of the smartest women Mandie knew, so she expected the slightly narrowed eyes, and the question of, "Why?"

Mandie didn't want to cause an alarm, and if she did, it wouldn't just stay within this house. Mom would text all of her friends, and the entire cove would be alight with the gossip before Mandie punched in at Soda Spectacular.

But she didn't want to lie. Mom dealt with a lot while Dad was gone in the summers, and she'd already spent most of yesterday bawling out Jamie for how she'd ignored everyone at beach day once Sawyer and his friend Eli had shown up.

Mandie had eyes, and she'd seen it. She didn't share a bedroom with Jamie anymore, so they hadn't talked much about it before Mom's lecturing had begun. But last night, afterward, Jamie had come into Mandie's room and slid into bed with her, and they'd talked then.

*Have you and Charlie been...you know,* Jamie had asked.

And Mandie could say with complete honesty that she and Charlie had not been intimate. *Yet,* her mind tacked onto the end of that thought, the way it had been for a few months now. It was just one of the things in the long line of ideas and thoughts racing through Mandie all the time. Just one of the things keeping her awake at night.

Charlie Kelton.

He was the most handsome boy Mandie had ever met, even after a year of college at NYU. She'd been with him all of that year, and no, she'd never been asked out by anyone else. That only proved to her that she would've endured the year alone, and for some reason, that felt too scary and too big for her to hold, think about, or carry.

He wanted to take their relationship to the next level, but they both had mothers with the eyes of an eagle and noses like bloodhounds. The very moment Mandie saw her mother after being with Charlie, Mom would know. Mandie just knew it.

So she didn't want to do it this summer. Even Charlie had agreed when she'd told him why. He'd said, *We should've stayed in the city like Ginny.*

But city living was expensive, and Mandie had missed the small-town island life here at Five Island Cove. Charlie wouldn't admit it, but she suspected he did too. The city— and college—had taken a big bite out of him, and she wasn't sure he'd quite recovered yet.

"Mandie," Mom barked.

She blinked and backed into the countertop behind her. "Sorry, I was just thinking about something."

"I asked why you wanted to know about Grandma Elmer."

Now she had her answer, but she still didn't want to hide anything from her mother. She sighed a great sigh and said, "You can't make this a big deal."

"Yeah, sure." Mom threw her a hooded look before she turned to make a pot of coffee. "I love it when you girls start conversations that way. Makes me really think it's not going to be a big deal." She pulled out the used filter from yesterday and tossed it in the trashcan.

Mandie moved out of the kitchen lest she get sprayed with gross coffee grounds next. "Tessa and I were cleaning out the big multi-purpose room in the basement at the library on Friday, and I found some papers with her name on them. That's all."

"That's all?" Her mom turned toward her, the task of setting coffee to brew completely forgotten. "What papers?"

"They were recipes," Mandie said. "It was harmless. We tossed them all in a box and put them in the storage room. But I saw the little stamp at the bottom, and the name tickled my memory. I meant to ask you about it when I got home, but you were on the phone with Dad." She did her best to act like this was no big deal—and how could it be? Recipes? They weren't dangerous.

Mom ducked her head and went back to making coffee. "I wonder how her recipes would end up in the library."

"Maybe Grandma donated some books or something, and they were stuck in there."

"Maybe." Her mom stayed quiet, and Mandie was sure that didn't mean anything good. She knew; too many thoughts could suffocate a person.

"I was just wondering," Mandie said with a half-shrug. "Do you want me to try to get them when I go today?"

"No, it's fine," Mom said. "We have the recipe binder, and I'm sure anything worth having is in there." She looked up and met Mandie's eyes, hers crinkling with a smile now. "Remember how I had to promise Grandma a kidney just to get that binder?" She shook her head and laughed, and Mandie smiled too. "For how hard she held onto them, I'm sure they're all there."

She slid the empty pot under the drip and said, "I'm going to go shower."

"I'll be leaving in five minutes," Mandie said.

"Okay, baby." Mom hugged her and held on tight. "I really don't want you getting involved in anything this summer." She pulled back and looked at Mandie with earnestness and worry. Her mom was a master worrier. Held a black belt in it. Gold medals. Wore a crown.

"This is supposed to be the best time of your life. A cute boyfriend. Good job. Hot beach days. You don't need to get involved in small-town politics and library programs."

"Okay," Mandie said, her voice pitching up. "I did— looking through old stuff is really fun for me, Mom. I loved going through the drawers and books and boxes in the library."

"Did you?"

"Yeah." Mandie smiled as she thought back to the single day she'd worked at the library. "I think I'm going to look at majors that involve history. Something. It's all fascinating to me. Old papers. Books. The secrets of the past." She beamed at her mother. "So I like the library job, and if that means I have to go look at some E-bikes for a possible book club, that's fine. I'm not getting involved in local politics."

"Okay." Her mom spoke in that same higher-pitched voice that meant she didn't really believe Mandie. But she did turn to go shower, and Mandie opened the fridge to pack herself a lunch. After all, she was trying to save money this summer, so she couldn't stop for lunch between jobs every day, the way she had on Friday.

She didn't have a car here in the cove either, and her mom needed the minivan during the day, so Mandie tossed her sandwich, an apple, and a miniature-sized bag of chips into a plastic grocery sack and put it in her backpack. Her purse already waited for her there, and Mandie slung the whole thing onto her back.

The bike she rode to work waited for her in the garage, and Mandie put in her earbuds before she set out for her first job. About halfway there, with the glorious morning sun shining down on her back, her phone rang.

Since the earbuds were connected to her phone, all she had to do to answer was tap one of them, which she reached up to do. "Hello?"

"Are you biking to work already?" Charlie asked.

"Yep." Mandie smiled to the route in front of her. "When's your first tour?"

"About ten minutes," her boyfriend said. "You're off at five?"

"Five-thirty," Mandie said, though she'd told him a half-dozen times.

"Five-thirty, right. So...do you want to go to Rocky Ridge tonight? I'm done at four, and I can shower and pick up dinner. Then I can grab you, and we'll ferry there."

He'd been wanting to have a cliffside dinner and watch the sun go down since they'd returned from school. They'd not found a time to do it, as Mandie had been on the job hunt pretty hard, and then there were their mothers—again.

"I think I can," Mandie said. "I'll just text my mom about it, but she shouldn't care now that I have this library job."

"Yes," Charlie said, clearly excited. "Okay, so I'll pick you up at the library at five-thirty."

"I'm just wearing shorts and my soda shirt this morning," she said. "I brought a cute blouse for the job at the library. Is that okay?"

"Should be fine," he said.

"We won't be swimming?"

"We're not going to the beach," he said. "Unless you want to, after the sun goes down. But I was thinking we'd be on the cliffs, not the shore."

"Okay," she said. "Tell me honest—do I need different shoes than my Converse? You're a mountain goat, but Charlie, I'm really not."

He laughed, and Mandie loved the sound of it. "Your Converse are fine, sweetheart. I can't wait to see you tonight."

She saw him almost every single day, though they'd only texted yesterday. Mandie wasn't terribly religious, but she had been known to go to Sunday services with a friend, or her mom and sister, or even Kristen sometimes. They hadn't gone yesterday, but they'd slept late, and Mom had made blueberry muffins for brunch, and they'd all laid together and watched movies in the afternoon.

Mom had worked a little in the evening, and that was when Mandie had retreated to the backyard, where her dad had put up a hammock. She'd drifted back and forth as she'd texted Charlie, and it had been a fantastic, easy, relaxing day.

"Can't wait to see you," she said, and the call ended. Mandie thought about Charlie for the rest of the ride to Soda Sensation, and then she had to remember all the flavor combinations. In downtimes, she thought about the recipes and papers they'd put in the boxes in the basement, and she determined she'd ask Tessa if she could take them home with her that night.

When she got to the library, Tessa greeted her with, "I can't stop thinking about your bicycle book club idea." She gestured her further into the office with a couple of other desks. Today, another woman worked at one of them, but Tessa had dragged over another chair.

"Let's go over it a little more, and we'll see if it's actually viable before we go see Shad."

"Okay," Mandie said. "I don't really know what else to say about it."

"I talked to Bonnie this morning, and she said if the participants pay a monthly fee—which is pretty standard for our programming—then we can use that fee to buy the books." Tessa wore pure excitement in her expression. "So I really want to do it. I love the idea of using video calls, so people from all the islands can attend, whether the ferries are running or not, whether they can leave their homes or not, all of that."

Mandie smiled at her enthusiasm. "Okay, so what do we need to work out?"

"The cost of the books." Tessa reached for a clipboard. "We have to be able to cover that with the fee. Someone to deliver the books, which is a personnel cost."

"I can do that," Mandie said. "As part of my job."

Tessa paused and looked at her. "Really?"

"Sure," Mandie said. "I don't have a car, and I'm too poor to to RideShare everywhere. I bike to work at the soda shop, and then here, and then home." She smiled at Tessa. "And an E-bike is far easier than pedaling. I could totally deliver the books." She let her thoughts run wild through her mind for a moment. "Probably not all in the same day. But maybe the south islands one day, and the northern ones another. Depending on how many registrations we have, of course."

"Sure," Tessa said. "We could have two delivery drivers— bikers."

"When would this start?"

"We definitely need a month to advertise it. Get the books ordered, delivered, and make sure people have time to read."

"So the beginning of July?"

"I was thinking the second week of the month," Tessa said. "A weeknight—mid-week. Tuesday, Wednesday, or Thursday. People seem to be less busy in the middle of the week."

"Sure," Mandie said, and the planning continued. Mandie didn't have a chance to ask about the recipes before they bustled over to City Hall to look at the E-bikes, and she enjoyed the wind in her hair as she rode one of them back.

Then they had to figure out where the library would store two E-bikes, and that took the rest of her time at the library. Before she knew it, Mandie was hugging Tessa and saying, "See you tomorrow," before rushing outside to load her bike into the back of Charlie's four-door sedan.

He wrestled with it, but they'd gotten it in the car before, so Mandie knew it could be done. Once he finished, he laughed and grabbed onto her. "Hey, beautiful girl." He pressed his smile to hers, and Mandie did love kissing Charlie. She couldn't believe he found her pretty enough to be with, or interesting enough to talk to for more than a few minutes. But he did, and Mandie loved how he simultaneously took care of her and let her be herself at the same time.

"Ready?" he asked. "Did you text your mom?"

Mandie swore under her breath. "I forgot." She pulled her phone out of her backpack and said, "I'll text her on the way. Say you surprised me." She tossed him a smile over the top of the car and then got in the passenger seat.

She quickly tapped out a message to her mom, and to her surprise, Mom responded with, *Okay, be safe. What time do you think you'll be home?*

*We're going to eat and watch the sunset,* Mandie told her. *And then the ferry ride back. Eleven? And before you say anything, it's fine, because I'm only working at the library tomorrow, and Tessa said I could come early at 11.*

She didn't wait for her mom to confirm before shoving her phone under her leg. "What did you tell your mom?"

"That we were going to Rocky Ridge for dinner." Charlie glanced over to her. "I told her we'd stop by my granddad's. I hope that's okay."

"It's just fine." Mandie waved her hand out the window, enjoying the breeze as it brushed her face and neck. She loved riding the ferry with Charlie's body pressing into her back, and by the time they'd stopped by his grandfather's and then continued on to the cliffs he'd had in mind, the sun had already started to sink in the west.

They sat seemingly on top of the world, and Mandie could see for miles and miles. Charlie had brought a couple of blankets, but he didn't spread them out. Instead, they used them as pads against the hard rocks, and Charlie sighed as he finally sat down.

"I used to come up where when we first moved to the cove."

"Oh, right," she said. "I forgot you lived here on Rocky Ridge for a minute."

"Just that one summer," he said. "When my parents got divorced, they sold the beach house."

"Yeah." Mandie smiled at him and took the can of diet cola he'd brought for her. "I haven't ever spent much time on Rocky Ridge," she said. "I didn't have any friends here, and I didn't see a reason to come."

"You didn't like the black sand beach?" he teased.

Mandie giggled and shook her head. "Only the...only couples went to the black sand beach," she said, shooting Charlie a look. "It was a pretty well-known make-out spot."

"Was it?" He looked over to her and then back to the western horizon. "I don't remember that."

"Come on." She nudged him with her shoulder, and he lifted his arm around her. "You had that girl who wanted you from the moment you started dating her."

He only chuckled, but Charlie didn't deny it. He'd been so much happier once he'd graduated from high school, and Mandie had enjoyed watching him grow into the person he was today.

"So...if I wanted to take you to the black sand beach to make-out, you wouldn't go?"

"No," Mandie said. "Have I ever agreed to kiss you in public?"

"Come on, Mandie," he said with a smile in his voice. "People kiss in public."

"Making out isn't kissing," she said.

He pressed his lips to the side of her neck, and she tilted her head away to give him better access. "I'm kissing you now."

"We're alone," she whispered. "Not down on some beach where another couple is only a few feet away."

"Is that what they do?" he asked, his lips sliding up to her ear.

"I don't know." Mandie cupped his face in her hand and brought his mouth to hers. "I've never been to the black sand beach, remember?"

"I want to take you right now," he said huskily. He kissed her again, and Mandie thought they might miss the sunset if they kept this up. But she didn't want to stop kissing him, and it was Charlie who finally pulled away.

"Where do you think we could be alone together?" he asked.

Mandie knew what he meant, and her pulse pounded in the vein of her neck. "I—I'm not sure."

"I wish our moms didn't work from home," he said.

"You work every day," Mandie said. "So that doesn't matter."

He slid one hand under the hem of her shirt while the other started to play with the buttons down the front. "Maybe we could plan something like this again, but instead of coming here, or to the black sand beach, we can check in to a hotel."

Mandie's throat closed, though she did want to be with Charlie in that way. "I'm nervous," she said as he ran his hand along her collarbone and under her bra strap.

"Me too," he said. "I've never been with a girl."

"You're so sure of everything, though," she whispered.

"We can't get a hotel. Everyone in the cove knows my mother."

"Out here on Rocky Ridge?" His breath trailed along her ear, and Mandie shivered.

"Yes," she murmured. "Even out here on Rocky Ridge."

"Maybe you're right," he said. "Maybe we should wait until we're back in the city."

"I'm not sure how to keep it a secret from my mom when I have to see her every single day." Mandie smiled at him and cradled his face again. "We'll be back in New York in three months."

"Feels like a lifetime," he whispered as he kissed her again. Mandie thought so too, but she didn't see a way around it, at least not here in Five Island Cove, when she had to look her mother in the eye several times a day.

No, this summer would go better if she showed up to work whenever she was scheduled and kept her hormones in check. So that was exactly what Mandie was going to do.

# Chapter Eight

Kristen Shields pointed to something on Tessa's screen. "That I and E need to be switched."

Tessa leaned closer to her computer, and a couple of seconds passed before she said, "I can't believe you saw that." She made the correction. "Maybe I should have Gail look at this too."

"It's always a good idea to have more than one person read your advertisement," Kristen said. "I'm just so happy you're doing this. Our community has needed a book club outside of the cliques for a long time."

"Do you really think people will sign up?" Tessa clicked around and printed her advertisement for the Cove Chronicles and the library circular, and after that, all she could do was hope and pray people would sign up.

She and Mandie had chosen a book they hoped would appeal to all ages—a popular novel Tessa had seen online, Bonnie had seen in her library chatter, and even Mandie had seen on her social media. Kristen herself had seen the book at the drugstore, and she planned to stop by on the way home today to get her copy.

*The Echoes of Avalon Park* was part memoir and part fiction, and everyone was buzzing about which parts were true and which weren't. They planned to run the advertisement alongside the cover of the book, and that had come from Kristen.

Bonnie had been working hard to bring more library programs to the cove, and the Chronicles gave her full color spots in prominent spots in their bi-weekly community flyers.

"This needs to be in today, right?" Kristen asked.

"Yes." Tessa got to her feet. "I just printed it, and I'm going to have Gail look at it. And we can check it on a hard copy." She moved over to the printer at the far end of the room and picked up the paper.

She studied it and came back over to Kristen. "I think it looks good." She handed the paper to Kristen, and she took her time reading over every word, every letter.

"I think it's ready," she said.

Tessa wrung her hands and paced away from Kristen again. She wished she could soothe the woman's worries, but she was still getting to know Tessa. She reminded Kristen of Eloise in some ways and Robin in others. She had the kindness of Kelli and Laurel, and she fit in better with the moms of young kids than the empty nesters, though she technically belonged more with Maddy, Alice, and Robin.

"Is fifteen dollars too much?" she asked. "I'm going to check the form one more time."

Both she and Kristen had submitted registrations to the form, and they'd come through flawlessly. Participants had the option to get a paperback or an eBook through the form, and Mandie had been working on the routes around the five islands for delivery of the books.

She wouldn't be able to truly iron everything flat until the registration window closed, but because of the topography of the islands here in the cove, the roads weren't laid out in a grid. They wove and curved and went wherever was easiest, and the buildings had been built up around them.

So her route would likely follow a general pattern no matter who signed up for the book club.

"Fifteen dollars isn't too much," Kristen said. "They get the book, Tessa, remember that."

"And the rest is for administration costs," she said.

"And refreshments," Kristen said.

"Yes. Oh, I forgot about the refreshments." Tessa looked away from her computer. "I literally just read the class blurb, which *said* refreshments." She shook her head and ran her hands through her hair. "I'm losing it."

"Guess what?" Mandie burst into the room wearing a cute sundress in white, yellow, orange, and red, with a cute crocheted shrug over it to cover her bare shoulders.

Tessa shot to her feet. "What?"

"I got Soda Sensation to donate the refreshments for our first book club meeting!" Mandie lifted both fists into the air in victory. "They're going to do their cookie of the month, a rice crispy treat—probably just the plain ones, though my boss said he could do the sprinkles if we wanted—and all the flavored water we want." She danced toward Kristen and Tessa, laughing.

Kristen loved the girl so much, and she drew Mandie into her arms as Tessa started to chuckle too. They formed a three-way hug, and Kristen was glad she'd offered to help with this part of Tessa's book club. She'd spent many hours writing class descriptions for circulars, as she'd run the Seafaring Girls program in Five Island Cove for a couple of decades.

Now, her daughter-in-law ran the program, and that made Kristen pull out of the huddle-hug. "Oh, my goodness. What time is it?" She looked around the office for a clock and didn't find one. Of course. Everyone had phones these days, and they used those to tell time. "I have to get to the lighthouse to babysit for Jean."

"It's two-fifteen," Mandie said.

Relief ran through Kristen. "Okay. I have another half-hour." She should set an alarm on her phone, so she didn't have thoughts like that which panicked her.

"Read over this," Tessa said, her smile still wide and bright. "We want to make sure it's comprehensive and succinct at the same time."

"And no typos," Kristen added.

Mandie looked over the blurb and handed the paper back. "It's amazing. How many people do you think will sign up?" They both looked at Tessa, whose smile slipped from her face again.

"I don't know," she said. "I should probably set a goal. Then I'll know if I need to adjust something for the next one."

"I really think a lot of it will depend on the book," Kristen said. "People are busy in the summer, too. Around holidays."

"Right," Tessa said. "Right, right, right." She started pacing again, and Kristen wanted to take her by the shoulders and tell her that she was doing a good job. Her worry about this echoed how AJ had acted when she'd first returned to the cove.

"I think it would absolutely amazing if we got twenty people signed up for our first book club." Tessa turned to face them. "And I'm not counting anyone I know, because I know you'll sign up, Kristen. And Robin, and Alice, and Jean, and all of them."

She looked past them and then strode toward her desk again. "Gail," she said. "Will you read over this before I submit it to the Chronicles?"

The shorter strawberry blonde took in the three of them, blinked a couple of times, and then took the paper from Tessa. "Sure," she said. She read through the description, which couldn't be longer than five hundred words, and added, "It's great, Tessa. I'm super excited for *The Echoes of Avalon Park*. I've been wanting to read that."

"I'm not counting any library personnel." Tessa took the paper back and plopped back into her seat. "I'm going to submit it. It'll run on Monday."

"Kristen," Mandie said. "Can I show you something before you go?"

"Sure thing, sweetie." She looked over to Tessa, who had multiple browser windows open. "We'll be right back."

"Okay," Tessa said, clearly distracted. Then when Kristen reached the door, she heard Tessa call, "Thank you, Kristen."

She followed Mandie out of the office and down the hall to the big, empty room that never seemed to get used.

"We've been cleaning out this room," Mandie said. "There are so many random things here, and Tessa said I could take home anything I wanted." She opened a door past a set of empty tables.

She flipped on the light switch and entered the room. It felt like an abandoned storage room, and Kristen detected some dampness in here. Mandie didn't seem to feel the chill or notice the dankness of the room, and she pulled a box from a shelf.

"Let's go out here," she said. "The light is better."

Kristen backed out of the room, and Mandie brought the box with her. She took off the lid and started pulling out old papers and books and notebooks. "I noticed something when Tessa and I were going through these last week. They're these old recipes."

She laid them out on the table and pointed to the bottom of the one closest to Kristen. She scanned it and found a recipe for New England Clam Chowder, then looked down to the stamp at the bottom. "Anna Elmer," she read.

Kristen's nerves immediately began to buzz at her. She picked up the papers and looked at them. The recipes had been hand-written, and she could picture the woman who'd written them. "I knew her."

"She's my great-grandmother," Mandie said. "So Tessa said I could keep the recipes." She didn't sound nervous or worried or afraid. In fact, she plucked the recipe from Kristen's hand. "I'm going to type them up for my grandma."

Kristen watched her smile and stack the papers together. There were probably a dozen of them, and she set them aside. "Then, I found these." She slid another sheaf of pages in front of Kristen. "They're letters, not recipes, and they're not signed. But I think the handwriting is the same."

Kristen picked up the top one, the paper feeling like doom in her hand. She'd read so many things in the past several years, things that had caused her reality to reform and reshape, that she didn't trust anything from the past.

She definitely held a letter, and it had been addressed to a man named Kenneth. The handwriting was feminine and flowery, but easily read.

"This is a love letter," she murmured.

"Yes," Mandie said, a hint of excitement in her voice. "That's what I thought. But she didn't sign it." She pulled the recipes closer and picked up the one for clam chowder again. "I swear it's the same handwriting."

She held it next to the letter in Kristen's hand, and she couldn't help looking over to it. Then back to the letter. The recipe. The letter.

She looked right at Mandie. "Honey, I don't know if I should tell you this."

"It's the same person, isn't it?" She wore joy in her expression, and Kristen did not want to be the one to squash that.

"I think so, yes," she said.

"These are my grandparents' love letters," she said. "I think that's *so* romantic." She took the letter back from Kristen, and she fought the urge to wipe her hands on her pants.

Kristen swallowed, and she thought the words as they came out of her mouth. "But Mandie, your grandfather's name was not Kenneth."

# Chapter Nine

"I just can't believe it," Tessa said as she stared at the spreadsheet of book club registrations. "There are forty-seven people signed up, Maddy. Registration just opened this morning." She lifted her eyes from her phone to look at her friend.

Maddy gave her a warm smile and reached for her margarita. She, Julia, and Tessa had met for drinks on this Monday night after work, and while Tessa didn't normally drink after work, today was a big day for her.

Plus, Maddy said she had news, and Tessa had some of her own. She reached for her drink and took a small sip. "In other news," she said. She couldn't help clearing her throat. "I ended things with Abe over the weekend."

"What?" Julia asked at the same time Maddy said, "No, you didn't."

"I did." Tessa nodded. "He's never going to move here." She lifted her drink and took a much bigger sip. She liked the fruitiness of it, and she liked the support of Julia as she covered Tessa's hand with hers.

"I'm so sorry, honey." Julia shook her head. "He was great. You two were good together."

"I thought so," Tessa said. "But he never comes here. I always go there, and I have a full-time job now."

"And your friends are here," Maddy said.

"And we hate Nantucket," Julia said dryly. "So many bad memories there."

Tessa nodded, as did Maddy. "I did meet Ben there," she said. "And I liked working with you, Jules."

They smiled at one another, and Maddy added, "You said you had news."

"Yeah." Julia took her sweet time sipping her drink and glancing around The Glass Dolphin, where they'd met. "Liam and I have started talking about marriage."

Maddy made a squeaking noise, and she nearly toppled her glass as she set her drink down. "What?"

"What?" Julia shot her a semi-poisoned look. "We've been dating for a while. Seven months."

"I didn't realize you'd...taken things to the next level." Maddy raised her eyebrows.

Julia waved her away. "I don't share intimate details. You never did." She shot a look over to Tessa. "Sorry, Tess. This feels like a slap in the face after your news." She wore a soft, sorry look. "I apologize. Let's talk about something else."

An awkward silence descended on them, and Tessa glanced around. "It's fine, you guys. I haven't seen him once this summer, and I don't even miss him."

"Of course you do," Maddy said. "And that's okay."

"How could I?" Tessa asked. "Do you know how long it's been since I've seen him?" She shook her head and finished her drink. "It's fine, Julia. I'm happy for you and Liam. Really. You get along with Ian great, and you deserve someone amazing in your life."

"We'll sort of be like Eloise and Aaron," Julia said with a particular glow about her. "Liam's a cop; Aaron's a cop. El owns Cliffside Inn; I work there."

"Yeah, why are you off today?" Maddy asked. "I thought you had Tuesdays off."

"Clara and I switched shifts today," Julia said. "Lena got an award in the morning meeting at the supermarket." She grinned and grinned. "They were both so excited, and El's planning a little something at the inn too."

A couple of beats of silence rained down on them again. "Clara didn't say anything," Tessa said.

"She's really private," Julia said.

"It drives Robin and Alice nuts," Maddy said. "I can see their point, but I also think everyone should get to share what they want, when they want." She shrugged and lifted her hand to the waitress. "Hey, Claudia, can we get some of the elk sliders and a basket of calamari?"

"Absolutely, Maddy. Comin' right up."

Maddy smiled and turned her attention back to Tessa and Julia. "I'm feeling lightheaded already." She giggled slightly, and she'd only had one drink. "Ben's at the station tonight, and I have to get back to Rocky Ridge alone."

"Why don't you stay with me?" Julia asked. "I told Ben

it was girls' night, and he's not expecting to see me or even hear from me."

"He won't want to know you got home safely?" Tessa asked with a grin. "I don't believe that."

"You could still stay with me," Julia said. "That would save you the last ferry ride—and you wouldn't have to go home alone." She raised her eyebrows at Maddy, who started nodding.

"You know what? That sounds fun."

"You can borrow something of mine for tomorrow," Julia said.

"I'll have time to go home in the morning," Maddy said. "Do you have pajamas for me?"

"Sure."

They turned their attention back to Tessa, and Julia said, "I'm so proud of you, Tessa. You're bringing ideas to life."

"Yeah," Tessa said, smiling. She didn't want to invite herself along for a sleepover, but she also didn't want to go home alone tonight. Perhaps if she had Abe there to take her into his arms and tell her how proud he was.

Her old life from New Jersey flashed through her mind. She could call her son, and he'd care. He'd congratulate her. Then the call would end—just like this evening of drinks and appetizers—and then Tessa would be left alone again.

The darkness surrounding her bungalow could creep so close when she was alone. The silence became something that drove her toward madness. She looked between Maddy and Julia, wondering if either of them would care if she tagged along.

Perhaps they had something private they wanted to talk about. Perhaps she wasn't as close to them as she'd imagined. Perhaps she was letting her thoughts derail her again.

"Hey," she said as the waitress arrived with their calamari and sliders. She smiled politely up at the woman, and they moved their drinks around to make room for the food.

"Any refills?" Claudia asked, and Maddy nodded.

Julia said she wanted a mojito, and Tessa said, "Ooh, that sounds good. Make that two." She still had half a drink left, and her brain buzzed slightly too. Her chest felt warm, and she looked at her friends once the waitress had left.

She reached for a slider, her attention focused there as she said, "Could I come stay with you too, Julia?" She looked up, every vulnerability inside her streaming out. "It's just such a happy day, and I don't want to go home to... nothing."

That was what she had to go home to—nothing. She'd never felt so lonely, even surrounded by two people who knew her so well and had been through so much with her.

To her relief, and maybe partial surprise, Julia didn't hesitate as she said, "Of course you can, sweetie. I've got an airbed I can set up. I use it when my boys come."

To Tessa's knowledge, Julia's sons had not come to Five Island Cove to visit her. Not even once. As she looked into Julia's eyes, she saw the flash of pain there, the quick way it whipped through her expression, and probably lashed at her soul.

"At the mention of children," Maddy said. "It's official, and Chelsea has authorized me to tell everyone—she and

Rob are engaged, and they're looking at a Christmas wedding." She beamed from every pore of her body. "Right here in the cove."

In that moment of time while Tessa drew breath, she saw that Julia already knew this. So this was just an announcement for her. As she smiled, she decided it didn't matter. "Maddy," she gushed. "That's so great. You must be thrilled."

"She's a bit wild," Maddy said with a laugh. "So yes, I'm thrilled." She bit into a slider, and Tessa turned her attention toward the food too.

She lived on Sanctuary with Julia, so she could stop by her own house and get her own pj's and a pillow. She met her friend's eyes. "I could just sleep on the couch."

"Or with me," Maddy said. "Julia's got a king and a queen in that house of hers."

"You could sleep with me too," Julia said. She grinned and grinned. "I'm so happy we're doing this."

"Me too." Maddy wiped her mouth. "Mm, Tess, how's Janey doing?"

The joviality drained right out of Tessa, but she trusted these women. "You know what? I see her and talk to her less than I did Abe." She coolly raised her mojito to her lips. The mint and burst of lime played well in her mouth, the burn of alcohol just what she needed to get the next sentence out. "So I don't know. I'm not really talking to my sister right now."

"Fair enough," Maddy said diplomatically.

Julia said nothing, because what was there to say? Tessa

pushed her sister out of her mind. She refused to let her memories of Nantucket Point come into her mind. She had a new life here, and she wanted to keep putting the bricks in place that would build her a fortress right here in the cove.

She had a full-time job now, and good friends, and she'd gotten her first major adult programming class off the ground in the first two weeks of her appointment. Now, maybe she could find someone like Julia and Maddy had. Someone to come home to at night and celebrate days like today with. Someone who wanted to be with her more than he wanted his deli on another island. Someone to love and cherish, and who would keep his promises and do the same for her.

Right now, she didn't have that, but as she lifted her glass in a toast Maddy made about their lives and careers, Tessa certainly had blessings to name and hope for a future she couldn't see yet.

THE WIND WHIPPED AT TESSA'S HAIR AS SHE GOT out of her car and immediately ducked down, her goal to get to the navy blue door of the lighthouse as fast as possible. The day had been lovely so far, but on this side of the island, and so close to the sea, the wind seemed to reign.

She didn't stop and knock, because Jean wouldn't expect her to. Inside, she huffed and straightened her blouse and then her hair while the wind screeched in a low-volume, high-pitched sound beyond the seam of the door.

"Jean," she called, bypassing the door on her left that went up to the lighthouse control center and deck, and instead went down the hall and then down the steps.

"Come down," Jean called, and as Tessa did, the scent of toasted oatmeal and chocolate wafted up to greet her. Two floors down, the warmth of a home met her, and Tessa smiled in the same way to Jean, who stood in the kitchen, an apron around her waist as she slid a spatula under a cookie and transferred it from sheet pan to wire rack.

"Hey," Tessa said. "The sea seems upset on this side of Diamond."

"She often is," Jean said with a smile. "Cookie?"

"They aren't for your Seafaring Girls?"

"They are, but I make bunches of them," she said. "Reuben has a real sweet tooth." She smiled with such happiness, and Tessa wondered what that would be like—to be so happy.

"Is Heidi awake?"

"She will be soon," Jean said. "I've got Parker here too." She nodded up toward the ceiling. "He's up with Reuben right now, but the scent of cookies will reach them both eventually."

"Oh, Kelli must be back at the yoga studio." Tessa pulled out one of only two barstools in the small space here at the base of the lighthouse and sat. She didn't hesitate to reach for a cookie, because Jean possessed serious skills in the realm of baking.

"Just once a week in the afternoon," Jean said. "So Parker comes here until his dad is done with work."

Tessa had taken a bite of the oatmeal chocolate chip cookie, the warmth of the cinnamon accompanying the chewy oatmeal and rich chocolate perfectly. She nodded, too much deliciousness in her mouth to speak.

"I'll get the map," she said, and she left the kitchen and went down the hall. Tessa had just finished her cookie had started contemplating eating another one when Jean returned. "It's probably a bit out of date, especially down on Pearl."

She put a large, posterboard-sized sheet of paper on the counter, and surprise whipped through Tessa the way the wind did outside. "I wasn't expecting it to be this big."

"It's five islands," Jean said as if that explained everything. "Reuben's father put this together, and he kept it up until he got sick. Since then, we haven't done as much with it." She pointed over to the other side of Diamond Island from the lighthouse. "See? The Glass Dolphin should be here, and it's not."

Certain landmarks had been colored in, like the lighthouse, City Hall, the south harbor port, every ferry station, the grocery store, the police station, and various places on other islands, including the Coast Guard station up on Rocky Ridge.

The map made her smile, and Tessa looked for The Cliffside Inn and didn't see it. She knew Eloise had recently revived the establishment, and it apparently hadn't been there before Reuben's father had passed away.

Her gaze stayed on Sanctuary, and she did find her beach bungalow, but the small grocer wasn't there, nor was there anything marking the outpost stations for fire and police that existed now.

"It's got all the roads," Jean said. "It should help you and Mandie map a route."

"Thank you," Tessa said. She didn't know the cove as well as Mandie, and she'd been gone for a year. "I can just roll it up?"

"Sure thing," Jean said just as Heidi started to fuss from down the hall. She turned that way, and Tessa looked back at the map. Leaning closer, she saw that some of the houses had been labeled with names.

A smile played with her mouth, because this was quintessentially small town, and while the cove felt like a bustling, lively place, Tessa reminded herself that it was summertime, and the cove was a completely different place in the winter.

None of the names meant much to her, but she wanted to show the map to Mandie, who'd grown up here and had generations of family members who had lived in Five Island Cove. She'd been thrilled to find recipes and letters from her ancestors, and Tessa closed her eyes to try to remember the name on the bottom of the pages, in that seal.

Heidi babbled as Jean brought her down the hall, and Tessa said, "Anna Elmer."

"Say hi to Auntie Tessa," Jean said, and Tessa turned away from the map to greet the darling girl.

She expected to find the dark-haired, chubby cheeked girl in her mother's arms, but Jean wasn't carrying her.

Instead, Heidi toddled along awkwardly, her arms straight out and a massive smile on her face.

"Jean," she said. "She's walking." Tessa looked at her friend in surprise.

"She just started this week," Jean said with obvious pride in her voice.

"She is the cutest." Tessa slid from the barstool and bent to pick up the little girl. "Yes, you're the cutest."

Heidi babbled and flailed her arms, and Jean took her and put her in a baby seat. "Let's eat," she said. "Then you can go upstairs with Daddy while my girls are here."

Tessa started to roll up the map, because she could see Jean had things to do. She'd show the map to Mandie and Robin, because it seemed like something she'd enjoy too, and then they'd get their bicycle book club route sorted out.

# Chapter Ten

J ulia Harper couldn't stop kissing her boyfriend. Something about kissing him at the police station felt forbidden, and she hadn't had a relationship this exciting in a long, long time. He finally broke the kiss with a chuckle and the whispered words, "What were we talking about?"

Her fingers ached from where she'd curled them around the triangular collar flaps on his police uniform, and Julia slowly released her grip. "I think you were saying you wanted me to move to Diamond Island and live with you and Ian when we get married."

"Mm, yes." Liam ducked his head, his shaggy blond hair falling across his forehead. "I think that was it." He looked at her with those dazzling blue eyes. "And? What do you think of that?"

"I think I've said how I feel about that," Julia said. Maybe not in words, but not everything had to be formed with consonants and vowels to be said. So much could be said with a sigh, a look between two people who knew each other well, or a kiss.

"I'm worried about Ian," she said next. "My friends seemed to think we're moving pretty fast. What does he think?"

"I think...you're probably right." He stepped away from her, but Julia stayed against the wall around the corner from the Chief's office where Liam had pressed her when she'd brought him lunch. "We should be realistic about the timeline."

"Has he said something?"

"He's at his mother's until the Fourth," he said. "So no, we haven't talked about it." He moved back toward the open floor filled with desks and activity, then turned back to her. "We've got a few more weeks alone, and then we'll go out with him again."

"He's sixteen," Julia said carefully. She didn't want to lecture Liam, but she had raised three boys through their teens while he hadn't. "It might just be too fast for him. We've only been dating for seven months, and boys don't always say what they're really thinking."

"Ian and I don't keep secrets from one another," Liam said. "It's our number one rule."

"And all children break their parents' rules." Julia looked up at him from underneath her lashes. "I'm not in a hurry, Liam. I want the best for your son."

"Thank you, sweetheart." He kissed her again, slowly this time, with plenty of passion but not quite as much spice. Someone cleared their throat, and Liam pulled away from her. He moved in front of her and said, "Hey, Foster."

Julia loved the way he protected her from prying eyes, and she carefully reached up to wipe her mouth. She needed to get to the ferry and get to Cliffside for her afternoon and evening shift, but she had a few more minutes for Liam to finish up his quick conversation with a fellow cop.

He turned back to her. "I'll meet you at the ferry at eight?" He slid his hand along her waist. "We'll have a late dinner and an early night, okay?"

"Sounds great," she murmured, and he kissed her one last time. Then he walked her out, his hand securely in hers. Julia loved being with him, and she practically floated to the ferry, then to her job.

She sighed happily as she entered the office she shared with Clara and Eloise, and thankfully, no one sat at the tables or desk to hear it. She drew in a breath and told herself, "You're at work now. Focus on the guests."

Julia worked check-in at The Cliffside Inn, and it was Thursday in the summertime. Eloise would have the entire inn turning over today, and Julia heard the industrial washing machines and dryers going as she changed out of her blouse and into The Cliffside Inn tee-shirt she wore with her black shorts.

Then, she moved into the kitchen and got the pre-made cookie dough from the fridge. As it started to warm, Julia went through her routine of making up several gallons of citrus water and then several more of lemonade and then several more of iced tea. As she stirred the last batch of that, Clara entered the kitchen.

"Julia," she said. "There are whales off the western side of the island."

She immediately abandoned her afternoon check-in prep and went with Clara, who should be leaving in just a few minutes. Outside, she gathered with Eloise, Billie, and Grace on the far side of the pool, all of them looking west.

"There's one that surges up," Grace said, her eyes shaded with both hands.

The three housekeepers had come out too, and Julia was one of the last to arrive at the watch party. She stood there with the others, all of them silently waiting to see if the whales would come up again.

They had to breathe, so Julia employed her patience as she watched the waves. "What kind of whales?" she asked.

"I think it's a humpback," Clara said.

All at once, the waves rippled, a hump surged, a full fluke came up and sure enough, the waters split, and another whale came lunging out of the ocean. Julia gasped while Grace cheered, and Billie shushed her. Pure delight streamed through Julia, because there was something simply magical about seeing something out of the water that normally stayed beneath the waves.

It was a whole different world down there, and Julia could admit to a trickle of fear of the ocean. Especially here on Five Island Cove, as it surrounded them on all sides, and the sea did not like to be tamed.

"What are you guys doing out here?" someone asked,

and Julia turned toward the familiar vo'
she strode toward them in a gorgeous b'
made precisely for her body. She loc
and she always had the best clothes c.

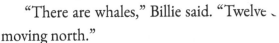

"There are whales," Billie said. "Twelve ˻
moving north."

"What are you doing here?" Eloise asked fondly as she gave Alice a quick hug. Alice did the same to Clara and then Julia, and the four of them stood on the edge of the world and watched the water.

"I had a client just down the hill," Alice said. "And I thought there might be cookies here." She smiled at Julia, who grinned back.

"There will be," she said. "In about twenty minutes, if I can drag myself away from the whales." None of them moved, and Julia kept searching the waters for the whales. "There are at least two of them."

"The best whale watching is up here," Alice said.

"There are some good spots on Rocky Ridge too," Eloise said. "Your dad's deck was amazing for things like this, remember?"

"Yes," Alice said quietly, and Julia didn't know the whole story there. She hadn't grown up in the cove the way Eloise and Alice had.

Neither of them expounded, and several seconds later, more humps surfaced, and Clara said, "There's a pair of flukes!" with plenty of excitement. Julia saw them both, as well as two more sprays as whale breath got blown out.

"Exciting," Eloise said. "I think I got that one for your

he lowered her phone and smiled at her girls. "All
. We have to get back to work, because we got that ship-
.nt for our pool. Girls?"

Billie turned away from the ocean in the distance, but Grace
didn't. Julia and Alice stayed with her for a few extra minutes
and one more whale sighting, and then Julia said, "Come on,
sweetie. You go help your mom, and I'll get the cookies going."

Grace came with her and Alice, and she went all the way
through the inn while Julia went into the kitchen. She
started scooping cookie dough while Alice leaned against
one of the stainless steel counters as her phone rang.

"Hey, son," she said.

Julia bent and put the oversized cookie sheet into the
oven, then pulled down another one. She set a timer and
started scooping again while Alice listened to Charlie.

Then she said, "Okay, whoa, whoa, whoa. Slow down,
Charlie."

Julia looked over at the urgency in her friend's voice. She
stopped scooping cookies and started over to her. Alice
pulled the phone from her ear and put it on speaker. Charlie's voice came through, full of animation and frustration.

"...a flood or whatever, and they just canceled my
contract for the full year." He paused, and Alice just blinked.
Julia hadn't heard the beginning of the conversation, but it
didn't sound good.

"Can they do that, Mom? I mean, can't we do something legal on them? It's going to be almost impossible to get
student housing this late in the game."

"You're right about that," Alice said with a sigh. "I'm not home to look at anything right now. You said you got an email?" She started swiping on her phone. "I'll have gotten it too. I get all of your and Ginny's emails with regards to school and deadlines and such."

"Yeah, an email," he said. "I saw it on my break." He let out a frustrated sigh. "Ginny's not going to have anywhere to live either. This is a nightmare."

"It's an apartment," Alice said calmly. "Don't over-react."

"I'm not over-reacting, Mom," Charlie said harshly. "I hate it when you tell me I'm over-reacting when I'm not. I just lost my student housing and it's the middle of June. There will be nothing available. *Nothing.* You know that, right?"

"Charlie," Alice said, her eyebrows bunched together as she hunched over her phone.

"You think I'm just like Dad."

She looked up then. "I do not."

"I have to go," Charlie said. "I have another tour starting in ten minutes."

"Charlie," Alice said again, but the call ended with a somewhat violent beep. She stared at her device and then met Julia's eyes.

Julia didn't know everything about Alice's ex-husband, but she'd been told a few things. She knew Frank had cheated on Alice, and she knew that Charlie looked just like his father. She'd never met Frank, but she herself had a son

117

who looked a lot like her ex, and it was hard to separate them sometimes.

That was, if she actually ever saw her sons, which she didn't. Not really, and a zip of sadness and longing cut through her.

"I don't think he's just like his father," Alice whispered.

Julia shoved aside her own feelings, took her phone from her, and wrapped Alice in a hug. "I know you don't, honey."

Alice gripped her in a show of emotion. "He's right," she whispered. "It will be difficult to find a decent student apartment at this point. And we need two of them for different genders."

"We'll figure it out," Julia said firmly. "Okay, Alice? We all know people in the city—heck, Maddy can probably put up Charlie and Ginny in a penthouse somewhere—and we'll help you figure this out."

Julia believed every word she said, because she had a friend group now that didn't back down from a challenge. They didn't backbite one another, and they rallied around one another even when they didn't agree.

A flooded student apartment?

"This is nothing," Julia said. "Do you want me to put it on the group text?"

"I need to talk to the twins first," Alice said as she stepped out of Julia's arms. She didn't sniffle, but her eyes definitely held more worry and concern than they had only minutes ago, while she waited for her cookies or watched the whales. "Then I will." She gave Julia a watery smile. "I better go. I'm sure Ginny will be calling soon too, and I want to get home and look at the contracts."

"Sure," Julia said just as the timer went off. "Do you want to take some cookies with you?"

"Yes," Alice said firmly. "I'll need them to get through my conversation with Charlie once he gets home."

"I'll load you up," Julia said, and she moved to get down a paper plate to do just that. After Alice left, she kept scooping cookies, her thoughts rotating around all the different pieces and people in her life.

Liam and Ian.

Alice and her twins.

Eloise and her girls here at the inn.

Tessa and Maddy. She had been worried about Tessa this week after hearing about her break-up with her boyfriend. She'd also asked to stay with Julia and Maddy this week, and the three of them had had a great time on Monday night, but Tessa hadn't ever done that before.

"So she's not doing as well as she'd like us all to believe," Julia murmured to herself as she switched cookie sheets, pulling out one that had perfectly browned and baked cookies and putting in one with raw dough.

Julia stopped for a moment and took a breath. She planted her hands against the cool tabletop in the kitchen. "Lord," she prayed aloud. "Bless us all this summer with whatever it is we need to thrive."

She didn't know everyone's exact situation, from Jean to AJ to Kelli, but she believed God did, and she could plead for her friends on their behalf.

# Chapter Eleven

B y the time Charlie was due home, Alice had started pacing in her office. She'd talked to Ginny, who was likewise upset. She'd spoken to Arthur, who'd advised her to let Charlie express himself without jumping in to correct him or tell him that his feelings were invalid.

She hadn't meant to do that, but looking back, she could see she had. She also knew what Arthur had not said out loud: She had to assure and then reassure Charlie that she did not think he was Frank. Not in any way.

That conversation alone made her stomach turn, and she looked out the front window to see if Charlie had pulled up yet. He hadn't, and her own irritation spiked. "He should be here by now," she said to herself.

She had not spoken to Frank about the children's flooded apartments. She had gone through the contracts, and she'd called the building manager for the affected apartments. An act of God made the contract null and void, and apparently, decades-old pipes were such a thing. Both Ginny and Charlie would get their deposits back, no questions asked, but that didn't solve the problem of having over one hundred and thirty NYU students now scrambling to find somewhere to live in just less than three months.

A door slammed somewhere in the house, and Alice spun to leave her office. "Charlie?"

"Yeah." He sounded tired and annoyed, and sure enough, after she'd gone down the hall and around the corner from her front office to the kitchen, she found her handsome son tossing his lunch box into the sink. He threw her a disgruntled look and added, "I don't want to talk about it tonight."

That wasn't going to fly, and there'd been a time when Alice would've let him brush by her and go upstairs to shower. Tonight was not that night, and she stood between the buffet and the dining room table—his only way out of the kitchen and to the steps behind her in the hall.

"We won't talk about the apartment," she said. "But we need to talk about what you said on the phone about me treating you like you're your father."

Charlie stayed in the kitchen, the peninsula between them. He said nothing, and the way he glared at her *did* remind her of Frank. He'd usually stay silent in the beginning of their disagreements as well, but once he got going, he could say the cruelest things.

"I do not think you're like your father."

"I was not over-reacting. Ginny called and left a voicemail of her crying."

"She cries," Alice said calmly. "You get angry."

"I'm not angry," Charlie argued back. "I'm frustrated. There's a difference, Mom, as *you've* told me so many times in my life."

"I know you are, honey." Alice moved toward him and took him into her arms, though it was clear he didn't want to hug her. "And you have every right to be." She stood at five-foot-ten, but Charlie still had a few inches of height on her. "But we'll figure this out, because that's what we do."

Charlie finally relaxed into her, but it didn't last long. He pulled away and backed into the corner, his arms folded. He was so much bigger than when he'd left here last fall to attend his first semester at NYU.

He'd grown into his personality, and his confidence had inflated and increased in all the best ways. Tears filled Alice's eyes, and she turned away and swiped at them. She never cried in front of her children, not even when she'd gone through her bitter and painful divorce, left all of her friends and acquaintances in the neighborhood she'd loved, and pulled her teens away from all they'd known to come make a life for them all here in Five Island Cove.

She hadn't cried in front of them, but Ginny and Charlie had surely seen the signs over the years. The puffy eyes in the morning. The wads of tissues that she dropped on the floor beside the bed that someone had come behind her and cleaned up.

They'd certainly seen her drink far too much, stop eating almost entirely, and they'd been around when her friends had intervened to prevent her from wasting away from both.

This summer, as he'd led kayaking tours, his muscles in his shoulders, chest, and arms had grown, and as Alice dared to look at him again, she found him watching her. He softened because of whatever he saw on her face, and Alice took a breath to steady herself.

"Your father lives in the city," she said.

"I am not living with him," Charlie stated flatly.

"Maddy is from New York," Alice continued. "We used to live very near there. Robin's mother has contacts there. We have options. We'll work together to figure this out."

Charlie nodded just once. "Okay."

Alice considered him for a moment. "How else do I treat you like you're Dad?"

"I don't know," he said, plenty of exhaustion in his voice. "I just know—I heard you tell Arthur a while ago that I remind you of him, and it's—I just—do you even know how hard I've worked to *not* be like him?"

"I—no," Alice said, going with truthful. "I didn't know it was something you even thought about."

"I know I look like him," Charlie said. "But I'm not him, Mom, and it's not fair for you to have this—this prejudice toward me."

"I don't," she said. "I absolutely do not." She wasn't sure how to make him believe her. The thing with Charlie was that he was very smart and very stubborn. "You're a wonderful young man, Charlie. I'm so proud of you. You work hard. You do great in college. I know you're nothing like your father in the ways that matter the most."

He nodded, but he said, "He works hard. He's smart."

"You're loyal and honest," Alice said. "You care about the people around you, and you understand that your actions impact other people. Your father still doesn't do any of those things."

The silence in the kitchen stretched, and Alice wasn't sure what to say into it. She'd never been sure with Charlie, but she loved him fiercely. She tried to think of what Kristen would say, because she always seemed to have the perfect thing to bring people together.

What would she say? Alice wondered as she gazed at her son. The house felt too cold, as the air conditioning had been fighting hard to ward off the mid-June warmth.

"Charlie—"

"I guess now is as good of time as any to tell you I'm in love with Mandie." He spoke in his regular low timbre, his tone even and slow. He'd been looking into the living room, but now he switched his gaze to hers.

Pure shock moved through Alice, and she had no words. Her mouth hung open, and Charlie half-smiled and scoffed as he shook his head. "I know you think I'm too young."

She did, but she didn't want to admit it. Robin's words from a couple of weeks ago flowed into her mind then, and Alice seized onto them.

"I am not going to argue with you on this," she said slowly. "I think you're a brilliant, capable, caring young man, and I think it's wonderful that you've found someone to love." She swallowed. "Have you told Mandie?"

He shook his head, his jaw tight. "I don't want you to tell Robin."

"Of course not," Alice promised. She moved toward him and took him by the shoulders. "How do you know you love her?"

"Mom."

"I'm not judging," she said. "I genuinely want to know what you're feeling. You never say stuff like this."

"Well." He drew in a breath and released it as Alice dropped her hands. She retreated to the other corner of the kitchen, on the other side of the sink, to give Charlie room to say what he needed to say.

"When I think about my future, she's always in it," he said. "When I think about all the firsts I'll have—first time graduating from college, first child being born, first time buying a house, first big job offer, all of that—she's there. She's the one I want to do all those things with."

Alice nodded, the thought of all of those things so beautiful. She'd never heard Charlie talk like this before, and she suddenly felt like perhaps she'd spent far too much time worrying about the wrong things when it came to her son. Too many lectures about sex and girls and school, when she could've been asking him about what he wanted his life to be. What dreams and goals he had, and how she could support him in achieving those.

"First time having sex?" she asked carefully.

"That too," he said. She looked over to him, and he dropped his head. "We haven't, Mom."

"Okay," she said in as normal of a tone as she could muster. "Do you think she loves you?"

"I don't know," he said. "I think I'm probably ahead of

126

her, to be honest. She really wants to graduate from college as the next step of her life, so I'm not real sure about marriage and all that."

Alice nodded, and such a thing would normally make her cheer internally. But not when she knew her son loved Mandie and wanted to be with her. Prolonging those dreams would only break his heart, and Alice certainly didn't want that either.

"Life is long," she said. "Though sometimes if feels like it's now or never, it rarely is."

"I know," he said, though Alice didn't see how he could. He sighed again and straightened from the countertop. "Can I go shower now?"

"Are you going out with Mandie tonight?"

"She got an extra shift at the soda shop," he said.

"So we'll go get a soda," Alice said. "Just to say hi."

Charlie looked at her, so many questions in his eyes. Alice just wanted to hug him close and tell him how much she loved him, so she reached for him again. "I love you, my son," she whispered. "Please forgive me for whatever I've done to make you think you're like your dad. I don't think that, and I absolutely don't mean to do that."

"Okay, Mom." He hugged her back, tight, and Alice's heart healed completely with that gesture. He stepped back and started to leave the kitchen. "You're handling this Mandie thing far better than I anticipated you would."

"You're choosing her," Alice said, making him pause and turn back to her, his eyes wide and again full of wonder. "She's a wonderful girl, with amazing parents, and

I just want to support you instead of pushing you further away."

She'd have to give Robin credit for those words very soon, because they made her son duck his head, sniffle, and then ask in a gruff voice, "I'm gonna go shower, and then can we get dinner to go with our soda?"

"Yes," Alice said, glad Charlie had started to leave the dining room. That way, he wouldn't be able to see her cry either. She turned to look out the window above the kitchen sink, and she sniffled and pulled back her emotions just as the garage door opened and Arthur walked in.

"I'm home," he called, and Alice turned to rush into his arms. "Oh, okay. Oh, boy." He held her tight. "The talk with Charlie didn't go well?"

"It did," Alice said, glad she had so many anchors in her life now. "He's showering, and then we're going to go to dinner." She stepped back and wiped her hair off her face as she centered her thoughts and feelings. "I'll talk fast."

# Chapter Twelve

R obin entered the library, feeling a bit underdressed in her beach cover up, though it wasn't like some others and could be seen through. She certainly didn't see many women in their beachwear, nor was anyone else currently carrying three oversized soda cups into a place full of paper. A place where no one spoke in louder than a whisper and surely eating and drinking were discouraged, if not completely against the rules.

Holding her head high and ignoring everyone who looked her way, she bustled past the check-out desk, the computer stations, and the magazine racks to the stairs in the corner.

Tessa and Mandie would be downstairs, and she'd brought drinks for them to get them through the last couple of hours of their day. She'd gotten up and gone running, the same way she always did.

She loved the weather early in the morning in the

summertime, and she was able to pound out her frustrations for the day before it even started. Then, she could see her girls out the door for their morning jobs, as Jaime had been picking up babysitting jobs this summer, and Mandie was trying to work as much as possible.

She'd then work in her home office on the weddings she had coming up—two in July, two in August, and a fifth in September—and then, Robin really tried to slow down and enjoy some relaxation time in the afternoon. Today, she'd gone to the beach with Kristen, Clara, and Lena, and they'd had a great couple of hours without the stress of packing lunches, monitoring teens and their boyfriends, or trying to keep up with all the conversations flying around.

She'd actually read a book before packing up and stopping by Soda Sensation and coming to the library. Her flip flops flipped and flopped against the cement steps, and Robin prayed she wouldn't trip and fall to her sticky, caffeinated death.

Down the stairs, she continued on into the big room where Mandie and Tessa were planning to hold their adult classes, and she came to a complete stop. "Wow," came out of her mouth before she could find something more eloquent to say.

The room had been transformed from a big, ugly, empty, stale space to a place Robin would like to come on a rainy day to do her reading. White bookshelves lined the far wall, with a break every grouping of three, where a comfy chair had been placed with a tiny table she could pull in front of her and balance a laptop on.

"That's amazing," she said. She had no idea if the plans included more shelves and books down here or not, but Robin liked the changes she saw so far. Mandie had really been enjoying her job here at the library, and the thought of her oldest daughter got Robin moving toward the other side of the room.

Across the hall and through a doorway, and she entered the shared office where she expected to find Tessa and Mandie. Sure enough, they stood at the back of the room, something spread out on the table in front of them. Robin's ears picked up the sound of their voices, but not the shapes of the letters, so she didn't understand what they were talking about.

Mandie heard or sensed her first, and she turned toward Robin at the same time she straightened. She took in the cover up and the soda pop and asked, "What are you doing here?"

She lifted the carrying tray of cups. "I brought refreshments."

"If that's Dr. Pepper with raspberry and coconut, you're going to be my favorite person in the whole world." Tessa looked a bit haggard, and Robin brandished the first cup toward her.

"I didn't even get diet."

"Bless you," Tessa said, plucking away the couple of inches of wrapper the workers at Soda Sensation had left on the straw.

Mandie smiled by the time Robin looked back to her. "What did you get me?"

"You're difficult to shop for," Robin said as she smiled back. "I went with Diet Mountain Dew, green apple, and pineapple."

"Mm, sour," Mandie said. "I love it." She took her cup and took a draw on the straw. "Mm, yes. Thank you, Momma."

Robin took her drink out of the carrying container and turned to find a trashcan. When she returned to the table, the others had resumed their tasks. Robin stood at Tessa's side and took in the map that nearly covered the whole table.

"This is amazing," she said. "Look at this thing." She looked to Tessa and then Mandie, realizing she'd interrupted them for a second time. "Did you make this?"

"I got it from Jean," Tessa said with a small curl playing with the corners of her mouth. "I guess Kristen's husband kept it up, so it hasn't been updated since he got sick and passed away."

Robin's chest trembled and threatened to crumble in on itself, but she took a breath, and her lungs pressed out against the emotion making her nervous. Scared? Worried? Robin wasn't sure what the chill in her blood represented, and she worked to remind herself that people weren't wholly one thing.

Hardly anyone was all good or all evil. Most people had some of both inside them, and all humans made mistakes. Some were bigger than others, and Robin hadn't known about any of Joel's until *after* his death. So much of the fabric of her life had been shredded then, and sometimes, in quick moments like the one she'd just had, she felt like she could be blown away with the slightest of breezes. Like she had no foundation anymore, and she didn't know who she was or how she'd gotten to this office in the basement of the library.

"The roads are mostly all the same," Mandie said. "We're going over the delivery route for the bicycle book club." She slid out some pages from beneath the map, as it spanned from top to bottom on the table.

"Did you show your mother the recipes you found?" Tessa asked.

Robin met her daughter's eyes, and something fearful flashed there. "She mentioned them," Robin said. "But I haven't seen them or heard more about it."

"Bonnie gave her approval to take them out of the library today," Tessa beamed at Mandie. "She filed all the paperwork and talked to her about it and everything."

Robin's pride swelled within her chest, and she let it beam out of her. Her own mother had never given Robin the accolades and validation she'd so sorely wanted, and she never wanted to make her own girls feel like that. "That's amazing, Mandie. Good job."

"They're your grandmother's," Mandie said. "There's eleven of them, and I'm not even sure if Grandma has them."

"I'm sure she does." Robin took a drink of her own diet cola laced with vanilla and cherry and added, "I'd love to see them, though."

"I'm bringing them home tonight," Mandie said, and she ducked her head and looked back at the maps. "I think I can do Rocky Ridge and Sanctuary in a couple of hours," she said. "That doesn't include the ferry rides, so that would take one day."

"Diamond will take one of your shifts," Tessa said. "We do have more sign-ups from people on this island than the others."

"How many have you got so far?" Robin asked.

"Registration closes tomorrow night," Tessa said. "But we have forty-seven people signed up." She wore the sunshine in her expression now, when it had been streaming from Robin only a moment ago. "I'm blown away—and they're not all women. There are a handful of men."

"Did you count us?" Robin asked, because Tessa had told them she wouldn't. At least not in her goal numbers.

"That's total," she said. "Minus you guys, there's still a lot more than twenty."

Robin switched her attention to Mandie. "And you can deliver all of those books?"

"It's going to take three days next week," Mandie said, barely glancing at her. "A day for the north islands, one for Diamond, and one for the southern islands." She bent and made a note on the paper in front of her. "It's an E-bike, Mom. I won't be pedaling."

"I remember," Robin said. "Is that why you ordered that helmet?"

"Bonnie insisted I wear one." Mandie stood up again. "I guess it's the smart thing to do; I just don't want to look dumb, and I feel like I can't see right with a helmet."

"I'm for the helmet too," Robin said, though she didn't

want to antagonize Mandie. They'd had this discussion already, and that was why Mandie had ordered her own helmet and had it sent to the house. She didn't like the one the library and town had provided, and she'd flatly refused to wear it.

"Tessa," someone said, and all three of them turned to the copper-haired woman sticking her head into the room. "Your shipment is here."

Tessa legit squealed, and she and Mandie abandoned their map and book club plans and headed for the door straightaway. Robin couldn't help but feel abandoned, and she called, "I have that dinner tasting tonight," after Mandie. "You and Jamie are on your own for dinner."

"I remember," Mandie said. "Thanks for the drinks, Mom!" Then she followed Tessa out of the office, leaving Robin there alone.

She looked back at the map, and then shifted it to pull out the papers hidden beneath it. This wasn't her daughter's handwriting, and it only took Robin reading one line— Hampton Fried Green Tomatoes—for her to know what she was looking at.

Her grandmother's New England recipes. A sense of nostalgia slithered through her now as she read through the quick list of ingredients and the directions for getting the perfect crisp on this fried food.

She'd eaten these before, at her grandmother's house, when she was a very little girl. Robin couldn't even place the memory on the timeline of her life that made sense, but it existed nonetheless.

At the bottom, she saw a seal that bore her grandmother's name, and Robin picked up the paper. "This is amazing." Her mother would definitely like to see these, and Robin hoped she could go with Mandie when she took them to show her.

She slid the bottom paper on top of the fried green tomato recipe and found one for Boston baked beans. A few seconds later, she said, "I have this recipe." And she did, but it had come from her mom's recipe box, and Robin had typed it up on her computer, printed it, and kept them in a binder above the microwave.

Having the original recipe, in hand-written ink by her ancestor brought the recipe to life in a whole new way.

Shifting the papers again, she expected to find another recipe. Instead, she found a letter, and it had been addressed to a man named Kenneth. Robin's heart beat faster, and then a little faster as she understood more of what she was reading.

"It's a love letter," she whispered. Her grandmother had not signed it, and in fact, save for the name at the top of the letter, no other names were used. Only initials.

Robin felt like she was reading something she shouldn't, and she glanced over her shoulder to the doorway. Tessa and Mandie hadn't returned. She went back to the letter and finished reading it, then she set it next to the recipe of the baked beans.

"Definitely the same handwriting," she murmured to herself. Mandie had not mentioned any letters at all, least of all love letters. Robin pulled her phone from her purse and snapped a picture of the letter.

She wasn't sure why; she only knew she wanted to be able to see it whenever she wanted to see it. A tug of adrenaline and guilt had her pulse pouncing as she shoved her phone back in her bag and turned to leave.

She did have to get home and shower the sunscreen off her skin. She needed to dress nicely for tonight's tasting, as she had to meet with a bride and her mother at one of the nicer restaurants in the cove for their menu tasting. It really needed to be finalized by next week if they wanted to stay on schedule, and Robin couldn't even imagine dealing with Kamilla—the mother—if the wedding date got pushed back again.

Her daughter had already moved it twice, and that caused a lot of work for everyone involved. Outside, she tossed her bag onto the passenger seat and started the van so the air conditioning would start to cool the interior of the vehicle.

She sent a quick text to Mandie, telling her she and Jamie could order pizza for dinner that night, and then she tapped to go back to the main screen of her texting app. She hadn't spent a lot of time with her mom this summer, despite both of them trying to rebuild their connection now.

For so long, it had just been Robin trying to reach out to her mother, but she'd gone on a cruise this past Christmas that had caused a great change within her. Seemingly, as Robin didn't really know what had been the impetus for her mother's change of heart.

She'd started seeing someone for the first time since the death of Robin's father, and Robin liked her boyfriend, Mitch, just fine. They'd been dating for six months now, and Robin wasn't sure if she'd be planning her mom's wedding anytime soon—or at all. Mitch had moved to the cove a couple of months ago, so their relationship wasn't long-distance anymore, she knew that.

Otherwise, Robin had kept busy with her wedding planning business, getting Duke off to Alaska, and mothering her girls. Of course she still saw her mother, but she hadn't been focusing her attention there as much as perhaps she should've.

Now, she texted her. *Have you spoken to Mandie about your mother's recipes?*

*Yes, she's planning to bring them this weekend*, her mom responded.

*Did she tell you about anything else?*

*Like what?*

Robin took a moment and pulled up the picture of the love letter. Something told her not to say anything, because Mandie obviously knew about the letters and hadn't even told Robin yet.

*Nothing*, Robin said. *I'm meeting with a potential bride on Saturday, but if I can come with her, I will.*

*I'm doing a waffle bar*, her mom said. *Both of the girls are coming, and Mitch will be here.*

*Sounds fun*, Robin said, her stomach swooping and pinching at the same time. Would she have ever gotten invited to this weekend's breakfast buffet? Maybe Mandie just hadn't mentioned it to her yet. *How are things with Mitch? Getting serious?*

*You know what? We have started talking about getting married. His condo is so expensive, but I'm far too old to have a live-in boyfriend.*

Robin felt the same, but she didn't say anything. Her mother had proven over and over that she could—and would—do what she wanted. *Big ceremony or small?*

*Something small,* her mom said. *I don't even know that I need anyone there.*

Robin's stomach lurched now. She tapped to call her mom, and when she said, "Hello, dear," in her cool-as-water voice, Robin said, "I'd like to be there. The girls would too."

"I suppose I could invite your family and Stu's."

"Yes," Robin said. "I suppose you could." Her pulse throbbed in her throat. "And I could plan a dinner. Something simple. At my house. Or yours."

"That's an idea," her mom said, and Robin recognized an old tactic of not wanting to agree to anything just yet.

"If I'm going to crash something this weekend, I don't have to come."

"Of course not," her mom said. "Mandie and I just confirmed this morning. She probably just hasn't had time to talk to you yet."

Robin thought about the love letter, and her throat turned dry. "Yeah, we have a few things to talk about," she said. "See you soon, Mom."

"Good-bye, dear."

The call ended, and Robin made the drive home almost

numbly. Once there, she told herself she had a couple of minutes before she had to get in the shower and start getting ready for her business evening.

She pulled out the photo album she kept on the tall bookcase in her office. Only a few flips landed her on pictures of her grandmother and grandfather. Her mother's parents. As she gazed at the woman with dark hair, perfectly pinned in place, and a smile to match, more memories marched through her mind.

She only had memories of her grandmother from when she was very young, because she'd disappeared after that. Robin couldn't quite recall if she'd left the cove or if she'd passed away, but her memory didn't cough up anything about a funeral, and her eyes dropped to the names at the bottom of the page.

*Wedding day* had been printed there, in neat block capital letters.

Anna and Ralph Elmer.

"Not Kenneth," Robin murmured, wondering what it all meant—and if she'd get any answers from her mother even if she found the courage to ask.

# Chapter Thirteen

~∞~

**M**andie's backpack felt like it weighed ten million pounds as she picked it up from the floor of the passenger side of the van. She had the recipes and letters memorized at this point, as she laid in bed at night and either texted Charlie or read the old handwriting on the weathered pages.

Her mom had rearranged a meeting this morning so she could come with Mandie and Jamie to breakfast, and that only added to the snakes currently hissing in Mandie's stomach. She didn't know how to bring up the love letters in front of her mom. Her grandmother was terrifying enough, and having them both in the same room brought a tremor to Mandie's shoulders as she walked up the sidewalk on a clear summer's day.

"Grandma," Jamie yelled as she entered the house ahead of Mandie.

"Why did you bring a bag?" her mom asked, and Mandie glanced over to her.

"I'm going to work from here, and then Charlie's picking me up from work, remember?" She lifted her backpack higher onto her shoulder. "So I've got my work clothes and my date clothes in here. My purse."

Her mother's eyes shuttered for a moment, and then she smiled. "I forgot. You're working from eleven to three?"

Mandie nodded. "Then Charlie and I are going to a movie, and then...I don't know after that. We might just go back to his house, because Alice said she might order from that taco truck if they have the citrus chicken this weekend."

She smiled at her mom, trying to be and act natural. "Is that okay?"

"It's all okay." Her mom slung her arm around her shoulders. "Has Charlie found an apartment in the city?"

Mandie shook her head. "He and Ginny can't seem to find one." She'd be in fits if she didn't have an apartment to move into in just over two months, but she'd been trying to remain upbeat and positive for both Charlie and Ginny. She spoke to Charlie's sister almost every day too, and if someone asked her to name her best friend, Mandie would say Ginny.

The scent of yeast and bacon reached her nose, and Mandie's stomach growled. "I'm starving."

"There you are," her grandma said from the back corner of the house, and Mandie left her bag by the front door. Maybe she wouldn't bring up the recipes or the letters today at all. She found them interesting, but literally everything fifty years or older intrigued her.

"Grandma," she said, smiling as she moved to hug her. Most of the time, Mandie wasn't sure she even knew her grandmother, but things had started to improve in the past several months. "You've been cooking this morning."

"Yes, I have." She smiled at her and indicated Mitch, her boyfriend. "You two remember each other, I'm sure."

"Of course," Mandie said diplomatically. Mitch wore bright eyes and a smile to match, and Mandie honestly wasn't sure how the two of them had gotten together. They seemed like such opposites, and she wondered what people thought when they saw her and Charlie together. To her, they had plenty in common, though they certainly had things where they didn't agree or tastes that didn't align.

Mom moved over to Mitch, and the two of them started laughing and talking. Mandie felt like an outsider here, and she wasn't even sure why. Jamie had folded herself right into the kitchen, and she currently removed a stout bottle of syrup from their grandma's microwave.

Mandie felt too big for her skin, and she ran her hand up her opposite arm. "Grandma," she said, deciding to get the recipes out right now. Get them out of the way.

"Let's eat," her grandma said, and apparently, she hadn't heard Mandie say anything. She ducked back to the front door and stooped to get the pages out of her backpack, and then she allowed herself to get swept up in preparing to eat.

She sat at the table next to Jamie, the pages like a stack of bricks in her lap. Her mom caught her eye, and she knew something immediately. Her eyebrows went up, and she'd gotten fully ready this morning with makeup and curled hair, as her meeting had been set for right after this.

Mandie shook her head slightly, and Grandma set a plate stacked with thick and fluffy Belgian waffles in the middle of the table. "We've kept them warm in the oven." She sat and gazed around at everyone.

Mandie had once thought her grandmother cold and uncaring. At the very least, she was proper, much the way Mandie supposed a queen would act. She still portrayed that persona for Mandie, but now that she was older, she could see her grandma as more of a human and less of a wax figure.

She'd also seen some of her flaws, as all human beings had them, and that had made her more approachable. She'd learned how to forgive from her mother, and Mandie glanced over to her again.

"I'll start," Mitch said, and he tipped a waffle onto Jamie's plate, then Mandie's, then, her mom's, and then his. He passed the plate to Grandma, and she gave him a kind and polite smile before tearing a waffle in half and putting only two rounded triangles on her plate.

Jamie attacked the fruit and cream while Mom took a much gentler approach to the butter. Mandie wanted fruit and cream too, and while she waited, her pulse flew up into the back of her throat.

She cleared it away and looked at her grandmother. "Grandma," she said. "I brought the recipes." She lifted the aged papers up above the table so everyone could see them.

"Oh, of course." Grandma's smile came instantly, and it

lit the whole room. She reached for them, and Mandie felt a ping of reluctance as she handed them over. She knew she'd get them back. "I wonder if I donated them accidentally." She glanced over to Mom. "Or what happened."

"I don't know, Mom," Mandie's mother said quietly. She finished doctoring up her waffle, and Mandie distracted herself by spooning on strawberries, bananas and blueberries and then topping it all with cream.

"Tessa couldn't find anything in the donation logs for the armoire," Mandie said.

"This is my mother's crab cake recipe." Grandma looked up with wonder in her eyes. "I'm not even sure I have this one."

"We have a crab cake recipe," Mom said.

"But I don't think it's this one." Grandma gave her a look and moved the pages.

Mandie couldn't take a bite of her waffle. "There's—" Her dry throat stuck together; she reached for her glass of orange juice and took an acidic swallow. "There were some letters there too," she said. "I'm not sure if they're from your mother, but the handwriting looks the same to me."

"Letters?" Grandma flipped another page. The whole room went quiet. Not even Jamie or Mitch dared to cut a piece of waffle and eat it. "Oh, I see."

"Mom," Mandie's mother said. "Let me see." She cut Mandie a look out of the corner of her eye, the gesture coming and going so fast Mandie couldn't quite read her expression. She didn't sound too surprised about the letters, though Mandie had not shown or mentioned them to her.

To Mandie's surprise, her grandma passed over the whole stack of papers, picked up her fork, and took a bite of completely dry waffle.

"Are these from your mom?" Mandie's mother asked, and Mandie's gaze volleyed between her mom and her grandmother.

"Yes," Grandma said simply. She held her head high and then higher, her neck seeming to lengthen with every passing moment. "She had an affair when I was—oh, I don't know. I think it had been going on for years before we found out." She looked over to Robin. "I had you, dear, but you were quite small when she decided to leave the cove."

Mandie had not expected her grandmother to come out and tell the truth. So much of her past interactions with her had been shrouded in secrecy. Mom hadn't spoken to her mother for a while over some secrets just last year.

"So she didn't pass away?" Mandie's mom asked.

"No." Grandma reached for the fruit spoon, thankfully, because Mandie wasn't sure how she'd even gotten that single bite of dry waffle down without choking it back up. "She had an affair with Kenneth Sherman, and he refused to acknowledge her publicly. She left the cove in shame, and we never heard from her again."

"Ever?" Jamie asked, looking over to Mandie.

"I think my brother tracked her down at some point," Grandma said. "I was—well, we all know how I was."

No one said anything, and Mandie regretted bringing up the letters. She should've just brought the recipes and let

Grandma enjoy them. She reached for the papers and took them from her mother without much of a fight.

She folded them carefully and neatly tucked them under her leg. "I'll type up the recipes and give them to you," she said. "And I'll preserve these papers, so we can enjoy them in the future."

"Not the letters," Grandma said. "I don't care to see those again." She looked down her nose at her waffle and poked a strawberry half and ate it.

Mandie exchanged a look with her mother, and both of them knew they would not be destroying the letters. They could keep them, preserve them even, and not show them to Grandma or talk about them again.

The problem was, Mandie wanted the whole story, and she'd only gotten the very tip of the iceberg.

*Kenneth Sherman,* she thought, and light bulbs burst to life in her mind. How many Shermans could there be in the cove?

Besides the Police Chief and his father, the Mayor.

---

"I LOVE THE WEEKEND." CHARLIE GRINNED AS HE dropped to the towel where Mandie had stayed while he'd gone swimming. He reached for her and brought her face to his. "Mm, I get to see you every day, and the sun today is phenomenal."

"It is," Mandie said against his lips. Then she sat up again, her gaze going out to the horizon. She'd enjoyed last night with him too, and today, they'd come to the beach during the quieter morning hours when everyone else sat in church.

She put her book away and lay down next to him. Charlie took her into his arms, and while salt water clung to him, Mandie didn't mind. "I love spending time with you," she whispered. "Anything on the apartments?"

"Nothing," he said with a sigh. "That one Ginny went and looked at with Erika yesterday is gone already."

"Already?"

"Already." His hand slid down to her elbow and back up to her bicep, then back down. "We're looking as if we can move in together, but student apartments don't allow males and females to cohabitate."

"Maybe you two can find a place that's not student housing."

Charlie didn't say anything for a moment, and then he said, "That's an idea."

"I have no idea how much a non-student apartment would be," she said. "Probably a lot."

"Maybe with the two of us sharing, we could afford it."

Mandie didn't know, and she didn't want anything to ruin today. She dropped the topic, and Charlie didn't continue it. He didn't say anything, and Mandie closed her eyes against the perfect blue sky, the glorious sunshine, and she listened to the beautiful sound of the waves.

"Mandie?" Charlie asked.

"Hmm?"

He didn't say anything, and Mandie tilted her head back to look at him. "Charlie?"

"I just—I need to tell you something, and I—you—" He exhaled and took in another breath. Mandie didn't like the tension radiating from him, and she wanted their carefree Sunday back.

"I'm in love with you," he whispered.

Mandie's heartbeat grew wings, and it flew right out of her body. She sat up and looked at him. "What?"

"You heard me." He gazed up at her, a smile slowly curving that mouth she loved. "And I don't want you to say anything unless you mean it."

Her foot wiggled and bounced as her thoughts took off, flying at five hundred miles per hour. They got away from her before she could catch a single one, and she blinked.

"I see you spinning." He pulled on her hand and said, "Lie back down, sweetheart. I was enjoying that."

She did settle into his arms again, because she'd been enjoying her place there too. "Charlie."

"Mandie, I'm fine."

"Of course I've thought about how I feel about you," she said. "You're the only person I want to spend my free time with. I—we've talked about so many things. Intimate things."

She watched a couple walk in front of them, hand-in-hand, talking. It could've easily been her and Charlie. They'd talked about being intimate—they both wanted to do that, though they haven't spoken of it since the sunset on Rocky Ridge.

"Yeah," he said.

She often needed more time to sort through things. To really analyze how she felt from all angles. To find a way to get her thoughts to slow enough for her to latch on to. But with this, she found she didn't need any of that.

A feeling rose within her, becoming brighter and brighter and stronger and stronger. She smiled as let the cleansing wash of love flow through her.

"And I love you," she said. She propped herself up on her elbow and looked at him. With those gorgeous eyes, he simply looked back at her. "I—" Mandie leaned down and touched her mouth to his.

She didn't normally kiss in public, and certainly not right on the beach for anyone and everyone to see. But she couldn't help kissing him now, and she couldn't stop either.

He kissed her carefully for a stroke or two, then deeper and with more passion. Mandie matched him move for move, and she pulled back and breathed, "I love you, Charlie."

"I love you too," he murmured back, and then he kissed her again.

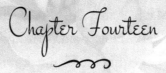

## Chapter Fourteen

E loise put a big bowl of salad on the table and glanced over to where Robin chatted with Aaron in the living room.

"Wild rice," Grace said as she put it on the table beside the grilled fish.

"Thank you, honey," Eloise said, smiling at the girl. "What else did you learn in your cooking class this week?" She smoothed the girl's honeyed hair off the side of her face, love for this child streaming through her.

Grace came alive all over again, as if she hadn't been bubbling and bouncing around the kitchen for the past hour as she made dinner for Robin and her girls. "It was all rice dishes," she said. "I've got to work on the risotto, because mine didn't turn out in class."

"Risotto is really hard," Robin said as she caught the tail end of the conversation. She held a glass of sparkling water with lime, as she didn't drink much. Eloise didn't either, and they both had children and jobs to keep up with.

She smiled at Grace. "Are you going to become a chef?"

Grace exchanged a glance with Eloise, who nodded slightly at her. "Maybe," she said. "I really like cooking."

"It's time to eat," Eloise said, sparing the thirteen-year-old from having her entire life planned out tonight. "Aaron, baby. It's time to eat."

He'd obviously gotten some sort of work text, because he'd been bent over his phone. He looked up now, and he moved to set his phone on the shelf, where it wouldn't bother them during dinner.

"What did my beauties make tonight?" He grinned as he approached the table, and Eloise couldn't stop the curvature of her mouth either.

"I made wild rice and fish," Grace said. "Billie and Addie and Ian caught them down in that bay where everyone gets fish." She smiled over to Billie as she came out of the office with Addie and Ian. None of them touched each other, but Eloise still examined them for any other signs of misconduct.

What she might find, she didn't know, but she felt like she had to look. "You guys ready?" she asked. "Find a spot."

"Over here," Billie said, and she moved down to the end of the table closest to where Eloise would sit. Mandie, Robin, and Jamie took the other side of the table, and Eloise shared the end with Grace, with Aaron down on the other end from her.

He seemed utterly relaxed and calm, and Eloise decided that had to be because of his police training, because her stomach had tied itself into a knot the moment Robin had called—called, not texted—to ask if Eloise, Aaron, and the girls would come over for dinner.

"Just you guys," Robin had chirped out in a totally false, cheerful tone.

"All of us?" Eloise had asked. Sure, they had beach days and backyard barbecues and ham dinners on Easter with their entire families. But those occurrences weren't nearly as often as the Wednesday lunches or the walks in the morning or any number of other get-togethers the women had with one another.

But Aaron was swamped this summer, and Eloise had thought it would be easier to have Robin and her girls here, to the northeast side of Diamond Island, at their house, than try to get Aaron off work on time and to someone's house for dinner.

He'd arrived mere minutes before Robin as it was, and she cast him a look from down the table, which she and the girls had put the leaf in to be able to accommodate everyone.

"Let's eat," Aaron said, and he reached for the platter of fish, which Grace had arranged with sprigs of thyme and rounds of lemon.

"Daddy, you take a wedge and squeeze it over the fish," Grace said. She half stood up. "And I made this dilly sauce to go with it. It's really good."

Billie reached for the salad, and Eloise took the bowl from her after she'd taken some. The food went around, and the conversations started. Jamie sat between Billie and Grace in age, and she wasn't in the same grade as the teens across from her. But she knew them, obviously, and they chit-chatted easily.

Mandie talked with Robin, and Aaron seemed to be listening to the teens down by him.

Eloise filled her plate with food while Grace flitted around to make sure everyone got the food, sauces, and seasonings they needed and wanted. When she finally returned to her seat, Eloise smiled at her and said, "It's great, Grace."

"Thanks."

Eloise turned her attention to Robin, whose knee she practically touched. "So," she said. "What's going on?"

Robin swallowed the food in her mouth and looked over to Mandie. Eloise didn't like that at all, and she really just wanted a nice, normal summer. The politics in Five Island Cove still smothered her personally, though tensions as a whole had gone down considerably in the past few months.

The town had genuinely tried to make improvements for the tourist season, and as far as Eloise could tell, they'd achieved a lot of them. There were more RideShare drivers than ever, and she hadn't had a single guest at the inn complain about long wait-times or the inability to get a flight in or out of the cove.

Aaron still didn't have all the cops he'd been funded for, but they seemed to have enough for now—mostly because he had young bucks who didn't mind working double shifts or picking up extra hours. Younger men, right out of the Academy, who didn't have wives or families waiting for them at home.

Mandie cleared her throat while Eloise speared a half of a cherry tomato. "We found some letters," she said.

"I don't want to see them," Eloise said instantly. Her reaction to finding things that had been hidden brought on a sense of trauma she hadn't had to deal with in a long time. She leaned back, away from her plate. "I really don't."

"It's not bad," Robin said.

"Finding letters is always bad," Eloise argued. "Remember the notes Kristen found after Joel died? Or the box of letters I found in the wall? Or what about all those mysterious emails we all got after the tsunami?"

She'd spoken too loud, and now the other conversations at the table had petered out. Billie, Addie, and Ian all looked at her, as did Aaron from down at the end of the table.

Her heart pounded against her ribcage, and her mouth felt too full of saliva. She swallowed, her adrenaline thrashing through her body. "Or the stuff Kelli found hidden in her yoga studio? Or the secrets that Laurel had to uncover to root out the drug problem here in the cove?" She looked around at the others now, as if challenging them all to disagree with her.

"Or the hidden things that brought Scott and Clara to the cove?" She shook her head. "The newspaper clippings that made Kristen doubt everything she thought she knew about the lighthouse? The ownership of it?"

Eloise shook her head. "No. No, thank you. I don't care about any letters you found."

Robin blinked, a familiar fire entering her gaze that told Eloise she wouldn't let this go. "It's about my grandmother," she said, and to Eloise's surprise, she swung her attention to Aaron. "And your grandfather."

Aaron sat there calmly, as usual. The only time Eloise saw him get upset at all was over the girls—or her—and she normally appreciated his even demeanor, his level head. He could get carried away in the bedroom too, but Eloise had no complaints about that either.

"My grandfather?" he asked. "Which one?"

"Kenneth Sherman," Mandie said, her voice croaking out of her mouth.

"My father's father," Aaron said.

"Right," Robin said. "My grandmother had an affair with him, then left the cove."

"All right," Aaron said easily, shooting a glance to Billie and then Grace. "Why does this matter, two generations later?"

"We've been doing a little bit of research," Mandie said carefully. "And we think she might've been pregnant when she left."

"No." Robin held up one hand. "We know she was pregnant. We know she delivered a baby boy in Boston. What we can't find is any record of either of them after that."

"So what are you saying?" Eloise asked. "What does this have to do with us?"

"Well," Robin said. "I guess I'd like to know if I'm related to Aaron."

Eloise's mind whirred, trying to match up the genealogical dots. "I don't—"

"You think my father has a half-sibling somewhere?" Aaron asked.

"Or he's their son," Robin said, holding her head high. "Which makes us...something."

"At least I'm not the only one who doesn't know what that would make you," Billie said.

Mandie actually smiled, and Eloise told herself to put her shoulders down. *Relax*, she coached herself. *They're not accusing you of anything.*

"I don't either," Mandie said. "But I guess if your dad's father is my grandmother's half-brother, then he's my half... cousin?"

"Yes," Robin said. "Once removed. Aaron would be my half-cousin, straight up."

Aaron actually smiled. "Wow. I have no idea how you figured that out."

Robin grinned down to him. "The Internet."

"Of course." He chuckled, but Eloise just wanted this conversation to die and for the talk to move on to something else.

"It sounds like you already know everything," Billie said.

"Except if Mayor Sherman is my half-uncle," Robin said, moving her gaze to her.

"Why does it matter?" Eloise asked.

"Because," Robin said. "Have you heard of that fertility doctor who fathered over a hundred children? And a whole bunch of them didn't leave town, and they live within a five-mile radius of each other. And they don't know they're related." She leaned forward, her expression more earnest now as she looked around at everyone. "What if they start dating? What if Aaron and I had dated in high school or gotten married? We grew up together, not knowing we were related."

"Okay," Eloise said. "I get it."

"It matters." Robin picked up her fork and stabbed a piece of lettuce. "The truth always matters." She shoved her salad in her mouth in a overdramatic way, about the way Robin did things she was passionate about.

"Okay," Aaron said. "What do we need to do?"

"You could take a DNA test," Mandie said, looking at her mom. "You both could. You could register on that same genetic website those kids of the fertility doctor did. Did you know that's how they found each other? All these matches popped up, and it showed that they all had the same dad."

A beat of silence filled the dining room, and then Grace asked, "How many were there?"

"A lot," Mandie said. "They sued him and everything. I don't really know what happened after that."

"It's a story for another time," Eloise said, shooting a look at Robin and Mandie.

"Well, I'm not going to do a website like that," Aaron said. "But we can take buccal swabs and send 'em to the lab on the mainland. With something like this, as it's non-priority, it might be a few weeks until we know."

Robin nodded like this was the answer she'd come here to get. "I can live with that."

"Come on down to the station in the morning then," he said. "Now, Ian. I hear you're on the committee that's plan-

ning the Homecoming Dance at the high school this year."
He pointed his fork toward Robin. "Did you know you're
sitting with a woman who's done that before? She might be
able to give you some pointers."

Eloise once again marveled at him—and at the way Ian's
face lit up as he turned toward Robin. "Really? Could I ask
you a few things?"

Robin loved attention like that, and she grinned and
grinned as she said, "Of course. Ask anything you want."

Eloise looked down the table to Aaron, falling in love
with him all over again as he smiled at her, and they had an
entire conversation in the space of a few seconds. She'd never
know if this revelation had bothered him while they sat there
and finished their meal. But she'd ask him later, when they
were alone behind a closed door, and then she'd get to the
truth.

Because as Robin had said, the truth mattered.

---

"So?" Eloise asked as she unbuttoned her
blouse. Aaron stood in the bathroom, brushing his teeth.
"What do you really think about you and Robin being
cousins?"

He spat and reached for the glass. "I think there are
worse things in the world."

Eloise pulled her pajama top over her head. "She's always
a bit dramatic, don't you think?"

He rinsed and flipped off the light as he came into the

bedroom. "Sure, but we know Robin. She's just intense about things she cares about." He smiled at her slightly and took her into his arms. "I mean, I didn't date her. I didn't marry her. So even if it is true, there's not been any harm in it." He pressed his lips to her cheek, then dropped them to her neck. "You smell nice."

He kissed her then, and Eloise responded eagerly. "You've been busy at work this summer."

"I know," he murmured. "But I'm not busy with anything right now."

"Are you really not worried about this?" she asked. "Your father is the Mayor. What if this has some impact on him?"

"It's an old story," he said as he slid his hands up her back. "It's not his fault he was born out of wedlock, to two adults having an affair." He pulled back. "I really don't see the scandal here, and besides, it's not like Robin will go on the news and make some damning announcement."

"No," Eloise murmured, her mind moving quickly through several scenarios. "You're right."

"Now, can you please focus?" he teased. "We haven't made love in a while, and I *need* you tonight."

Eloise smiled back at him. "Oh, you do, huh?"

"Yes," he whispered. "Desperately." He kissed her again, and Eloise did love the way he cherished her. He was right; it didn't really matter if it turned out that he and Robin were related. If anything, then Eloise would be related through marriage to one of her very best friends in the whole world.

It would be nice to know the truth, and they would know that soon enough.

# Chapter Fifteen

Mandie couldn't stop smiling as she wheeled the E-bike off the ferry at Rocky Ridge. She hadn't been here since Charlie had brought her here to watch the sunset. She hadn't had to cart the fourteen paperback books she'd deliver today, because Tessa had had them shipped from the library to the police and emergency services outpost here on the island.

She'd pick them up there and do the route she'd mapped out for Rocky Ridge and Sanctuary Island. Tomorrow, she'd deliver another fifteen books to people on Diamond Island, and then she only had to do eleven for Pearl and Bell Islands.

That was only forty books, and their final registration had ended at sixty-two. The other twenty-two participants had opted to get a digital copy of the book, and Tessa was sending those today with a few clicks of her mouse.

"She definitely got the easier job," Mandie said to herself

as she went past the line of people queuing up at the Ride-Share podium.

But she didn't mind. She strapped the helmet on her head and mounted the E-bike. She'd already ridden it a couple of times, because it accelerated differently than the pedal-bike she'd been using to get around this summer.

The wind flew in her face, and Mandie had never felt so free. She did love riding a bike, and there wasn't anywhere better than the cove. Her flurry of thoughts landed on Charlie, and where they might end up if they kept dating, graduated college, got married, and actually started their lives together as one.

Since he'd told her he loved her, Mandie couldn't fall asleep at night without hearing it and smiling about it. She often giggled too, then felt silly for being so giddy. But she loved him too, and she saw no reason they wouldn't keep dating, graduate from college, get married, and actually start their lives together as one.

Charlie wanted to go into pharmaceuticals, and Mandie had no idea how long it would take him to get that degree. She wanted to graduate too, but such a thing felt like such a long way off.

Her parents would want her to just go ahead and get married if she and Charlie were going to stay together, because they'd see no reason not to. Mandie could admit she couldn't really see a reason not to either, other than she hadn't anticipated falling in love so soon in her life.

"Maybe we could live together," she said aloud, the thought just manifesting itself and flowing out of her mouth. Then she laughed at herself, because if she thought her parents would flip out over her and Charlie getting married sooner rather than later—or never—they certainly wouldn't be on board for the two of them living together without being married.

But he didn't have an apartment—and neither did Ginny. Her ideas started to swirl and paint the sky with color, but Mandie didn't let any of them cross her vocal cords.

She arrived at the station and went inside. "Hey," she said to the man sitting there. He looked up, then jumped to his feet, his eyes widening. Mandie had pulled her helmet off outside, and her hair could be matted to her forehead for all she knew.

"Hello, there," he said. "What can I help you with?"

Mandie casually reached up and pushed her hair back. Nope, not matted. "I'm, uh, here for the books? I'm Mandie Grover with the library."

"Mandie Grover with the library," he repeated, and he relaxed against the side of the desk. "We don't get many pretty girls coming in here."

Mandie smiled at him. "Well, today you've got one. I should have some books here that I need to deliver."

"Yeah, I think we've got them over here." He moved over to a counter in front of the window, all of the things he wore on his body clinking and wrinkling and making noise.

"How do you stand to wear all of that all day?" she asked.

He picked up the box of books and faced her. "You get used to it, I suppose." He gave her a dazzling smile, a dimple appearing in his right cheek. "Here you go."

"Thanks." Mandie took the box from him and peered inside. "Can I bring the box back to you? I'm on a bike, and I can't carry it."

"Sure. I'll help you get loaded up." He took the box back from her and motioned for her to go outside first. She held the door for him, noting his flirtatious smile as he went by.

"The E-bike there," she said. "We had it fitted with a container on the back for the books."

"I see that." The cop took a few steps toward the bike. "What's all this for?"

"The bicycle book club," she said proudly. "It's our first one, and we have over sixty people signed up."

"Wow." He balanced the box on the seat and opened the compartment that had been affixed to the front handlebars. "There's not sixty books in this box."

"Nope." She smiled as he started transferring the blue-covered books to the compartment. "I'm only doing Rocky Ridge and Sanctuary today. Some people opted for eBooks. That kind of thing."

"Ah, I see." He finished up and lowered the box. "Well, there you go, Miss."

"Thank you." She dropped her gaze to the name badge on his chest. "Officer Mallroy."

"It's Dex," he said. "Could I get your number? It can get lonely out here on Rocky Ridge, and I'd love to take you to dinner after a long day of no pretty girls coming into this outpost." He grinned, and he was smooth. And cute.

Mandie smiled and shook her head. "I'm sorry. I'm seeing someone."

"Ah." He nodded, a slight flush crawling into his face. "Lucky guy." He backed away and saluted her. "Have a great day, Mandie."

"You too, Officer." Mandie re-mounted her E-bike and got on her way. If she'd been single, she'd have given him her number. Gone out with him. Seen if they had a spark hot enough to build a relationship over.

But as it was, she wasn't single, and she rather liked the fire she and Charlie had been building for the past couple of years. It was nice to be called pretty, and it was flattering to have another man look at her.

But looking would be all that happened, and Mandie merrily went on her way, delivering the books for the first ever bicycle book club in Five Island Cove.

"IT WAS AMAZING," SHE SAID LATER THAT EVENING. She reached for a breadstick and broke it in half. "I don't think I've ever lived a better day."

Charlie chuckled as he took a breadstick from the basket that had just been brought too. All they'd ordered here at Seafarers was bread and salad, as they couldn't afford entrées. He certainly couldn't, not if he and Ginny were really going to try to get an apartment together in the city. She'd been looking for such a thing now, and it sure would be cheaper if they could stomach living together in a studio.

But Mandie didn't want to ask about the apartment hunt, as they talked about it all the time, and surely Charlie had grown weary of it. "Mm, I love this Alfredo sauce," she said instead. She beamed at him from across the table. "Thank you for bringing me here. It's the perfect ending to a perfect day."

"Biking around the northern islands is the perfect day," he said, not phrasing it as a question. "Good to know."

"You know what I mean. This is exciting. It's a new program here in the cove—one I've helped with, Charlie."

"I know, baby doll." He smiled at her and dipped his bread in the Alfredo sauce too. "You should always have bread and salad when you want it."

"Yes, sir," she agreed, and she let the radiance she felt flow from her "You should."

They ate for a minute in silence, and then Charlie said, "Ginny called this afternoon."

"Did she?"

He nodded, and he'd grown quiet. Not just in voice, but in every other way. Mandie had seen him shrink into himself before, and she didn't like it. He always came out of his shell again for her, and she simply waited for him to say whatever he needed to say next.

"There's a one-bedroom apartment," he said. "One bath. Six hundred square feet."

"Wow," Mandie said. "That's downright huge."

"Big enough for a full-sized couch," he said. "One with a bed in it." He cleared his throat and glanced out of the booth. He looked at whatever out there, and then he sighed as he returned his attention to her. "We can't afford it."

"I wouldn't think so," she said carefully. "Families live in one-bedroom apartments in New York City."

"We could if...maybe...if we had a roommate."

Mandie stopped chewing, though she'd just taken another bite of her breadstick. "A roommate?" she said around the food in her mouth. "Who would you--?"

His eyebrows went up, and Mandie quickly started chewing so she could swallow and speak properly. She didn't chew enough, and the chunk of bread slid down her throat painfully and then got stuck.

She coughed and reached for her glass of water.

"Oh, come on." Charlie grinned at her, but he wasn't as relaxed as he normally was. "You're milking this."

She cleared her throat. "I am not."

"I should've texted you," he said. "To give you time to think about it before you had to talk to me about it in person."

"It's not a crime to think about things," Mandie said.

"I know." He reached across the table and took both of her hands in his. She was the one peering out of the booth now, trying to find something to focus on for a moment. "Ginny and I need an apartment. I want to be with you. You and I—I mean, we said we loved each other last week. Why shouldn't we live together?"

"I can think of a few reasons," Mandie said. "And they're named Alice, Robin, and Duke." She pulled her hands away and leaned back into the cushioned seat of the booth. Neither of them said anything, and she'd lost her appetite for bread and fattening sauces.

"It was just an idea," he said. "A bad one, I can see."

Mandie pulled her gaze back to him as she folded her arms across herself in an attempt to protect herself. "How much more than my student housing would it be? Because it has to be more."

"Only about seventy dollars a month," he said. "It's not a big apartment. My dad has said he'd subsidize it for us."

Her eyebrows went up this time. "You're going to take money from your dad?" That totally surprised her, because Charlie had not wanted much to do with his father since the divorce. Since he'd moved to Five Island Cove.

He lifted one shoulder in a shrug, and he was so sexy when he did that. His mind worked overtime too, but he hid it better. Mandie drew in a long breath, knowing he saw it. "Seventy dollars isn't that much."

"No," he said.

She uncinched her arms from across her chest and reached for her bread again. "Who's going to sleep on the couch? You?"

His dark eyes glinted. "I hope not," he said quietly. "I'm assuming Ginny would."

"You haven't talked with her about it? Who does she think will be your roommate and where would you all sleep?"

"We didn't have much time this afternoon," he said. "I had maybe four minutes before my tour began, and she was rushing across the city to work."

"So how did you leave it?"

"I said we better start thinking about who we could ask to live with us." He looked up as the waitress brought their bowl of salad.

"Anything else I can get for you two?"

"No, thank you," Charlie said with a smile.

"I'll get you more bread." She grinned back at him and tucked her hair behind her ear, which was a silly move, as she'd pulled her hair back into a ponytail.

"Who do you think she'll suggest?" Mandie asked.

"I honestly don't know. She had a couple of roommates last year she liked. Maybe one of them."

"So maybe she thinks you'll be sleeping on the couch." Mandie let him tong up a plate of salad, and he put all the tomatoes and a whole heap of croutons on it. Then he slid it across the table to her in a sweet gesture that reminded her of how well he took care of her. Of why she'd fallen in love with him.

"Do you think she'd mind living with us?" Mandie asked. "I can't believe I even said that out loud." She forked up some salad and slid a crouton onto the utensil too. "I mean, we're together Charlie. We'll be...sleeping together. With your sister just down the hall on the couch? It's weird."

"Is it?"

"Yes," she said emphatically. "It is." She put her salad in

177

her mouth, and the tartness of the dressing making a party there. "Mm, I love this stuff."

Charlie took his own bite of salad, and he nodded. "Me too."

"How are we--?"

"Let's just sit on it for a few days," he said, his expression turning a touch sharp. "Okay? We don't have to know every detail today, nor do we need to know how every moment will look if it does happen. All right?"

Mandie's chest stung, but she nodded. "You're right." She took another bite of salad as his eyes softened.

"Mandie, I'm sorry." He hung his head. "You just tend to get ahead of yourself sometimes, and I can feel you quietly freaking out."

"You just asked me to live with you and your sister," she said. "I can't even imagine what my mother will say."

"I'm going to talk to mine about it soon," he said. "She said she'll support me—us—in anything, and I guess we'll see if that's true or not."

Mandie stared openly at him. "You're—she said that?"

"When I told her I was in love with you." He took another bite of salad and wiped his breadstick along the dressing on the edge of the bowl before he looked at her again. "Your mom might not be as upset as you're imagining."

She took another bite of dinner, contemplating what he'd said. "You might be right."

"And that kills you, doesn't it?"

She matched the grin on his face with one of her own. "No," she said. "I like it when you remind me my crazy thoughts might not be warranted." She reached across the table and covered his hand this time. "But I do still need to think about this."

"And I need to talk to Ginny," he said. "We don't have to say anything to anyone yet. It's just an idea, and it could be a really bad one." He turned his hand over and laced his fingers through hers. As he squeezed, he said, "Promise me you won't be up at night, thinking about this."

She gave him a soft smile. "I promise."

"All right." He looked out into the restaurant again. "Now, what's taking so long to get that extra bread?"

Mandie giggled, because he was so cute—and she wanted extra bread too.

*Living with him?* she thought, her mind already going back into overdrive. *How is it that you thought that today while delivering the books and then he brings it up tonight?*

Mandie wasn't a huge believer in fate, but this felt like a huge coincidence. She also hadn't realized how much further ahead of her he was. Talking to his mom about their relationship, being prepared to bring up something as delicate as living together, all of it.

She needed to do the same, and that would require a level of courage she didn't know she had. So, for tonight, she ate bread and salad and kissed Charlie outside the restaurant before he took her home, because he did calm her and open new pathways in her mind.

When he pulled up to her house, he leaned across the

console and kissed her again. "I love you, baby doll. See you tomorrow."

Mandie looked right at him, and she had enough courage to say, "I love you too, Charlie. Thanks for tonight." She meant the food, but also simply his company, for driving her around, for being him.

For loving her.

# Chapter Sixteen

T essa entered the basement room in the library, but she'd transformed it in the past six weeks since beginning as the Assistant Director. Now, the far wall held bookcases full of beautiful volumes, with comfortable chairs set up for reading and relaxing.

The Wi-Fi had gotten an upgrade so it worked down here, and the most recent edition had been a grouping of couches that Tessa had moved this way and then that until they sat in exactly the right spot.

She'd brought in lamps and put in bright LED bulbs, so this room didn't feel like it was underground. Each couch had an end table on either side of it, and she'd brought in succulents, because they were easy to care for, unique, and small enough that patrons could set their phones or bottles of water beside them.

Yes, she'd convinced Bonnie to allow patrons to have water in the library, though she'd seen a few women down here with their tumblers of diet cola too. She'd said nothing, even with them in plain sight, because she was just so happy people had started to use what she'd created for them.

This was an adults-only room, and no children's books, activities, or furniture existed down here. So adults could handle having bottled water, and in fact, Tessa had gotten approval for a vending machine that sold it—and they'd sold out within three days when the supplier wouldn't be back for a week.

Her nerves buzzed with anticipation, because the book club would begin in just another hour. She'd wanted to simply stay at work to get everything set up, but Bonnie had shooed her out of the library about three p.m. Her and Mandie both, with Dusky the cat meowing his agreement.

So she'd gone home. She'd paced in the beach bungalow, and she'd texted Maddy and Julia, asking them if they'd please come a little early in case she needed any last-minute help getting set up.

She'd changed out of her professional slacks and blouse and into a denim skirt with a matching top. She loved the jean look, and this outfit wasn't made of the stiffer denim, but something soft and brushed that made her feel elegant and rich.

"Like Alice," she murmured to herself. "Alice must feel like this everywhere she goes." The thought made her smile, and she launched into action. Mandie's boss would be here with the refreshments in a half-hour, and Tessa needed to have the tables ready for him.

She pulled them out of the storage room where they'd

THE BICYCLE BOOK CLUB

moved all the books they couldn't get rid of in the sale, and she'd just finished with the third one when the door opened.

Mandie and Robin walked in, and they both wore a pretty dress. Robin's was a soft blue that complimented her eyes, and it had sleeves and an appropriate neckline for a woman about to turn fifty. Mandie's white dress held soaring butterflies in all different colors, barely had straps, and made her look like a million bucks.

"Don't worry," she said. "I have my shawl. I just need to grab it out of the office." She didn't slow as she went by Tessa, her pursuit of her crocheted coverup obvious. Robin did, though, and she eased into Tessa's arms.

"This place is amazing," she said. "I've never seen it like this before."

"It's a work in progress," she said. "I want more book-shelves for the opposite wall, and then we'll need more seat-ing, of course."

"I'm sure Bonnie loves all the budget request forms you're submitting."

Tessa grinned and grinned. "She loves them, yes." She surveyed the room again. "Tables are up for refreshments. I need to get the seating done, and I want to include the couches."

"We came early so we could get a soft seat," Robin said.

"And to help," Mandie added as she returned to the room with her shoulders covered now. "Charlie's only a minute behind us, and let's let him do the heavy lifting."

"Good idea," Robin said as she moved over to one of the

couches and put her purse on the end cushion. "I bet me, Alice, Maddy, and Julia can cram all onto this one."

"The front is here," Tessa said, moving to stand directly across from the tables she'd set up, directly in front of the camera broadcasting the book club to the outer islands. "So that couch doesn't have to move, but the others will."

"This table goes here, right?" Mandie asked as she flopped the fourth and last one onto its side. "This is where the books and signage goes?"

"Yes," Tessa said. "I brought it out and put it on the chair over there." She went to get it while Robin helped Mandie with the table.

Charlie arrived, and he wore a pair of khaki shorts and a button-up shirt in deep blue at the bottom that faded to white by his shoulder. "Hello, Tessa," he said pleasantly.

"Hello, there." She smiled at him and nodded to the couches. "We need that group broken open. So three of those have to move, as do the lamps."

"I can carry a lamp," Mandie said, and she beamed at Charlie and kissed him quickly on the mouth. A peck, if that, but Tessa could see the spark between them. She couldn't let that get out of the control here, or all the dry pages of the books would go up in an inferno.

She set up the welcome signs and the book poster she'd made for tonight's club. Then, she started helping Robin and Mandie set up chairs to go with the couches as Charlie pushed them this way and that.

"Hello," a man's voice boomed, and Tessa raised her head to find a tall tow-headed man carrying an enormous dispenser of water with oranges, lemons, and limes stuck to the outside.

She went to meet him at the tables, her heartbeat thudding strangely in her chest. It had to be because this was so real now. It had been a concept for so long, but the moment was literally here.

"You must be David," she said.

"Dave will do." He smiled at her and extended his hand. "And you're Tessa."

"Yes, sir." She shook his hand, something zinging up her arm and lodging in her elbow. She blinked, not sure if she could trust anything tonight. Not with her nerves already at the heightened end of excitement.

She cleared her throat and pulled her hand back, looking at the water to give herself something besides Dave's handsome face to focus on. "Thank you so much for doing this. I've got signs for you too." She gestured to the room as a whole behind her. "Back there. I'll make sure we thank you vocally too, right at the beginning."

"It's my pleasure," he said, smiling in a symmetrical way, with two neat rows of white teeth. Tessa definitely recognized the attraction moving through her, but she had no idea what to do about it. She wasn't as young as she'd once been, and it had been a while since she'd flirted with a man to let him know she was interested in him.

She'd never really done that with Abe at all, and besides, she didn't even know if Dave was single or not. She also wasn't sure how old he was, but he had to be close to forty.

*He better be forty,* she thought. Or she'd feel like she was having improper thoughts.

"I'll—uh—I've got something else to do," he said, and Tessa realized neither of them had moved.

"The cookies," she said. "I hope I left you enough room."

"There are three tables here." He looked at them, and Tessa did the same, just now realizing how much space they had. "It's cookies and rice crispy treats."

"Do you need help bringing them in?"

"No, I—yes." He smiled at her. "Yes, I absolutely need help bringing them in. Can they spare you in here?"

"It's setting up chairs," she said. "I think they'll be fine." She pushed her hair back and blew out her breath. "Plus, I could use a minute outside of this room." She pressed both palms over her stomach. "I'm so nervous."

Dave took in the room, and then he looked right at her. Right into her eyes. "It sure seems like you're completely prepared, and you don't need to worry if you're prepared."

Tessa narrowed her eyes and smiled at him. "Are you one of those preppers?"

He tilted his head back and laughed. The sound of it filled the room and made Tessa think the word *boisterous.*

She laughed a little too, simply because his was so infectious, but no one heard it. Not even her. Dave looked at her, all glitter and stars, and he asked, "Should we?"

"Yes," she said. "Let's sneak out while we can." She went with him, only taking a moment to tell Mandie she'd be right back.

"No problem," she said. "Hey, Mister Shepherd."

"Hi, Mandie." Dave let Tessa go upstairs first, and she wasn't sure if she liked that or not. She'd been a little sweaty downstairs, and climbing sixteen of them only added to that. She tried to control her breathing, so he wouldn't hear her panting, and thankfully, by the time he came to her side, they'd reached the exit.

She wasn't sure why she expected the outdoor air to cool her down. The evening had reached the pinnacle of heat, and the sun wouldn't go down for hours. Tessa breathed in the air, trying to catch a hint of breeze or salt, but she didn't get either.

"Don't worry," he said. "I left the van running, so the AC's on."

"I wasn't worried," Tessa said. She went with him to the pink-painted van parked against the curb. "Do you actually drive this?" She giggled at the curly lettering along the side of it, the giant cartoon soda cup with eyes bringing her such joy.

"Yes," he said. "It takes a real man to drive a pink van."

"Your, uh, wife doesn't drive it?"

"No, she doesn't," Dave said, and Tessa's smile flattened. "Because she's an ex-wife, and she lives in North Carolina now." He gave her a flash of a smile, and she couldn't tell if pain accompanied it or not.

"I'm sorry," Tessa said. "I didn't mean to bring up something hard."

"It's not hard," he said as he pulled open the back doors

of the van. Cool air flowed out, and Tessa saw there were two trays: one full of cookies shaped like trees and frosted with bright green foliage on the top and a stripe of brown for the trunk.

"My goodness," Tessa said. "Those are the cutest cookies in the world."

"Mandie said the book was *The Echoes of Avalon Park*," Dave said. "I looked up the cover, and since it has all those trees on it, I figured this might be good." He pulled the tray out and handed it to her. He then slid the one with rice crispy treats on it from the built-in rack, and Tessa realized in that moment that he could've carried both of these in by himself.

She turned to go back inside as he said, "I'll come back out for the lemonade and tea."

"I'm not helping with those," she said. "They'll be heavy, and I'm already sweating like a cow."

"A beautiful cow," he said.

Tessa gasped and turned back to him just as he slammed the doors to the van. He then stepped up onto the curb, apparently not realizing she hadn't continued walking. "Oh." He nearly hit her, and Tessa blinked at him.

"Did you just call me...a cow?"

"No." His face blanked and then started to turn red. "I mean, it was a compliment. You're not a cow. I think—I—I think you're *beautiful*, and I'm really hoping you're not married and don't have a boyfriend, because I'm not married and don't have a girlfriend, and I'd like to go out with you."

All of his words rushed over one another, and they raced past Tessa's eardrums and into her brain. "Well," she said, the world spinning a little too fast now. "All right."

"All right?" Dave smiled at her "Yes, all right. Tomorrow night? Are you available?"

"Yes," Tessa whispered. "Tomorrow's fine."

"So I'll get your number before I go tonight," he said. "And I'll text you for your address. Six? Is that too early? What time do you get off here?"

"Five," she said. "I live on Sanctuary, though. Where are you?"

"Here on Diamond," he said.

"You don't need to come pick me up then," she said, and she managed to get her feet to turn and head back to the library. Dave fell into step beside her, and Tessa liked that. "We can meet somewhere."

"I'll see where we can get into," he said. "It's the height of tour season, and the islands are full. If it's somewhere on Sanctuary or Rocky Ridge, I'll come get you."

"You've got yourself a deal, Mister Shepherd." Tessa threw him a smile and a light laugh, and then they re-entered the library. She tacked her professionalism back in place and led the way downstairs and into the big room.

Others had arrived in her absence, and Tessa felt too hot all over again. She carried the tree-shaped sugar cookies over to the table and slid the tray into place. "Thank you, Dave."

"I can't wait to see you again," he murmured. "Your number?"

Tessa looked over her shoulder to where Julia stood with

Maddy, Robin and Alice. Her ribcage collapsed inward, squeezing all of her organs too tightly. Then she decided she was certainly old enough to give a handsome man her phone number. She didn't have to be embarrassed, and she'd tell everyone the moment she could anyway.

So she smiled and rattled off the number while Dave typed it into his phone. "Great," he said, and then he shoved his phone in his back pocket and added, "I'll bring in the rest of the drinks and have you sign something, and then I'll be out of your hair."

"Mandie's going to keep the containers here until tomorrow," Tessa said. "Right?"

"Yes, right." Dave seemed a tiny bit flustered too, and he turned in a full circle before he headed back to the door to get the rest of the drinks.

Tessa stood there and watched him, which was a big mistake. By the time Dave disappeared through the door, all of her friends were watching her. She swallowed and spun away from them. Maybe they'd have mercy and go easy on her, because tonight was her first book club.

"So," Robin said.

"You were staring at the drink guy," Julia said.

"He's really handsome," Maddy added.

Alice said nothing, but that didn't mean she hadn't said volumes.

"It's nothing," Tessa said as she picked up one of the crispy treats with bright, multi-colored sprinkles on it. "He only asked me on a date, and I only said yes."

She grinned at her friends; they grinned back; Tessa took

a bite of the rice crispy treat and said, "Now, come on. I need to find the signs for Soda Sensation for this table, and then I need to throw up, and then it's time to start book club."

# Chapter Seventeen

AJ felt like she belonged with the women loitering around in the beautiful basement room at the library, but at the same time, she kept looking around for someone else to stand with.

She wasn't sure why. She and Kelli had more in common now than ever before, and AJ sometimes loaded up Asher in his stroller, took the ferry to Bell Island, and went walking with Kelli, Daphne, and Parker before the sun got too high in the sky.

Then, she'd board another ferry and go see her sister and her dad on Pearl before coming back home. It could take almost the whole day, and then Asher would sleep. AJ could work on an article or searching for something freelance.

This summer, Matt's daughter Lisa had come to stay with them, and honestly, AJ's days seemed to be melting away like a candle that had been lit for too long. She wasn't sure why she felt like a crooked piece in a puzzle, especially since she didn't even know what picture she was trying to make.

"Ladies," Tessa said into a mic. "If you could find a seat, please. We're about to begin."

The conversation seemed to swell up, not down, and a mass of legs moved women closer to the chairs. AJ found herself flowing with them, talking to a woman who lived only one block over from her.

"Great to meet you, Kate," she said as she followed Alice and Kelli down the row. She ended up getting the last seat, and she wasn't sure why, but that made her feel like an outsider. Of course, Robin had gotten them as close to the front of the room as possible, and that meant the second row. Five feet across the aisle, more women filled the seats, and AJ certainly wasn't on the outside of anything.

"First, I want to thank the Library Director, Bonnie Lancomb. She's the one who wanted programming for adults, and I'm going to do my best to bring it to you."

"Woo!" someone yelled from down the row where AJ sat, and she leaned forward and peered down to see who it was. Alice, of course. The woman didn't mind eyes on her, and she did want to champion everyone.

"I'm Tessa Simmons, and I couldn't have done any of this without my fearless assistant—and the brains behind the bicycle book club—Mandie Grover." She started clapping, and that got the room doing the same thing.

Mandie smiled and smiled, her face growing redder and redder by the moment. She finally ducked out of the way, and Tessa stepped back to the mic. "We want to thank all of you for signing up for this book club, and I hope we'll have a lively discussion tonight. We want to thank David at Soda Sensation for our refreshments, and I'm excited to kick off our first library-sponsored book club with *The Echoes of Avalon Park!*"

The crowd erupted into applause and cheering again, and the vibe here made AJ's pulse skip several beats. She drew in a breath trying to contain all the energy of this event in a single moment, and she wanted to soar on it.

Just fly up into the sky and drift around, looking at everyone below as little ants, tiny specs in the grand scheme of things.

AJ exhaled and came back to earth just as Tessa said, "Okay, I think we should start with some of the suggested questions, and we'll see where the discussion takes us." She smiled around at everyone and lifted her phone to her sightline. "So let's begin where all good books do—in chapter one."

A COUPLE OF HOURS LATER, AJ WASN'T SURE IF SHE was riding on a sugar high or just so up in the clouds from real, adult discussion. She hadn't been enthused by the idea of a book club. She'd found it mundane. Boring. The same thing that happened in thousands of towns and cities across the United States, Canada, and other countries.

But she stood with a plastic cup of iced tea and her second cookie of the evening, with three other women, none of whom were from her core group of friends. "So what do you really think about that chapter with the cardinal?" Kate asked.

The four of them stood there, and AJ glanced around and finally said, "I think the cardinal is real. I know she uses it throughout the book as sort of a symbol—"

"Like the only color in the snowy landscape," a woman named Anna said.

"Right." AJ took a tiny bite of her cookie. "But I think this woman had rows and rows of bird feeders, and I think she knows cardinals better than anyone." She grinned around at the group.

"I found it a powerful symbol," Holly said. "I could actually see the crimson-ness of it among all the black and white on the page."

AJ nodded. "I agree. When I was reading it—and this is so dumb—but I'd actually stand at the window and look for cardinals." She trilled out a laugh. "We don't even have them here, and certainly not in the summer." She shook her head, feeling more like the person she wanted to be in that moment than she had in a while.

"I found it a little symbolic of us as women," Kate said, and she had a softer voice, one that didn't say much but what she said carried power. "We flit around here and there, looking for the best things in life."

"The best man," Holly said.

"Trying to raise the best kids," Anna added.

AJ just nodded, because she hadn't realized how much she wanted to be the perfect wife and mother until reading this book. She normally didn't love long-form prose, preferring articles and short stories over anything novel-length.

But this book had read like a string of articles, and she had found herself guessing at what was true and what wasn't. She'd honestly felt like that these past five or six years of her life since she'd returned to the cove. There had been so many secrets uncovered and mysteries brought to life.

There'd been different personalities and opinions, and AJ had sifted through so much. She'd come out a winner in some ways, and she'd had to reform and transform herself in ways she hadn't even dreamed she could.

"But in the end, we have to nourish ourselves first, before we can take off," Kate said. "Before we can take care of others." She'd chosen lemonade, and she lifted her cup and drained the last of it.

"Interesting," AJ said. "I didn't think that about the cardinal."

"No?" Kate smiled at her, and she didn't seem judgmental or even challenging. "What did you think it represented?"

"Oh, gosh." She drew in a big breath and let it flow right back out. "I really liked the allusion to the fact that a cardinal always showed up right when she needed that ray of hope." AJ swallowed. "I'm not terribly religious, but it felt like a tiny piece of heaven shining its light down into the dark situation happening on the page."

She hugged herself, her plastic cup crinkling a little bit. "And I felt that if God cared about the author in that way, then maybe, in the story of my life, I should be looking for and expecting cardinals to show up and remind me of the fact that...I don't know."

"That all is not lost," Holly murmured. "I sort of felt like that."

"Yeah," Anna said. "I looked for cardinals too, though it's not like I really have anything to complain about." She twisted and tossed her empty cup in the trash can. "Sometimes regular life can just feel heavy. It's the monotony of it."

"Feels gray," Kate murmured.

"The same thing every day," AJ added. "And the cardinal can break up that sameness with something different."

"What are you ladies talking about here?" Robin asked as she edged in beside AJ.

"Cardinals," Holly said. "How's Duke doing in Alaska?"

AJ wasn't surprised that she knew Robin. A lot of people in the cove knew her; she'd lived here for her entire life. "He's catching a lot of fish," Robin said with a smile. She looked at Anna. "I'm sorry; I don't know you. I'm Robin Grover."

"Anna Maxwell," she said, and the two women shook hands.

Robin moved her gaze to Kate, and said, "I think you're..."

"Kate Bryan," AJ said. "Kate, this is Robin. She's one of my best friends."

Robin beamed at her and put her arm around AJ's waist. She did love Robin, though they didn't agree on everything. AJ had learned that she didn't have to agree with someone on everything in order to love them.

Someone's phone started to chime, and Kate pulled hers from her purse. "That's my alarm to..." She trailed off, but because of AJ's height and proximity to Kate, she could see her phone. The alarm had been set and it said in big capital letters: TIME FOR MEDICATION.

Kate silenced the alarm and glanced up. "I have to get home." She flashed smiles all around before she left, and AJ really didn't want her to go without making sure she was okay.

"I'll be right back." She stepped away from the group and hurried after Kate. She had bustled right out of the library, not getting caught by anyone else as she went. AJ wasn't sure why, but something told her to keep going. Get to Kate and make sure she didn't need any help.

"Kate," she called as she burst out of the library. The hour had passed nine, but the sun still hung low in the western sky, casting plenty of light over the cove.

Her friend turned, her blonde hair swinging as she did. She finally did pause, and she seemed a bit frustrated by AJ's intrusion. Still, AJ continued forward, her strides long and strong, the way they'd once been when she muscled her way into locker rooms to speak to elite athletes.

"AJ," she said.

"I just—want to make sure you're okay."

"I just need to get home," she said.

"Is it your medication that you need to take?" AJ cocked her head, really looking at Kate and letting her journalist eyes do the examination. "There's something—I'm worried about you."

"It's—" She exhaled heavily and pulled her hair back into a ponytail. She scraped it back and back and then let all the hair drop. "My son. He has to have his medication at the same time every day, and I'm the only one who can do it."

"Do you want me to come with you?"

"No," Kate said quickly. "I'm okay." She offered a tight smile and stepped into AJ. "Everything will be okay. I just need to go."

"Okay," AJ said, though she still had some alarms going off. "Can I put my number in your phone, so you can call me if you need to?"

"Okay." Kate handed over her phone, and AJ quickly tapped her number into it.

"Any time," she said. "I have people I can leave my son with and be at your house in minutes."

Kate looked like she might cry for a moment, and then she nodded curtly and got in her minivan. AJ stood near it and looked inside, and she saw the mess in the van. Kate clearly had more than one child, as she had two car seat bases in the middle row.

And no last row at all, but a place for a wheelchair.

AJ's gaze flew back to the driver's door, but Kate had already gotten behind the wheel and started to back out. AJ put a smile on her face and lifted her hand in a wave as Kate went by her, and she watched the blue vehicle drive away.

"She needs a cardinal," AJ murmured to herself, and as the taillights of Kate's van disappeared, she vowed she'd find a way to give Kate some joy.

# Chapter Eighteen

A lice stood from her table in the courtroom as the bailiff led the way in. The judge followed him, and Alice held very still, the tips of her fingers pressed into the wood in front of her.

She'd had quite a few cases that weren't getting settled outside of hearings, and Alice had bought two more skirt suits so the two judges in Five Island Cove wouldn't learn the rotation of her wardrobe.

Today, she stood before Judge Leo Wiley, and she'd been in his courtroom four times this summer already. "Thank you," he said as he sat, and Alice nodded to her client, a single mother named Susan Marvin.

Everyone settled down, and the judge said, "I've reviewed this case, and it's my understanding that Mister Marvin wants full custody, claiming that Miss Marvin can't adequately care for the children while she's at work."

That was about the gist of it, but as Alice knew—and Judge Wiley knew too—most familial situations couldn't be boiled down to a single sentence, even if it was a compound one.

"Miss Rice?"

"Yes, Your Honor," Alice said, looking right at him. "My client has had to get a full-time job to support herself following the divorce, as it was her and Mister Marvin's previous arrangement for him to work and she'd stay home with the children. So without that, of course she needs employment."

She looked down at the perfectly prepared papers in front of her. "Miss Marvin has adequate child care in the form of her mother, who watches the children—in her own home, I might add—three times each week, and she's arranged for a neighbor to take the kids on the other two days."

"It's this neighbor to which my client objects," the lawyer at the opposing table said, his voice nearly a monotone. "She's a hoarder, and it's an unsafe environment for two children under the age of ten."

"Miss Richards is not a hoarder, Your Honor," Alice said, and she lifted another paper. She indicated it to the bailiff, and he came forward to get it. "I have personally visited her home, and I had social services do the same. I have their report here. There is no harm happening to those children while Miss Marvin is at work."

She waited a few beats while the bailiff delivered the

paper to the judge. While Judge Wiley scanned it, Alice took a breath. "Mister Marvin simply doesn't like that his ex-wife now has a job that sustains her and that she doesn't need to rely on him so fully. Plus, he still has to pay his child support and spousal maintenance, and this is merely a ploy to reduce his expenses at Miss Marvin's expense."

Alice looked up to the judge, who met her eyes. "He's victimizing her again, and he's using his children as weapons."

"Okay, Miss Rice," Judge Wiley said in a tired voice. "Mister Holt?"

"Mister Marvin has a genuine concern for his children at the neighbor's house, Your Honor."

"Did you call social services?" Judge Wiley asked.

"No, Your Honor."

"What evidence do you have that Miss Richards is an unfit caretaker?"

"She has six cats," Holt said. "And Lily, Mister Marvin's daughter, is allergic to cats."

"Lily has medication for her mild—very mild—allergy to cats," Alice said.

"And the hoarding?" Judge Wiley asked.

"The place is a mess," Holt said.

"So is mine," the judge said dryly. He sighed and looked down at his bench. "This report from social services is pretty thorough." He looked up and surveyed the lawyers in front of him. "I see no reason to change the current custody arrangement. I did, however, see that Mister Marvin is now six days behind on his monthly payments, and if those aren't submitted by the end of the day, Miss Marvin will have grounds to file a complaint with the court."

Alice hid her smile as she stood to show respect to the court. Everyone filed out, and Alice waited until Holt and his client left before she allowed her client to go past her and toward the door.

"Okay," she said once they'd reached the stairs that led down to the sidewalk. "Let me know if anything else comes up—or if he doesn't transfer that money by five o'clock tonight." She gave Susan a stern look. "Okay?"

"Okay. Thank you, Alice." She hugged her quickly, and they separated. Alice sighed as she got behind the wheel of her SUV, and she pulled her phone out of her briefcase. She'd missed a call from Ginny, and her heartbeat bobbed in the back of her throat.

She tapped to return the call, and when her daughter said, "Hey, Mom," Alice nearly choked on her own breath.

"Did you get an apartment?" Alice asked.

"No." Ginny didn't sound too terribly upset about it either. "That one I applied for is gone already."

Of course it was. That had been how things had been going all summer. Alice had been living in a state of constant worry, and she'd found just as many apartments as Ginny and Charlie combined. Nothing had worked out, and school started in less than a month.

Charlie definitely seemed worried, but no one else seemed to be. Probably because Ginny could continue to stay with Frank, and she'd had a great job all summer.

"So what's up?" she asked her daughter.

"I just wanted to call and tell you...I met someone this week."

Alice allowed some of her cares about the apartment situation and the weight of her caseload to slide away as she smiled. "Did you? What's his name?"

"Don't laugh."

"Why would I laugh at his name?"

"It's—I don't know."

"Then tell me his name."

"Bob," Ginny said, and she giggled. "He's a little older than me, but not that much older, and he's so cute, Mom."

"You brought up his age," Alice said calmly. "So please define what 'a little older' means."

"He's, uh, twenty-four."

"Oh." Alice's voice came out a bit like she's inhaled helium. "Is he in college?"

"Yes," Ginny said. "He's a student at Harvard Law School."

Alice scoffed. "I went to Harvard, Ginny."

"Yeah, and you've told me how hard it is to get into a million times," Ginny said. "He's leaving the city in a few weeks, but we've still been out a couple of times, and I thought I better tell you before Dad did."

"You think he'd tell me?"

"I know you guys talk about me all the time," Ginny said with another laugh. "So yes. I figured next time you called him in a panic over the apartment, he might tell you."

"He might," Alice agreed, but she wasn't going to admit that she'd specifically been calling and texting Frank this summer to get regular updates on Ginny. Truth be told, Ginny texted or called her nearly every day anyway, but Alice didn't always get the full story from her. She wanted a parental perspective on Ginny's summer activities, and Frank had provided that.

"So I wanted you to know," Ginny said. "We're going out again tonight, and I'll get a selfie and send it to you."

"I'd love that," Alice said as she looked out her side window. "Love you, Ginny-girl."

"Love you too, Mom. I'm off this afternoon, and I'm looking for apartments. Charlie sent me a couple too."

"Sounds good," Alice said, and the call ended. She took a couple of breaths, then connected her phone to the radio in her car. As she pulled away from City Hall and the courthouse, she fought with herself over whether she should call Frank or not. She decided against it, and called Arthur instead.

"I won," she said when her husband answered, and Arthur cheered for her.

"I'll bring home tacos," he said, and that made Alice smile. She'd give it a few more days, and then she might have to take this apartment problem by the horns.

---

A WEEK LATER, THE SECOND BICYCLE BOOK CLUB loomed when Alice called her ex-husband. The novel sat on Alice's desk, and she hadn't even cracked it open yet. She wasn't sure she'd attend the meeting tomorrow night, but she wanted to support Tessa and Mandie.

"Hey," she said as brightly as she could when he answered. She paced in front of her desk in her office, her anxiety at an all-time high. She'd been to the Wednesday lunches this summer, and all of her friends knew of her situation. They'd all offered their support and contacts, and still, Charlie and Ginny didn't have anywhere to live in the city.

"Hello, Alice," Frank said in a very diplomatic voice. "I have five minutes before my next appointment."

She rolled her eyes but hoped it would stay out of her tone. "I just need to know what we're going to do about this lack of a place for Charlie to live." Her frustration over the situation reared and she couldn't keep the sigh inside as she settled to a stop in front of the window. "They start school in three weeks, and he has nowhere to live. Could he possibly stay with you?"

"They got a place," Frank said nonchalantly, as if he hadn't been worried at all.

"They—what?"

"They got an apartment a couple of days ago," Frank said, and something scratched on his end of the line. He said something to someone while Alice still reeled over the fact that her children had gotten an apartment and hadn't told her.

"Can they afford it?" she asked. "Or are we subsidizing them as we've discussed?"

"They got a roommate," he said. "I'm sorry, Alice, I have to go. Charlie knows all about it. He'll tell you."

The line went silent, and Alice lowered her phone. She stared out the window, not really recognizing the landscape in front of her. "They got an apartment?" she asked herself aloud. "And a roommate?"

And that naturally led to the next question—who? *Who* was going to be living with her children in New York City?

# Chapter Nineteen

M andie stood at the front of the boat, the ocean wind pulling at her clothes, her sunhat, her hair. She grinned and grinned into it, because she hadn't had an afternoon off in a while. She'd been working so hard on the book club, and their second one was tomorrow night.

Tessa had been seeing Mandie's boss, and that seemed to be going well, though Mandie didn't pry into either of their personal lives. Soda Sensation hadn't catered for tomorrow night's event, because Maddy had gotten The Glass Dolphin to do finger appetizers.

"This is amazing," she said as she turned back to Charlie. They weren't going super-fast, as he'd managed to get his boss's houseboat for the afternoon and evening.

"Yeah?" Charlie joined her at the front of the boat, his arms snaking around her midsection as he pressed into her back. "You're enjoying it?"

"Yes." She smiled to the south sea. "And I know you got something special for dinner."

"You do?" He nuzzled her neck. "How do you know that?"

Mandie leaned back into his touch, a thrill moving down both arms as it ran up her spine. "I could smell it when we first got on the boat." She ran her hands up his arms. "What did you get?"

"Are you hungry?" he asked, his lips right against her ear.

"A little," she said. "But it's not dinnertime yet."

"I thought we'd anchor first," he said. "Then I don't have to worry about currents or anything like that while we eat."

Mandie turned in his arms. "I'm going to tell my mom about the apartment," she said. She ran her hands up his chest. "We have to tell them before your mother finds out from your dad."

"I know." Charlie sighed and gazed past her to the water beyond. "I'll tell my mom in the morning."

She nodded. "Me too." They'd been over and over how their parents would take the news, but Ginny and Charlie couldn't afford an apartment on their own, and it all made logical sense in her head.

Charlie kissed her, and Mandie sure enjoyed the heat of the sun on the side of her face as it danced and combined with the heat inside her. It built with Charlie's touch, his body heat also mingling in the mix.

"I love you," he whispered as he slid his hands down her sides.

She smiled as her skin tingled with the touch of his lips against her collarbone. "Mm, I love you too."

"Come on," he whispered, and he took her hand and led her back toward where he'd been steering the boat. He checked it as he went by, and then he kept a firm hold on her hand as he went downstairs.

The hallway narrowed, making Mandie feel a bit boxed in. "It's cozy down here," she said.

"Yeah." Charlie opened a door and stood in the doorway. Mandie moved to his side and looked inside.

A big bed filled most of the room, but she could've walked around all of it but the headboard. She swallowed. "Wow," she said. "Cozy."

Charlie kissed her again, this time with a bit more urgency. She kissed him back, her pulse hammering and pounding and ricocheting through her body.

"Charlie," she gasped, and he pulled back.

"No one is expecting us until late tonight," he said. "I want—I thought—"

Mandie knew what he wanted and what he thought. She wanted and thought the same things. "I just—it's daytime."

He smiled at her. "That's what you're worried about?"

"I—" Mandie didn't know how to articulate her fears to him. "I've never been naked in front of a boy," she whispered.

Charlie gazed at her, his smile gone. He didn't try to kiss her. He pushed a lock of her hair back off the side of her neck and bent down. "Okay. Why don't you change into your swim suit and meet me up top again?"

"Charlie," she said as he slid away from her and back down the narrow hall.

"I'm not going to pressure you," he said quietly. He turned back to her. "When you're ready, then well, I'll be ready too." He gave her a smile and went up the steps two at a time.

A pit opened up in Mandie's stomach, and she groaned as she went into the bedroom and closed the door. The comforter on the bed was a dark blue, and her backpack sat there. She'd packed her swimming suit and a coverup, plenty of sunscreen, and a few snacks though Charlie had said he'd have an amazing dinner for them.

She collapsed on the bed. "He does everything right," she said. He texted her sweet things. He brought her the things she liked best—soda when she needed it after work, and her favorite foods when they went out to eat. He held her when she didn't want to talk, and he talked when she wanted to hash things out.

"We're going to be living together in a few weeks, for crying out loud," she said to herself. "And what? Your first time is going to be with Ginny sleeping on the couch fifteen feet away?"

She shook her head, frustrated with herself. "You already have to have a hard conversation with your mother." She stripped out of her shorts and tank top and shimmied into her swimming suit.

Feeling nervous about facing Charlie again, she took a few minutes to braid her hair, thinking about what it would be like to be with him. Really with him, here in this room, with nothing between them but how they felt about one another.

The boat slowed, and Mandie took that as her cue to go up top and face him. She pulled her cover-up on and re-set her hat on her head, then headed upstairs. She looked around when she arrived, the dazzling blue sky above and all the gorgeous glinting water surrounding them.

"It's South Port," she said. The harbor where big ships could dock with their supplies sat a bit behind them, with a few other boats dotting the calmer waters closer to the southern shore of Diamond Island.

"Yep," Charlie said. "Not far enough for the ferries to bother us. Great for fishing and swimming." He lifted a couple of poles as he moved away from the driving components of the house boat. "What do you want to do first?"

"Swimming," she said as she took the poles. "The fish won't be biting until tonight."

"If you say so," he said with a smile. "Fisherman's daughter." He kissed her quickly and moved by as he pulled his shirt off. "Want me to slather you with your sunscreen?"

"Yes, please," she said, and she slid her shoulders out of her cover-up. She let it drop to the bench seat at the back of the deck area, and she handed him the tube of sunscreen. "It works better than the spray-on stuff."

"That stuff works for me," he said.

"Yeah, but you tan, and I burn."

He creamed up his hands and then started rubbing the sunscreen into her shoulders. "You know," he said in that same quiet voice he'd used down below. "This swimming suit doesn't leave a whole lot to my imagination."

Mandie dipped her chin and let him keep slathering up her back. Yes, the whole thing needed to be protected, save for a tiny strip where her bra-top strap went. She wore shorts on the bottom, and they were high-waisted to hold in some of her tummy, but they didn't go down too far at all.

Her whole leg extended down, and Mandie's blood rushed to all of her extremities. "Charlie," she said without looking up.

"Done," he said over her, and he handed her back her bottle of sunscreen and brushed by her. "Will you spray my back?" He was acting totally normal, but nothing felt normal between them to her.

She sprayed his back and rubbed it into his gloriously tan skin, and then she slid her hand into his. "I want to," she said.

"I know you want to, baby," he said. "That doesn't mean you're ready, and I'm not going to be that boyfriend. Okay? There will be other times."

She nodded, and they jumped off the back of the houseboat, both of them laughing and shrieking. She floated on her back with her hand in Charlie's, and they climbed back onto the boat, where he brought up dinner.

"For you, my love," he said, his voice back to that deep joviality she was used to. "Salmon filet with rice pilaf and lemon green beans, with a blackberry reduction sauce."

"Charlie," she said. "This is from The Glass Dolphin."

"Yes, ma'am," he said as he slid her plate in front of her.

"I got the steak and shrimp." He sat down across from her, the sun still blazing as it lowered on her right.

"This is perfect." Mandie smiled at him and added, "You know, I'd love you even if you didn't get me fancy dinners."

"I know," he said. "But wait until dessert." He grinned and cut into his steak. It still had a pink center, though it certainly couldn't be hot any longer. Her fish wasn't, but he'd warmed it slightly, and Mandie had no complaints about any of it.

"I'll miss working at the library," she said. "Guess I'll have to find something in the city, especially with the new apartment."

"Have you heard anything from the applications you put in at the university?" He ignored his phone as it rang, but Mandie looked over to it.

"Not yet," she said. "You?"

His phone stopped ringing as he nodded. "Yeah, I've got a video interview with University Press next week."

"That's great, babe." Mandie grinned at him. "I'm going to change my major to History."

Charlie looked at her, his eyebrows up in a classic look of surprise. "You are?"

She grinned at him. "Yes," she said. "I am. You're the first person I've told. I'm thinking Ancient Artifacts or something."

He chuckled and shook his head. "You know a few letters from sixty years ago don't qualify as 'ancient,' right?"

She laughed too, her gaze connecting with his. She really did love him, and she knew he'd orchestrated this evening to be absolute perfection, so they could be together. He'd provided a safe, private place for them, with things she enjoyed—swimming, the sky, the sun, the ocean, and fishing.

He'd probably have lit candles if it was dark yet or he thought he could get away with having fire on a boat.

"Charlie," she said as his phone rang again.

He sighed as he got up and went over to his clothes on the bench seat. "It's my mom." He silenced it this time. "I'll just text her really quick." He did that, then shoved it under his T-shirt and came back to the table.

Mandie got to her feet and said, "Will the food keep?"

"Keep?"

She ran her hands up his bare chest. "Yeah. Keep." She leaned in and up to kiss him, and Charlie got the message pretty quickly. He sucked in a breath through his nose and kissed her back. Deeper and then deeper, and Mandie's hands slid to the waistband of his swimming trunks.

"Come on," he said huskily, and he took her hand and led her decisively downstairs.

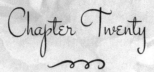

# Chapter Twenty

R obin had just added cream to her coffee when she heard footsteps overhead. She'd skipped her run this morning, because she needed an off-day every now and then. She'd survived three of her summer weddings so far, with one more later this month.

"Then, you'll be moving Mandie back to the city," she said to herself and the depths of her mug while her oldest daughter came downstairs.

"Morning," Mandie said, her eyes flitting to the fridge. "I don't have much time this morning, so I'm just going to grab a protein shake."

"Okay," Robin said. She watched her daughter, and Mandie did seem a little off-kilter. Her movements almost seemed nervous, and Robin wasn't sure what to make of that. She'd gone out with Charlie yesterday afternoon, and she'd stood in the doorway of Robin's bedroom and whispered, "I'm home, Mama," when she'd come in late last night.

"You okay, honey?" she asked.

Mandie nodded, and a moment later she sighed. She slammed the bottle of her protein shake onto the counter. "Mom, I have to tell you something."

"All right." Robin calmly lifted her coffee mug to her lips. "Should I be drinking for this?" She tried to offer Mandie a smile, but her daughter had unshed tears in her eyes. So no coffee.

"Hey," she said gently, setting the mug aside completely. "Come tell me everything." She got to her feet and rounded the island to take Mandie into her arms.

"I'm going to call out of work," she said, and Mandie pulled away to do that. "Can we just lay in bed and talk for a few minutes?"

"Sure," Robin said, and she went down the hall to the master suite. This one was so much bigger than their last house, and Robin had put a recliner in the corner that she mostly draped her clothes over these days.

She waited for Mandie to climb into bed, and since she was dressed and ready for work, it wasn't quite as casual as the other times they'd laid in her bed and talked. But the room was dim and cool and quiet, and Robin slid back between the sheets too.

"Tell me everything," she murmured. "Whatever it is, it'll be okay."

Mandie sniffled, then said, "It's not even bad stuff. I'm

not really upset by it. There's just a lot...and I know you're not going to like some of it."

"Mandie, you are an adult, sweetheart. Our roles are shifting, and I just want to support you. I just want you to be happy." She reached over and smoothed her hand down the side of her daughter's face.

"I'll start with the easiest one," she said. "I'm changing my major to History. Going through all the stuff in the library has been really fun for me, and I don't know. There's just something about old, forgotten things I like."

"Okay," Robin said, determined to wait for more. Her thoughts raged through her mind, the way the ocean did in high winds, but she held her tongue.

"I'm moving into an apartment with Charlie and Ginny," she said next, and that really rendered Robin mute. "It's a one-bedroom, and with the three of us paying, we can afford it."

"I—wow." She didn't want to start in with the questions immediately, though she had plenty building up behind her tongue.

Mandie turned her head and looked at Robin, her eyes wide. "The couch in the living room folds out to a queen-sized bed. Ginny's going to sleep there. Charlie and I—" She swallowed. "We—I love him, Mom. He loves me. We've talked about living together anyway, and this—it helps him and Ginny, and I feel good about it."

Robin nodded, not sure how to speak anymore. Everything balled up tight, like a pair of socks that had been stuffed inside one another and then tumbled in the dryer, fusing them together.

She had questions here too—like what would Mandie do with the apartment she had? Could the contract even be sold? What did this new apartment have in it? Would the teens need a bunch of furniture?

Then she reminded herself that while yes, Mandie was a teenager, she was also an adult.

"We—" Mandie looked back to the ceiling, her nerves pouring from her now. Robin had always been able to sense her daughter's mood, which was how she'd known something was off in the kitchen. "We were finally intimate last night."

Robin nodded now too, her own emotions rearing up and flooding her eyes with tears. "Okay," she whispered, though she wasn't sure if it was entirely okay. She wasn't going to ask too many questions about that, because both she and Alice had lectured their teenagers relentlessly as they'd grown up.

They knew about sex, about condoms, about all of it. It would do no good to lecture now. What she'd said earlier held true: Mandie was an adult, and Robin's role as her mother had changed. Violently.

She might not like the changes, because Robin did like being in control of every situation. She liked people and things to be predictable, with all the details planned out and done to the T. She liked being in charge, with what she said passing as law.

Again, that had changed, and Robin had to trust

Mandie. She had to believe in her. She had to support her in any decisions she made—including the three she'd listed in the past five minutes.

If she'd learned anything as a wife and mother, it was that she couldn't control another human being. Duke wanted and needed to be in Alaska every summer, and nothing Robin did could mitigate that situation.

She'd had a lot of talks with her daughters, but in the end, they each got to choose their paths in life. Mandie was her own person, and all Robin could do was hope and pray that her daughter made the smartest decisions possible.

"We used protection," Mandie said. "We don't want a baby right now."

"Are you going to marry him?"

"Yes," Mandie whispered. "I don't know when, and I want you to plan it. I want to get married here in the cove, on the most gorgeous of days, with Dad here to walk me down the aisle, and...yeah."

Robin nodded slightly to herself, as Mandie had closed her eyes, probably with visions of her forthcoming wedding parading through her head.

"When?" she asked, because Mandie's version sounded like a summer wedding, and that meant next year at the earliest.

"We don't know," Mandie said. "At least next summer. If then."

Robin frowned then, and she checked to see if Mandie was watching her. She wasn't, thankfully. She didn't understand living together perpetually. Why not get married, if the love and commitment were there?

But she said nothing, because she wasn't the one who'd be twenty in another few months, and she didn't get to make Mandie's decisions for her. It made her chest quake and shake, but she had lessons to learn here too.

She'd never been the parent of an adult child, and this was an untraveled road for her. It would have bumps and ruts and hills and valleys, and Robin couldn't dictate any of it. She desperately wished Duke were here, and she'd call him as soon as Mandie deemed their morning talk over.

How she'd tell him everything Mandie had just said, she didn't know. She'd likely do what she'd always done—she'd open her mouth and say what lingered in her heart.

"Are you upset?" Mandie whispered.

"No," Robin said, the truth flowing right out of her mouth. "I'm still processing, because you gave me three pretty big things, but once I get through it all, I don't think I'll be anywhere near upset."

She turned onto her side and gazed at her daughter. "You found a good man who you love. What's upsetting about that?"

Mandie rolled and faced her too. "We're nineteen."

"Yeah," Robin said. "Yep, you sure are." She smiled at Mandie. "But even young hearts know how to love."

"I know you don't approve of living together before marriage."

Robin didn't know how to defend herself, and then she decided she didn't have to. "I just want you to be happy, honey. I want him to commit if he's going to get the privilege of sleeping with you every night."

"He has," Mandie said. "He loves me, Mom. I know it. I feel it. He says it all the time."

"Okay." She smiled again, and a slip of sadness did pull through her. It was sad, seeing her daughter all grown up and making her own decisions. She didn't need Robin the way she once had, and that *was* sad.

Robin had so enjoyed raising and mothering her girls, and it broke her heart that this phase of being their mother in the way she knew how had ended. At least with Mandie, but Jamie was right behind her.

But watching her girls grow into smart, capable women was also exciting. Satisfying. Wonderful.

She reached over and cradled Mandie's face again. "I love you."

"I love you too, Mom."

Mandie stayed for a few more minutes, but she didn't say anything else. "I better go. No one picked up my shift."

"And you just stayed?" Robin watched as she rolled out of bed and fixed her T-shirt.

"I said I'd be late." She came around the bed and leaned over to hug Robin. "I'll see you tonight? At book club?"

"Yes," Robin murmured, wondering what she was going to do with her day now. Everything had just been let out of the box, and then those boxes had been overturned, tossed about, ripped apart.

There was no going back, and Robin felt wild and out of control. She stayed in bed, as she hadn't changed out of her pajamas yet, and when she heard Mandie leave, she rolled onto her other side and reached for her phone.

She couldn't wait to hear her husband's voice, and as his line rang, she prayed, "Come on, baby. Pick up."

He did with a, "Hey, sweetheart? How's my favorite girl?"

Robin let her tears out then, because she just wanted him here. She wanted him to hold her close and tell her she wasn't losing Mandie. That these were crucial and important steps their daughter needed to take—and should be taking.

But it still felt very much like losing her.

"Robin?" Duke asked, the static or noise or wind on his end of the line dying. "Baby, are you there?"

"Yes," she choked out. "I'm here." She drew in a breath and tried to steady everything inside her. It didn't completely work, but she didn't have to be bold and strong for Duke. He was the one person she could be vulnerable and completely messy with.

"It's so good to hear your voice," she said.

"What's wrong?" he asked.

Robin smiled to herself, though tears still ran down her face. "Nothing's wrong," she said. "Our baby grew up, Duke, and she's making all kinds of adult decisions."

A pause came over the line, and Robin could just see her handsome husband's face all frowned and puckered as he thought about what she'd said. "Adult decisions?" he asked slowly. "Like what kind of adult decisions?"

"The kind that come with being in love with a man,"

Robin whispered, because that was the best way to put it. "Hurry home, my love. I miss you."

"I'll be there to move Mandie back into her dorm," he said. "It's only a few more weeks, sweetheart."

"About that," Robin said, and the story poured out of her from there. About halfway through it, she thought of Alice and what Charlie had potentially told her.

And Robin suddenly knew what to do with her day. Because her husband wasn't here, she'd spend it with her best friend.

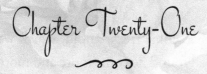

# Chapter Twenty-One

Kelli had just finished her yoga classes for the morning when her phone chimed. Her pulse bobbed, her first thought about Daphne, the baby girl she'd had only five months ago. Then, her brain kicked in and reminded her that she'd hired two women to act as daycare here at Whole Soul.

She'd dedicated a room and the backyard to the endeavor, and anyone who wanted to take an exercise or yoga class at the studio could bring their children for an additional fee. Kelli wasn't trying to make money on it; she'd priced the fee at exactly what she needed to pay her new employees.

So Daphne was safe.

This had to be about something else, and she wiped the sweat from her forehead with one hand as she picked up her phone with the other.

"Great class, Kelli, thanks," someone said, and she looked up.

"Yeah, sure, Margot. Thanks for coming." She smiled the older woman out of the room, and then only she remained.

The text had come from Robin, which wasn't unusual. While Kelli had found her time more and more limited since having Daphne, she still spoke with her friends frequently. Maybe she didn't make the trip to Diamond for the Wednesday lunches as often.

"Or ever," she murmured to herself. She'd gone to a couple of the beach days, but having a new baby, running her studio, dedicating her spare time to her new husband, and having Parker here all summer left Kelli with little energy, time, or gumption to do much more than what she already did.

And most of what she did happened on Bell Island, not Diamond. Shad, her husband, went to work on Diamond every day, and he took Parker to the lighthouse or a friend's house a couple of days per week. Otherwise, Kelli had enrolled him in swimming lessons held here on Bell, a drawing class that a woman did out of her house here on Bell, and an online driver's education course, though he wouldn't be fifteen for several more months.

She just needed him to stay busy, as she normally didn't have him in the summertime, and school and after-school soccer had kept the teenager out of trouble in the months she did have him.

*Summer Sand Pact*, Robin had said. *We need to do it.*

*Just the five of us. One day next week? The week after that? Who's available when?*

No one had answered yet, and Kelli would need to get to her desk to see what she had going on. Daphne had an appointment next week, and the doctor's office was just down the street from City Hall. Perhaps she could take the baby and then Shad could take a half-day off work and get Daphne home.

Kelli's heart twisted, because she knew why Robin had texted. "Just the five of them" barely existed anymore. Kelli found herself gravitating toward AJ, of course, but Laurel and Jean as well. The four of them had small children all under the age of two, and Kelli needed those moms in her life.

It had been such a long time since Parker was a baby, and so much had changed. Just the equipment and toys available now blew Kelli's mind. AJ would ride the ferry and go walking with Kelli sometimes, and she liked that.

Her phone worked, and she texted and called her friends all the time. But actually getting together with them and spending time? It hadn't happened as much as Kelli would've liked. And certainly not enough to maintain the strong friendships she'd rekindled with her high school friends in the past six or seven years.

She couldn't believe she'd returned to Five Island Cove at all, and she left the studio where she'd been teaching and headed around the corners of the house to her office, which sat tucked behind the biggest studio.

Robby's cardio explosion class should be starting in

another ten minutes, and Kelli would be able to hear the pumping bass through the wall. She didn't mind it, and she'd taken the most popular class here at Whole Soul a few times. It really was like a cardio explosion.

Now, however, she faced her two-foot by three-foot desk calendar, her goal to find a whole day to pamper herself. Get away from the kids, her husband, her studio, her day-to-day life here on Bell Island.

*Maybe a pedicure,* she thought, but she reminded herself it was summertime, and that meant thousands more people on the islands. The salons would all be booked.

Her phone chimed again, and AJ had said, *Maybe we should say what days we can't do it instead. I can any day next week except Tuesday, for example.*

*I have a client on Tuesday and I'm due in court on Thursday morning,* Alice said. *But I could be out to Rocky Ridge probably by eleven. It's a nine a.m. hearing, and it'll be fast.*

Kelli taught yoga every morning, but if she was going to take the whole day off and pamper herself, she just needed to choose a day and get someone to cover her two classes. Not only that, but Daphne's appointment was on Tuesday, and they obviously wouldn't do it then.

*Just tell me when, and I'll arrange to be there,* Eloise said. She ran a very busy inn on Sanctuary Island, but she had help. She could probably just tell Clara or Julia she'd be gone for the day, and they'd cover for her.

*I'm the same,* Kelli said. *I just need to know so I can get someone to take my yoga classes. Then I can come for the whole day.*

*Okay,* Robin said. *Wednesday, then.*

*It's the monthly lunch on Wednesday,* Alice said almost on top of her. *Clara chose The Harbor House, remember?*

*Okay, so not Wednesday,* Robin said. *Monday? Or Friday? Which is easier for you, El?*

"Both will be hard for El," Kelli said. People came for the weekend, and they checked in on Fridays and out on Mondays. Eloise had six rooms at the inn, and she tried to make it as personal as possible, from homemade chocolate chip cookies available in the afternoon, to a wide spread of breakfast foods in the morning.

Kelli knew, because she and Shad had escaped to Cliffside Inn for a few nights before their baby had come. She loved the views from the cliffs on Sanctuary, and she adored the black sand beaches on Rocky Ridge. It had been a while since she'd been further north than Diamond, and she suddenly couldn't wait to go.

While they waited for Eloise to respond, Kelli texted her husband. *The ladies and I are doing a get-away day next week. Either Monday or Friday. Which is easier for you?*

*Friday,* Shad said. *Almost everyone is taking Fridays off this summer.*

She nodded to herself, because she knew that. Shad had been going in late to work on Fridays, if he went at all. He'd taken Parker sailing last week, and as she sat there and looked at her phone, she remembered he'd planned to take everyone to The Block for lunch tomorrow. It was a new-ish restaurant that had opened on Pearl last year, and he'd gone with some people from work and wanted Kelli to try the fried Brussels sprouts and the fiesta corn dip.

He claimed she'd love them both, and she loved him for finding things she'd enjoy and taking her to sample them.

*For next week, Friday,* Eloise said.

*Friday works great for me,* Kelli tapped out quickly. *Shad barely works on Fridays.*

*Just the five of us?* AJ asked. *So I can ask Jean or Laurel to babysit Asher?*

*Do we want them to know we're getting together without them?*

Alice's question brought the whole group text to a standstill. Even Kelli didn't know what to say. She normally sat back in situations like these anyway, and she certainly wouldn't be the first to respond.

As the seconds ticked by, she wondered if Robin had dropped and broken her phone. It would usually be her firing back, never one to hold her opinion if she had one. AJ was a bit like that too, though marriage and motherhood had softened her. She still spoke her mind, and she'd be riveted to her phone, awaiting an answer. After all, she had to find a babysitter.

Eloise might be busy, but she might simply be playing Kelli's hand—and waiting. She did that a lot too, but when she spoke, it was usually with wisdom and power and a level head.

*I think everyone knows we get together as smaller groups,*

Eloise said. *For example, today I'm going to lunch with Clara, Jean, and Kristen.*

*Maddy, Julia, Alice, and I are taking the whale and dolphin tour*, Robin said.

Kelli's heart started to pound. One, locals didn't normally go on the touristy tours, unless they were entertaining out-of-towners. Two, Kelli suddenly felt like she'd been replaced with Maddy and Julia.

The next text came from AJ, and it wasn't on the group text. *They're going on the dolphin tour, huh? Wonder why we didn't get invited.*

She also felt like the ladies from Nantucket had taken over some of the spots she and Kelli had used to occupy, but every time they talked about this, they came to the same conclusion: They liked their moms group. They liked their original high school friend group. They liked getting together for the Wednesday lunches with everyone.

And in short, Kelli reminded herself of the most important thing—she had a place with any and all of the women she'd befriended here in Five Island Cove. She did. She had to show up and participate, but there weren't a finite number of spaces.

"You haven't been showing up and participating," she told herself.

*It was last-minute*, Alice said. *I just needed a day off.*

*Don't we all?* AJ sent to the group, and Kelli pulled in a harsh breath.

*I just got invited this morning*, Eloise said. *Kristen was taking her daughters out, and Clara mentioned it. She knows how overworked I am, and she invited me.*

*No one's mad*, Kelli typed out, but she couldn't bring herself to send it.

*You're welcome to come*, Alice sent. *The tour leaves at noon, and we're getting a late lunch afterward.* She didn't offer any explanation as to how Julia and Maddy—who both had full-time jobs—had come to be invited when no one else knew about their dolphin tour.

Robby's exercise class music started to pump, and Kelli got to her feet and left her phone on the desk. "They have the same type of group as AJ and I do with our moms group. They're the moms who have grown children. It's normal. It's fine."

She went outside, where Cami and Pam had taken the children for their morning recess time. Some drifted on the swings. Some ran around together. Some jumped rope. Daphne had been put in a sling and she looked out at the world from where Pam stood overseeing the toddlers in the sand box.

Kelli breathed in the serenity of the shade, the peaceful-ness back here, the simpleness of life. She didn't have to think about the squabble happening in her texts, or arranging childcare, or anything.

On winter days, when no one stood on the deck where she did, Kelli might be able to hear the water lapping from the shore, which was about a ten-minute walk from her studio. But today, she couldn't hear it above the laughter and babble of the children.

She wondered if her absence on the texts would be noted, and she sighed as she turned back to the house where she'd grown up, and which she'd converted into her yoga studio. She wanted her place with her friends, and that meant she couldn't sit back and stay silent.

Several more texts had come in while she'd been outside, and Kelli didn't care about any of them. Robin had said where they'd go for lunch and that all were invited.

AJ had made excuses for why she couldn't come. Eloise had said to have fun at lunch, and she'd send pictures of her lunch that day. AJ had texted off the main string a couple more times. Kelli wanted to agree with her, but it would have to wait.

*Summer Sand Pact*, she typed. *Friday. What time should we plan to meet on Rocky Ridge? Anyone want to meet me on Diamond to ride the ferry together? I've arranged to leave Daphne with Shad the whole day, and my classes at the studio are covered.*

*Let's meet for the ten-twenty ferry on Diamond*, Eloise said. *I'll meet you, Kelli.*

*So will I*, AJ said.

*Ten-twenty ferry on Diamond*, Robin said. *I'll be there.*

*So will I*, Alice said.

She navigated over to the texts from AJ, and instead of typing, she called.

"Just ignore me," AJ said. "I know I'm being irrational."

"You're not," Kelli said. "I—my heart stopped when Robin said they were doing that tour."

"I know we have our group too." AJ sighed. "In fact,

let's get lunch today. Asher and I will come to Bell. I'll call Laurel and see if she can come. Jean's obviously going to Sanctuary with her mom."

Kelli nodded and paced in her office. "Why aren't we mad at Kristen, Clara, and Jean?"

"They're...family." AJ sounded uncertain, but she'd really hit on the truth.

"Yeah, so it's okay for them to go out together and exclude the rest of us," Kelli said. "I just—I know you're struggling with the different relationships we have. I am too. But we're closer to each other than the other ladies. They're closer to each other than us."

"I'm fine with it being Alice and Robin," AJ said. "I don't know why the four of them bother me."

"Because it used to be the four of us," Kelli whispered. "Or five, with El."

"I love my life," AJ whispered.

"So do I." Kelli drew in a breath. "I can be done here for today, and I've already got Daph with me. I can be on Diamond in probably forty minutes."

"I'll get Asher ready," AJ said. "And call Laurel. Maybe we can just hit a food truck and enjoy the sunshine. Let the kids play at the park or the beach."

"Sounds amazing," Kelli said. "See you soon." The call ended, and she moved over to the cabinet in the corner and pulled out a big bag. She transferred everything from the diaper bag, stuck in her purse, and turned back to the cupboard for sunscreen.

She tapped for a RideShare, and the moment she got the

confirmation, her phone rang. Robin's name sat there, and Kelli hesitated. She didn't want holes in her friendships, but she wasn't sure she wanted to hear Robin's reasoning for anything.

Her RideShare notification beeped, saying her ride was only a minute away, and Kelli grabbed her bag. She had to get Daphne and talk to Robby, who'd be in charge until Kelli returned later that day.

So she swiped Robin's call away, and she'd text her once she got on the ferry and had more time.

# Chapter Twenty-Two

Julia lifted her head from her phone and faced into the beauty of the world before her. She wasn't sure why Alice had changed the location of their lunch, and then why Robin had done it again. She didn't really mind, because she was just enjoying her day off.

She'd awakened to the sound of Liam chuckling as he slid into bed with her. He hadn't stayed over, as he had his son to take care of, and he put Ian first in all things. But he had to be to work early, and Julia did not, so she'd still been asleep.

Giggling, she'd kissed him despite her worry over morning breath, and he'd spent twenty minutes with her, making her eggs and bacon and coffee. She hadn't eaten since, and her stomach craved some food.

On the horizon, Rocky Ridge loomed, and Julia had never eaten at any of the restaurants up on the northernmost island in Five Island Cove. She wasn't even sure what she could get to eat here, but Robin had said she'd heard of a new fish 'n chips shop, and she wanted to try it.

"What's Liam doing this afternoon?" Maddy asked as Julia's phone buzzed again.

"He just got off," Julia said. "He's going to pick up Ian from work, and I think they're going to go running on the beach."

"So nothing you want to do."

Julia laughed and shook her head. "Heavens, no. But Ian wants to run track next year, and Liam has to get in his workout anyway. It's something they can do together." Julia beamed at Maddy and leaned her head against her shoulder. "How's Ben?"

"Amazing." Maddy sighed. "We're thinking of moving to Diamond Island."

"Really? I though he had to be close to the Coast Guard station."

"When he's on-call, he stays there." Maddy straightened as the ferry station came into view and the ferry slowed. "When he's not on-call, he doesn't need to be on Rocky Ridge, and I go to Diamond almost every day."

"Even Sanctuary would be closer."

"Sanctuary would have permanent neighbors," Maddy said.

Julia looked fully at her friend. "You're lonely up there."

"Yes," Maddy said, not even trying to disguise it. "I do like jumping on the Nantucket steamer for some shopping, but I don't want to do that alone."

Julia let that sit for a moment, because she didn't want

to dismiss Maddy's feelings. "At least the wedding plans are going well."

Maddy smiled. "Yeah," she said. "I'm thrilled for Chelsea, and I can't wait to get to the city to meet Robert. She sends me pictures all the time, and he seems to adore her."

"That's the dream," Julia murmured.

"Like you and Liam." Maddy gave her a nudge.

"Oh, she's talking about Liam now." Alice sidled up to them at the railing. "Robin will be upset she missed this."

"I missed something?" Robin appeared on the other side of Maddy, and she wore a sweatshirt as if cold. Julia supposed the wind on the ferry could drop the temperature enough to warrant such a thing, but not on such a glorious August afternoon.

"You didn't miss anything," Julia said. An awkward silence followed, and Julia wasn't sure what she was supposed to say.

"So, what would I have missed?" Robin asked.

Julia glanced down to her. "Why did we have to come to Rocky Ridge for lunch?"

Robin's blue eyes skated past Julia to Alice, and Julia looked over to her too. "Alice?"

"We know there are some other groups of our friends going to lunch today," she said smoothly. "And we don't want to run into them, plain and simple."

Julia volleyed her gaze to Maddy and Robin. "Who else is going out?"

Robin swallowed and cleared her throat. "Kristen is

taking her daughter and daughter-in-law out on Sanctuary. Eloise is going with them."

"Okay," Maddy said slowly. "Who else?"

"We don't know," Robin said, dropping her head. "But we think AJ and Kelli are probably upset that we did the tour and lunch today, and I'd really rather just not be on Diamond."

"Are we a problem?" Julia asked.

"No, of course not," Alice said dismissively, but she was a lawyer and could probably make something wrong sound right. "Things just get dicey sometimes. It has nothing to do with you guys."

"I like Kelli and AJ," Maddy said.

"Me too," Julia added. Her lungs crackled a little bit as she breathed in all the way. "I didn't know they didn't want us to...be around."

"They don't feel like that," Alice said quickly. "They like you just fine."

"I honestly think this is just one of those things," Robin said, clear irritation in her voice. "They have little kids in their late forties. We don't. It's normal and natural for us to hang out, because we're in the same phase of life. It's one hundred percent normal for Kristen to take her daughters out for lunch, and for Clara to invite El."

"I've gone out with El and Clara," Julia said. "We work together." She folded her arms, trying to protect herself a little. "I didn't know it was causing a problem."

"It's not," Alice insisted. The ferry docked, and she turned to disembark.

Julia exchanged a look with Maddy, but she didn't know what else to do. They'd had a mini sleepover with Tessa and hadn't invited anyone else.

"Let's just go to lunch," Maddy said. "I like Robin and Alice—and all of them."

"I do too."

The four of them got off the ferry and joined the Ride-Share line. "So I have some news," Alice said, her eyes glued to Robin. She switched them to Maddy and Julia. "The reason Robin and I just needed a day away today is because our children are moving in together when they go back to college."

Julia worked hard not to gasp. "Charlie and Mandie?"

"They're in love," Robin stated simply. "They've slept together." She looked away and drew in a deep breath, which lifted her shoulders. "Mandie says they'll get married, but they're not sure when."

"Charlie loves her," Alice said tenderly, and Julia looked between the two of them. Nothing but love filled her heart and mind, and she reached for Alice's hand.

"They love each other," she whispered. "That's so sweet."

Alice swiped at her eyes with her free hand. "I just wish we were having this conversation in five years."

Robin sniffled too, and then she pulled everything tight. "I am not upset about this," she said. "Julia's right. They love each other, and it's sweet."

"Yes." Alice drew in a long breath and then whooshed it all out. "And we got to see three whales today, and a whole school of dolphins, and now, we're going to stuff ourselves with fish and chips."

Julia smiled and linked her arm through Alice's. "I think I'm in love with Liam, so there's that."

"Oh, wow." Alice started to giggle. "You're moving as fast as me and Arthur."

Robin chortled. "I don't think anyone can move that fast." She gave Alice a withering look and then started to laugh too. "You guys know she married him willy-nilly, right? Just because her friends were getting married."

"Willy-nilly?" Alice demanded. "That is not true."

"It's so true," Robin said between her giggles. "Her and Kelli both. They decided on Laurel's wedding day to get married in my back yard only a week later."

"It was *two* weeks later," Alice said.

"Only because Duke came home, and I wouldn't allow the weddings to be the very next day."

"She's a stickler sometimes." Alice grinned at her, and Julia felt the love between them expand and expand.

"At least you guys know you'll have good in-laws," she said.

Robin reached for the door handle on the SUV that pulled up, as it was their turn for a ride. "And today, we're going to have an amazing lunch." She ducked into the car, and Maddy followed her.

Julia filled the back seat as Alice got in the front. "I hope so," she said. "I'm starving."

"We want to go to that new fish 'n chips place," Robin said to the driver. "I'm not sure where it is."

"It's not open yet," he said, and the whole world froze.

"It's not open yet?" Alice asked. "Are you sure? We saw reviews online."

"Those are from their Long Island store," the man said. "I can take you by where it is, but I'm ninety-nine percent sure they don't open until Labor Day." He put the car in gear, because he couldn't keep blocking the RideShare lane. "Too bad too, them missing the summer swell."

"Let's just go to my house," Maddy said. "I can put something together."

"Is there anywhere else to eat?" Alice asked.

"You can't cook for us on your day off," Robin said.

"I don't actually cook at The Glass Dolphin," Maddy said.

"There's the diner at Topside," the driver said.

"My house," Maddy said decisively. She rattled off the address, and the driver started the drive through the cliffs to her house. "We don't want to eat at that diner." She shook her head. "Ben and I went there once, and trust me, even if all I have at my place is cold cereal, it'll be better than that place."

"Plus, we have the appetizers at book club tonight," Julia said.

"Oh, my goodness," Robin said, sucking in her breath. "I forgot about book club tonight."

"I'm so tired," Alice said.

"Well, I have coffee and tea," Maddy said firmly. "Because we're all going to that book club tonight. And we're going to sit with all of our other friends, because we're not going to let cracks break us apart."

"And Tessa needs us there," Julia said. "There aren't as many registrations this time."

"We don't really count," Robin said.

"We do too," Julia argued back. "My money and name counts for something." She folded her arms again and shook her hair over her shoulders.

"Oh, you've riled up Julia," Maddy teased.

"I'm not riled up."

"So when will you and Liam get married?" Robin asked. "I don't need to plan it or anything, but I'd love to attend."

"Oh, the whole cove will attend," Maddy said. "Liam's a police officer. Laurel's posted some pictures of her wedding on social media. Felt like the whole force was there."

"Well, Paul is Aaron's second," Alice said.

"Liam leads the detective team," Julia said, as if he she needed to defend him or make him seem better somehow. "I'm sure he'll have the whole force there." She leaned forward and looked past Maddy. "I'll talk to Liam about when," she said. "Because I would love to have you plan it. We're—well, he's wanting to make sure things are okay with Ian before we really move forward."

"Teenagers are tough," Alice murmured.

The driver pulled up to Maddy's house, and the women started piling out. Julia spread her arms wide, feeling the whole of the earth beneath her feet. "I want to get married in the summer," she called to the skies above.

She drew in as much oxygen as she could as her friends

giggled and laughed behind her. "Come on, Julia," Maddy said. "Let's go see what I have to eat."

Julia smiled at the world before her, the ocean she could see on three sides, the cloudless sky, the beauty of the rocks and earth and everything. She'd once thought she'd have her restart, her refresh, her second chance, in Nantucket.

But now she knew that the job in Nantucket had just been a stepping stone to get to Five Island Cove. She belonged here, and she couldn't wait to keep making her life here. With Liam. With Ian.

She exhaled and turned to go inside with her friends. As she approached Maddy, she said, "Now I just have to figure out how to become more involved in my sons' lives."

"Oh, honey," she said. "I know that's been a roadblock you don't know how to get by."

"I'm just going to keep beating down their doors," Julia said, though a pinch of pain cascaded through her stomach. "I don't want them to forget I'm here, and that I love them."

"Your boys?" Alice asked, as Julia had just rounded the corner to enter the kitchen when she'd spoken the last sentence.

"Yes," Julia said. "We don't just give up, do we?"

"No," Robin said as she straightened from where she'd been leaning into the fridge. "We don't. And look. Maddy has lime seltzer water, and I can make mock-mojitos with these." She held up a few bright green cans of soda.

"Mint in the narrow drawer," Maddy said. "And Ben's on his way with the station leftovers. They had lasagna and garlic bread today."

"Mm, cooking from a military base," Alice said.

"They're better than firemen," Maddy said. "I promise. I've never eaten better than since I married Ben, and my ex is a senator." She grinned from ear to ear, and Julia's mouth watered.

"How long until he gets here with the food? I haven't eaten since Liam stopped by to make me breakfast before he went to work."

A silence filled the house, and it took a few beats of it before Julia realized what she'd said. "I mean—"

"Oh, Liam's stopping by to make you breakfast before work?" Maddy teased. "Did he wake you up in bed too?" She laughed as she joined Robin in the kitchen and got down glasses for their mocktails.

"Cops have to go in early," Alice said. "You must be starving." She walked over to the fridge. "I'll get you a snack."

"Oh, please," Maddy said, still giggling. "Ben will be here in ten minutes."

"Ten minutes," Julia complained. She got to her feet and headed for Maddy's couch. "I'm going to lie down. Bring me a drink when they're ready."

Everyone laughed, and that lifted Julia's heart. She was good friends with these women, and she loved them.

All of them, even the ones that weren't in the same phase of life as her, and she was so glad she'd moved to Five Island Cove when the opportunity had come up.

Now, she just had to survive book club with everyone,

when she'd just learned that she might be the cause of a splinter in the group.

# Chapter Twenty-Three

Tessa left her bedroom and stalked forward as if she had entered a fashion show and had just stepped onto the runway.

"There she is," Eloise said, as she'd stopped by after leaving the inn and caught Tessa getting ready for her date. Julia had come over specifically to loan Tessa a new dress, because she'd been out with David almost a dozen times now, and she'd worn everything worth wearing already.

She didn't have time to go shopping, and Julia had said she had "the perfect thing" for tonight's Summer Soiree on the beach.

"Wow," Billie said, turning from where she'd perched on the coffee able. "Miss Tessa, you look fantastic in that."

Tessa felt fantastic in the bright purple dress. It flowed around her legs like silky water, and she'd squeezed herself into her shapewear to boost her chest and slim her tummy.

"I think the neckline is a little low for me, but I'm not ruling it out."

"The neckline is perfect," Julia said. "You're just not used to showing that much."

"Exactly." Tessa pulled the shoulders of the dress back, but then the garment didn't sit or hang right. "I think it's fine, and I'll get used to it. I just...I'm not a cleavage woman."

"Tonight you are." Julia grinned at her. "It's perfect, Tess. Really."

"El?" she asked.

"It's stunning," Eloise said. "Do you feel good in it?"

"I really do." Tessa smiled and did a little twirl before she did her model-walk back toward the bedroom. She paused at the doorway, put her hand on her hip, and posed for everyone, a Very Serious Look on her face. The ladies watching her laughed and laughed, and Tessa felt lighter than she had all summer.

She returned to the living room of her small beach bungalow and sighed happily. "Thanks, everyone. He'll be here soon, so you don't need to hang around."

"Oh, but we do," Eloise said as she put another cracker in her mouth. "I want to see what Handsome Dave is wearing to the beach party tonight."

"I can still go with Ian, right, El?" Billie asked.

"Yeah," Eloise said. "We won't miss the next ferry." She smiled at Billie. "Grace, are you coming with me and Dad?"

"Yeah," Grace said, and she didn't seem happy about it.

Eloise didn't question her further, but she did watch the younger girl for an extra moment.

"You look fabulous," Julia said as she got up. She kissed Tessa on the cheek. "You are fabulous. I'll maybe see you there. I'm bumming along with Liam as he works."

"We're doing the same with Aaron," Eloise said. "So if you're on the outskirts of the Soiree, you'll see us." She smiled at Tessa and added, "Let's go, girls. Tessa wants to greet her date in private, I can tell."

"I would too," Billie grumbled. Everyone left, and Tessa's nerves fired in the resulting silence. She wasn't sure why. She'd been out with Dave several times now. He was a sweet man, if a bit on the shy side. Sometimes their conversations died and neither of them knew how to revive them.

The silence between them didn't bother her, but she wondered if they were truly compatible if they couldn't even talk for a couple of hours after being apart all day, or even for a couple of days.

Not only that, but he hadn't kissed her yet, and Tessa had started obsessively carrying mints and peppermint gum, which she used immediately following dinner. Dave seemed almost like a scared rabbit, a squirrelly squirrel, and any moves that had been made had been done by Tessa.

"So maybe you'll just have to kiss him if you want to kiss him," she told herself as she stood by the back sliding doors. The beach extended from there, and a sense of beauty filled her.

A knock sounded on her front door, and she spun toward it. Her heartbeat sprinted up her throat, and she pulled her dress up again. It just settled back down over her chest, and Tessa told herself to "be confident. Do what feels natural."

She closed the distance to the door and opened it. Dave stood there in a pair of blue shorts and a polo in pale yellow. He'd cleaned up around his beard, and his blue eyes shone at her the way the sunshine glinted off the azure waters.

"Hey, there," he said, his gaze sweeping down the length of her body. If they'd been headed to dinner and a dance, she'd be wearing heels. But tonight, they'd be on the beach, and Tessa wore sandals that would easily navigate the sand.

Dave's eyes met Tessa's again. "You look amazing."

"Thank you." Tessa smiled at him. "I just need to grab my purse." She turned, her brain misfiring at her. She had no idea where her purse had been put. "I think it's in my bedroom." She started that way. "Come in."

Behind her, she heard the door close just as she bustled into her bedroom. Sure enough, her purse sat on her bureau. She'd barely made it home before Julia and Eloise had come by, and she snatched the purse and spun to go back out into the main part of the house.

Dave waited over by the island that gave separation to the spaces in the large, open room, and when he turned toward her, he once again seemed nervous. Tessa didn't want this tension between them anymore.

"David," she said as kindly as she could given her frustration with things. "Do you like me?"

Dave swallowed. "Of course I do, Tessa."

"You always seem so nervous around me," she said. "I

mean, you loosen up eventually, but I'm just not sure how to get that part of you sooner."

"I don't know," he said. "I guess I'm still trying to believe that someone as amazing and as beautiful as you wants to go out with me."

She smiled at the compliment. "I want to do more than just go out with you," she said. "I have friends I can go to the Summer Soiree with. I want to go with my boyfriend."

"I am your boyfriend."

"I want you to touch me when you get here," she said, and she heard the frustration in her tone. "I want you to kiss me. I want *you* to hold *my* hand." Tessa wasn't sure if she was trying to ruin this or improve it.

Dave's gaze dropped to her lips, and Tessa eased closer to him. He did slide his hand along her waist, and he murmured, "I want to touch you when I see you. I want to kiss you. I want to hold your hand."

"Then do it," she whispered.

Dave's hand on her back became firmer, and he brought her closer in a single moment of time. He didn't hesitate, and she expected him to. She expected his kiss to be as hesitant as he'd been, but the instant his lips touched hers, a radiant heat swirled through her, exploding and popping in all directions.

He stroked his mouth against hers in perfect precision. His lips were soft and firm at the same time, demanding and giving back what he got. Tessa kissed him back, feeling a bit more lightheaded with every moment that passed.

She had never been kissed like this, and Dave kept at it

for several long moments before he pulled away. Tessa gasped for air, her chest pitching up and falling down, just like Dave's did.

When she'd caught her breath, she whispered, "Incredible." She opened her eyes and looked at him. He didn't smile. He didn't speak. "So you *really* like me."

"Yes, ma'am," he whispered.

"Don't hold back with me, okay?"

"Okay." He drew a breath and backed up a half-step. "Are you ready? Should we go?"

"Yes," Tessa said. "Have you been to this Soiree before?"

"No." He took her hand, and they walked toward the door. "They've never had it before. It's new, as part of the Safer, Cleaner Beach Initiative."

"Sure," Tessa said. "I've got a couple of girlfriends who'll be there with their cops."

"The cove's been doing events like this to get more people to the beach, but in a more controlled way. To show them the beaches are safe and clean. It's a good tourism move."

"There's been some controversy around increasing tourism," Tessa said.

"Yeah, there always is," Dave agreed. "It can be hard to keep staff during really busy times, but then, once everyone goes back to school and their normal lives, then we have people we don't need. It's a constant up and down."

"Ah, I can see that," Tessa said. They walked the short distance to the ferry and boarded the one she assumed Eloise and her girls were on. Tessa didn't look around for her, though. She wanted to be present with Dave, and enjoy the feeling of his fingers between hers.

She knew he'd lived in the cove for a couple of decades now. He'd been divorced for eight years. He only had one child—a daughter—who'd left the cove to attend college in Connecticut who he spoke to often.

He'd owned Soda Sensation for twelve years after working at the airport as a runway technician, his favorite food was a really juicy mushroom Swiss burger, and he had a big, boisterous laugh that made Tessa happy in a way nothing else ever had.

Oh, and now she knew he could kiss her like she'd never been kissed before, and she sighed as she laid her head against his shoulder and they faced into the wind as the ferry pulled away from the dock.

"What do you want to do with your life?" she asked.

He gave her question some thought, and Tessa liked that about him. He didn't speak to impress her; he said what he really thought, and he often took a few seconds to think about it first.

"I think I'm doing it," he said. "I own my own business. I live in the most beautiful place in the world. And now that I have you..." He trailed off. "I'm not alone anymore, so I'm not really sure what else I need."

"Mm."

"It feels almost selfish to ask for more, you know?"

"Yeah," Tessa said.

"What do you want to do with your life?" he asked. "Are you doing it?"

"I've always loved working at libraries," she said. "I used to have a beautiful yard in New Jersey. I'd like to get back to gardening, maybe. But otherwise, I think so. I have amazing friends who are important to me. I live in a great place that has everything I need, and I do love my job now that it's settled down a little bit."

He chuckled but didn't argue.

"And yes," she said. "Now we're together, and it feels good so far."

"Sorry I frustrated you with my nervousness." He pressed his lips against her temple, and Tessa leaned into it.

"You don't need to apologize. I hope I didn't come across as pushy or too strong."

"Not at all."

The conversation moved to a story that had happened at his soda shack that afternoon, and Tessa laughed as the ferry pulled up to Diamond. Everyone seemed to be convening on this island tonight, as the cove had done a great job of getting the word out about tonight's very public Soiree.

The line for the RideShare was long, but they chatted while they waited, and they ended up sharing a car with another couple. They got out on the beach, where music blasted, a couple of big blow-up toys had been inflated, and all the food trucks had gathered.

Down the sand a bit, the city had games set up, including horseshoes and volleyball nets for at least a hundred yards. Then the boutique took over, and that interested Tessa the most. Shopping on the beach with her boyfriend, the scent of fair foods hanging in the air, and the distant pounding of music—it was what summer nights were made for.

As they walked down the boardwalk in that direction, Dave asked, "What are you going to do about Mandie leaving?"

Tessa sighed out her breath. "Well, she has to be replaced. She does so much for me that I simply can't absorb. So Bonnie's already listed the position on the job boards."

"Any applicants?"

"I don't know," Tessa said. "She said she'd let me sit in on any interviews, but I haven't heard anything." A hint of worry touched her mind, but Tessa pushed it away. It was the Summer Soiree, and she wasn't going to let anything ruin tonight.

"She's at least one you won't have to let go, right?" She smiled over to Dave, and he chuckled as he nodded.

"Right. I'm going to miss her, though. She's a hard worker."

"She's the best," Tessa agreed. "I think she and Charlie are planning to be here tonight." She edged to the far side of the boardwalk as a large group of teens coming the opposite direction threatened to push her and Dave right off the path.

"I think everyone in the cove is going to be here tonight," Dave said, both hands on her body to balance her. "Honestly, I've gone face-blind already."

Tessa smiled, because he'd told her that with all the people he served, he stopped looking at their faces about fifteen minutes in. "It's overwhelming, isn't it?"

"I'm kind of wishing we'd just stayed on your beach," he said. "It's as nice as this one, would be quiet, and we'd still be together."

"Yes, but then we wouldn't be able to go shopping," she said. "Or get ice cream. Or one of those deep fried cheese sticks."

"Cheese sticks?" Dave tipped his head back and let loose that laugh. "No, sweetheart. If we're eating anything fried tonight, it's fish."

"Fish?" Tessa scoffed. "How very boring. So coastal town." She danced ahead of him still holding his hand. "You know what you need to try? That Southern barbecue that went in a couple of years ago."

"Barbecue? I like barbecue. You think I don't know how to eat barbecue?"

"I think everyone in Five Island Cove is a little obsessed with fish," she said. "Seafood. All of it."

"We're literally surrounded by the sea," he teased. "If you don't like fish, what'll you eat in a crisis?"

"I like fish just fine," Tessa said. "I simply think we could all stand to branch out a little bit. Keep some other restaurants in business."

"That barbecue place has been there for a few years," he said. "It's doing just fine."

"But that Korean place went out of business after like six months."

"That's because no one should be eating kimchi," he teased.

Tessa swatted at his chest and then settled back to his side. "There's fireworks later."

"I bet we could see them from your beach," he said.

"My beach faces northwest," she reminded him.

"But Sanctuary sits higher than Diamond," he said. "We'd be able to see them."

"You're not much of a people-person, are you, Dave?"

"I see so many people every single day," he said.

Tessa could hear the exhaustion in his voice, and she realized that he'd only come here—that he'd brought her here—tonight, because *she* wanted to attend the Summer Soiree. "Can we just walk around the booths for a little bit?" she asked. "And I hear they're releasing fireflies when it gets dark, and I've always wanted to see one."

"You've never seen a firefly?"

"No." She grinned up at him. "Just a couple of hours, and then I'll take you back to my beach, and we can watch the fireworks from there. Get ahead of the ferry crowds."

"Well, we definitely can't leave until you've seen a firefly." He squeezed her hand, and Tessa knew he'd like to leave right then. But he played a good sport and let her walk around the boutique so she could buy tea towels she didn't need, and a little notebook she'd never write in.

The sun settled in the western sky when he bought her the fried cheese stick she wanted, and they got ice cream on the way to the RideShare line. Full darkness had settled by the time she keyed her way back into her bungalow, and she tossed her purse onto the couch and led the way straight out the back door again.

"Ah," he said as he sagged into the lounger on her back patio.

She giggled. "You didn't even make it to the sand."

"I've had enough of walking through sand." He grabbed her hand as she went by, and he hauled her onto his lap.

Tessa squealed in a way she was sure she never had before, not even as a much younger woman. "We'll miss the fireworks," she said as he started kissing her neck. "You can't even see them from here. There's an eave above us."

"Truth be told, Tess." He touched his lips to hers. "I don't care about the fireworks in the sky nearly as much as the ones we've got between us."

"Oh, you don't, huh?"

"No, ma'am." He kissed her as completely as he had standing in her kitchen. "Sorry we left before they brought out the fireflies."

"I'm not worried about it," she pressed her cheek to his. "I know you'll get me a firefly one day." She leaned back and looked at him, no teasing glint or playful quality to her voice. "You will, won't you?"

"I absolutely will," he promised her, and Tessa let herself fall a little bit in love with him as he kissed her again.

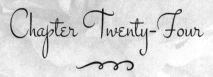

# Chapter Twenty-Four

Eloise hefted the bag of food into the backseat of her car as Billie got behind the wheel. "Grace," she said. "Can you watch this? It can't tip over."

"Okay." Grace slid over to the middle of the seat and put her hand on top of the Styrofoam containers Eloise had brought from Sanctuary. It was their dinner, and Eloise just wanted an easy evening at home with her family.

She and Aaron had a trip planned to Boston, just the two of them, once the summer tourist season died down. October in New England awaited, and she'd been listening to Clara tell stories of the leaves in Vermont for a couple of weeks now.

They hadn't had a vacation in, well, ever. Besides their honeymoon, that was, and Eloise needed some time with her husband.

Time away from Cliffside, and away from Five Island Cove, to be honest.

The girls were staying with Aaron's parents, and Aaron had promised to leave his work phones—both of them—at home.

Eloise got in the passenger seat and looked over to Billie. "You got your seat in the right place?"

"Yes." She gripped the steering wheel tightly and looked like she might choke to death before they pulled into the driveway.

"Mirrors," Eloise said gently. Billie had been doing a summer driver's education course, and Eloise had been spending many a lunch hour with Billie behind the wheel.

Billie dutifully checked the mirrors and adjusted the one on her side. Eloise said nothing, because she had pre-sets she could put back with the press of a button.

"Ready." She looked over to Eloise, who merely nodded. She'd coached the girl through how to get started, and Billie could do it herself.

"Go on," Eloise finally murmured when Billie still sat there.

Billie startled and reached to put the car in gear. She had a back-up camera, but she still looked over her shoulder, and Eloise couldn't help checking her rear-view mirror too.

She backed out successfully, and she got the sedan moving toward the exit of the ferry parking lot. The drive home happened easily, and the Styrofoam containers in the backseat barely made a squeak as Billie drove carefully home, and Eloise said, "Amazing job, honey," as Billie put the car in park in their driveway.

The girl looked at Eloise with her gorgeous blue eyes, wide and full of hope. "I did okay?"

"It was perfection," Eloise said. "So next, you'll work on increasing your speed. It's okay to drive the speed limit. The car will still stop." She smiled at Billie and twisted to look at Grace. "Let's take your dad dinner."

They all piled out of the car and went inside the house. Aaron's police cruiser sat in the driveway, so Eloise knew he'd be home. She didn't see him upon immediate entry, but she herded the girls past the dining room table and into the kitchen.

They set everything down, and Eloise bustled around putting her purse away and pulling the containers out of plastic bags.

"Aaron?" she called.

"In the office," he answered, and she glanced over to the door. It sat open only an inch or two, and Eloise eyed it for a moment.

"Mom, it's Ian," Billie said. Eloise glanced to her to find her holding her phone up. "Do I have a couple of minutes?"

"Yep." Eloise nodded, and Billie's face split into a grin as she spun toward the front door.

Grace had settled onto the couch with a notebook, and Eloise turned her attention to the office.

She knocked once as she opened the door, but Aaron didn't turn from his desk against the far wall. Eloise came in here often enough to see the changes on his bulletin and white boards, but they didn't like the girls coming in.

"Baby?" She wrapped her arms over his shoulders, and he sighed and leaned back into her. "What's wrong?"

"I lost two cops today," he said.

Her heartbeat seized. "I didn't hear anything on the radio."

"They're quitting," he said. "Not a death or anything."

She rounded him and settled onto his lap. "Maybe lead with 'two of my officers quit today' instead of 'I lost.'" She smiled at him, and he briefly returned it.

"Sorry, my love." He kissed her gently, then pulled back and added, "The DNA came back."

Eloise' pulse sped this time, and she searched her husband's face. He looked worn along the edges, and Eloise wondered how much longer he could be the Chief of Police here in Five Island Cove.

"And?"

"Robin and I are related." His eyes closed as he sighed. "I didn't think I'd care, but it turns out I do."

She stroked her hand down the side of his face. "I'm sorry, baby."

"I just feel...I don't know." He looked away. "Lost, maybe? It doesn't make sense to me. I know who I am. My parents are still my parents. This is a generation removed from me, and yet, I suddenly feel like I'm standing on shattered ground."

"I understand," Eloise whispered. She'd been through something similar a few years ago, when she'd learned things about her brother and father she hadn't known. Things that had rocked her to the core foundation of who she was.

"I know you do." He leaned his forehead against hers. "I love you, El. You are my rock. My anchor. The safety inside any storm raging in my life."

Eloise smiled internally, because she didn't want to diminish his feelings. She'd longed for a relationship like what she had with Aaron, and sometimes, she still couldn't believe she had the love of this good man.

"We brought dinner," she said. "Your daughters are still your daughters. That hasn't changed."

He looked at her, and Eloise did let herself smile then. "Your mom and dad are still your mom and dad. That hasn't changed. In fact, your grandmother is still your grandmother. That hasn't changed."

"She had to have known," he said. "It's not like *she* was the one who carried another man's baby, and it was him who didn't know. She had to have, I don't know, adopted my dad. I mean, she *knew* she wasn't pregnant."

Eloise nodded and cradled his face in both her hands. "Blood means something, but we both know real relationships can overcome that. Right?"

He nodded, but she continued. "I mean, look at your beautiful girls. I am not their mother. They know that, and yet, I'm here every day for them. I'm teaching Billie how to drive, and she's asking me if she can go talk to Ian before dinner, and she calls *me* Mom."

He smiled softly and nodded again. "I know, El. You're right."

"They have their mother's blood, but she's *not* their

277

mother. Family relationships are very long, and we have to be patient and build them brick by brick."

"They won't go back to Carol," he said.

"They might," Eloise said. "As adults, they might both have this need to know who she is. They might really want to understand more than they've been able to as children. Billie especially."

"It won't change how she feels about you," Aaron said. "You *are* her mother, and you're right. Blood is only so thick. The people we choose to spend our time with willingly, the people we sacrifice for, the people we serve—they're who becomes our family."

"Right." Eloise slid from his lap, glad for all of these reminders. She extended her hand toward him. "Now, come on. Dinner's cold, and Billie's been on the phone with Ian for ten minutes already."

He put his hand in hers and stood. Aaron lifted her fingers to his lips and kissed each one. "I love you," he said again.

"And I love you." She led him out of the office and left him in the kitchen. "Grace, dinner." She continued toward the front door as the girl set aside her notebook and slid from the couch. She started saying something to Aaron as Eloise opened the front door.

She expected to find Billie sitting in the rocking chair on the front porch, her phone at her ear and her face glowing as she talked to Ian Clearwater. They weren't dating, but they liked each other.

Her feet came to a complete standstill, and her mouth

had opened to call Billie in for dinner—but no sound came out.

For Billie wasn't on the phone with Ian. She stood in the boy's arms at the bottom of the few steps that led from porch to sidewalk.

Kissing him.

"Bills?" Aaron called, and Eloise panicked.

"Billie," she barked, and Ian jumped back from Billie. "Time for dinner."

Billie looked dazed as she turned toward Eloise. The sound of Aaron's boots thudded on the floor behind Eloise, who still stood in the doorway, hopefully blocking the teens in front of her.

"Ian, you better go," Eloise said. She reached her hand toward Billie. "Your dad is calling us for dinner."

Billie's face cleared, and her eyes sharpened again. She looked at Ian, who had started backing down the front sidewalk. "Bye," she said, and then she flew up the steps to Eloise.

Their eyes never left one another, and Eloise couldn't imagine the questions she was firing at her daughter. "You better have some stories for us at dinner."

"Bills," Aaron said. "El says the driving is going great. Do you want to go out with me after dinner? Some night driving practice."

Billie tore her gaze from Eloise and looked at her father. "Yeah, sure," she said smoothly. "That sounds fun."

They all returned to the house and sat down to dinner. The tension trapped under the roof had rendered them all silent, and Grace looked around at everyone and said, "Fine. I'll go first. Tyler Fonnesbeck asked me to the movies, and I said I'd go. I was going to fake sick on Friday and stay home from the inn and sneak out and go with him."

Tears filled her eyes. "I really want to go, and maybe Billie can come to the same movie but sit away from us." She looked over to her sister with such hope on her face.

Aaron looked at Grace, his eyebrows sky-high. "Tyler Fonnesbeck? Son of Leann and Don? She works as Paul's assistant secretary?"

"Yes, sir." Grace dropped her chin and wiped at her face.

"I'll go with you, Gracie," Billie said quietly. "But I won't be alone. I'll invite Ian to go with me. We can double."

"Double?" Aaron's gaze flew to Billie. "I thought you and Ian weren't dating. *Just friends*, I believe, were the exact words you used."

"Yes, well." Billie shook her long hair over her shoulders, then reached back and gathered it into a ponytail. "Things change."

"They do?" Aaron looked at Eloise, who gave him a small smile.

"They do, honey," Eloise said. "Tell them how things have changed for you."

"I kissed him," Billie blurted out. She looked wildly from Eloise to Aaron. "Just now. Outside."

Aaron had opened his mouth to say something, but it snapped shut immediately.

"Just now," Eloise said. "First time?" She studied Billie, who nodded. She didn't have a habit to lie, but she did like to keep things a secret until she'd been found out. Aaron had tried to tell her that staying silent about something was akin to lying, but Billie was still learning.

"So things change," Billie said.

"What about Addie?" Eloise asked.

"She likes Quinn now."

"Well," Aaron said as he scooped up some noodles and rice. "El, do you have anything to tell us before I go?"

She smiled at him, because he was handling this kissing very well. "No, baby," she said. "You go on ahead and tell everyone what you found out today."

Her smile slipped, because finding out his family dynamics had changed certainly wasn't something to make light of. It wasn't the same as Grace's first date or Billie kissing a cute boy she liked.

Sometimes, she wished she could solidly hold the past in the past. Sometimes, she truly believed it deserved no place in the future.

At the same time, Eloise also believed that sometimes the past could shape a person into exactly the type of person they needed to be. They could help others with their experiences and knowledge and empathy.

She wasn't sure how to categorize different events into different buckets, so she simply waited for Aaron to tell his story. That was all someone could do—tell their story to those they loved and cling to them.

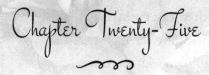

# Chapter Twenty-Five

A lice rang her father's doorbell and tried the knob. "Dad," she called as she stepped into the house.

"On the deck," he yelled through the house. Alice went through the living room and kitchen and stepped back outside to join her father. As she did, she got reminded of how much she'd loved growing up on Rocky Ridge. She loved this view, though for a while there, she'd blamed the ocean for the loss of her mother.

When that had gotten too hard, as the water lapped and waved around her constantly, she'd blamed her father.

Thankfully, she'd found a way to move past that, and Alice could come here and only see the good again. "Hey, Dad."

He put his arm around her. "Darla's got a kite."

Alice looked back into the sea of blue in front of her. Bright azure sky, which faded down to robin's egg blue right before it kissed the ocean, which shone a light navy against the black sand beach.

"Where?"

"Over yonder." Her dad nodded toward her right, and Alice looked that way, eventually finding a bright yellow and red diamond flapping through the blue.

"I haven't flown a kite in forever."

"She goes down every once in a while." He removed his arm from her shoulders and leaned against the railing again. "How are the kids? Ready to move back to the city?"

"Yes," she said. She'd already told her father and Darla that Charlie, Ginny, and Mandie would be living together in the city. No one seemed to have too much of a reaction to the news, but Alice still had an internal struggle warring within her.

"You've done such a good job with those kids, Alice."

She looked at her dad, because he didn't dole out compliments that often. "Thank you, Dad." She took in a big breath of the clear, clean air here. "The ladies are going to be here soon. It's okay if we tromp through your house and go down to the beach from here?"

"Anytime." He gave her a smile. "Darla even made orange scones and iced tea for when you guys are done with your Pact."

Alice leaned into him again and hugged his arm. "She's the best, isn't she?"

"She sure is."

The doorbell rang again, and Alice turned to go get it. She'd congregate everyone here in the house until they'd all

THE BICYCLE BOOK CLUB

arrived, but she assumed all four of them would be standing on the stoop.

The ferries ran to Rocky Ridge every twenty-five minutes, and they'd agreed to meet at eleven-thirty today, because that gave them time to arrive on the eleven-fifteen ferry, catch a RideShare, and be at Alice's father's house at that time.

Sure enough, Alice opened the door to find Robin saying, "...open the door. She knows we're coming."

Alice grinned at her, then Eloise, AJ, and Kelli. "You could've just walked in."

"Told you," Robin said as she stepped up into the house first.

"You're in a bad mood," Alice said. "This should be fun."

"I'm not in a bad mood." Robin gave her a glare and moved out of the way so others could enter too. "It's a work thing, and I'll deal with it after we do this."

"A venue canceled on her," Eloise said as she entered. "She'll be fine for this."

Alice nodded and switched her gaze to AJ. "Lisa has Asher today?"

She smiled and nodded and something inside Alice told her to hug AJ. So she grabbed onto her the moment she entered the house and held her tightly. "It's so good to see you."

"It's nice to be seen," AJ whispered, and she moved out of the way so Alice could hug Kelli.

"You look amazing, Kelli."

"The yoga has been amazing in helping me to lose the baby weight," Kelli said. She smiled at Alice as she pulled away. "I know you can't, but you would love yoga."

"I would," Alice said. "I do. I did some yoga classes with some of the Hampton wives." And now that Alice thought about it, that was why she hadn't' done it since leaving The Hamptons. She'd wanted to be someone completely different than who'd she'd been in that house in The Hamptons, and that extended all the way down to something as simple as a yoga class.

Her heartbeat skipped as she closed the door and turned to face her friends. She'd wanted them all here for this Summer Sand Pact renewal, because everything going on in their lives had started with the five of them oh-so-long ago, and Alice wanted that foundation to be strong, impenetrable, and solid.

They all looked to her, and Alice pasted a smile on her face. "Darla made orange scones and iced tea for later," she said. "Unless we want to take them down to the beach now."

Robin carried a huge bag over her shoulder, and she shifted it. "I got everyone's order from Mort's."

"So we'll have them as post-Pact refreshments," Alice said. "Everyone ready?" She picked up her own beach bag and led the way out the back door. "We're heading down, Dad."

"Okay," he said. "Have fun."

Alice hoped it would be fun, and she listened to her friends say hello to her father as they went by. She'd once counted the steps down to the beach and back up, and she knew the back-and-forth staircase had ninety-four steps.

She'd once thought of herself kept captive by those ninety-four steps, and she'd fled down them many times for escape.

The black sand beach glittered and welcomed her, and a pull of relaxation brought her shoulders away from her ears where they'd been bunched since she'd boarded the ferry from Diamond Island.

Her dad had already brought down the umbrellas and a flash of love moved through her. She set up her chair in the shade of one, and she'd already talked to Robin about not sitting right beside her.

So she wasn't surprised to find Robin behind everyone, bringing up the rear of the group, with several steps still to descend. Kelli sat right next to Alice, and the five of them made a rainbow shape in the shade by the time everyone had settled down.

Robin took charge, as Robin was wont to do, and she started handing out their lunches.

Alice took hers with a murmured, "Thank you, Robin," and pulled the plastic fork out of the plastic container of seafood salad. She loved this stuff, and she'd only eat it from Mort's and only every so often.

"I brought wine," AJ said as she lifted a bottle from her bag. "Kelli has agreed to get me home today, but I'm only going to have one drink, so it should be fine."

"I'm not drinking," Kelli said. "Since I'm still breastfeeding." She lifted her tuna BLT to her lips and took a bite. She groaned and added, "I love this sandwich so much."

Eloise smiled over to her and then Alice. "I'll take a glass of wine. Billie has started dating Ian Clearwater, and Grace went on a date with a very nice, very cute boy last weekend." She took a deep breath and popped a French fry into her mouth. "I don't know how those of you who've raised teenagers have survived."

Robin laughed lightly. "It's not easy."

"Day by day," Alice said. "And listening to your gut."

"There's a lot of that, too," Robin said, exchanging a glance with Alice. "I still do that, even for my young adult child. Sometimes I feel like I should say something, and sometimes my brain screams at me to hold my tongue."

"Can you actually do that?" AJ asked, her eyebrows quirked.

"Hey," Alice said, but AJ laughed.

"I'm kidding, Robin." She grinned at everyone. "If I'm half the mother you are, Asher will probably win the Nobel Peace Prize."

Alice sank back into her seat, recognizing she didn't need to protect Robin. Or AJ, Kelli, or El. They *knew* each other, and each of them could stand up for themselves.

"Let's do news then," Robin said. "Since El sort of already started."

Alice caught the "sort of," but she didn't challenge it or demand that Eloise tell them everything. She'd tucked into her first piece of fried fish, so she obviously wouldn't be talking again for a minute.

"I'll go," Alice said, clearing her throat. "It's sort of Robin's news too. Our children." She gestured between her and Robin on the other end of the rainbow. "Are moving in together in a few weeks. Charlie and Mandie are probably going to get married at some point. She'll never be able to get rid of me." She grinned at her best friend and then drank in the reactions of her friends.

"Wow," Eloise said around her halibut and tartar sauce.

"They're going to live together?" AJ asked.

"You lived with Matt before you got married," Robin said.

"Yeah, but—" AJ looked at Kelli. "That's me."

"We are going to be nothing but supportive of them," Robin said. "I personally want Mandie to tell me whatever she's comfortable telling me. Ask me whatever she needs to ask me. And I know you guys are a big part of her life too, and you can do what you want, but if she comes to you and asks you something, I hope you'll just be loving and kind and answer as honestly as you can."

"What would she ask?" Kelli asked.

"I don't know," Robin said. "But she asked Kristen what she thought about her living with Charlie last weekend while we were there for Sunday brunch. Thankfully, I'd already told her, and Kristen handled it well, the way she always does."

They sat there in a moment of silence, and Alice's mind had seemingly recalled every fond experience with Kristen she'd ever had over the years. "Kristen is so great," she murmured.

"She's the best," Kelli agreed. "Very accepting. Very loving."

"That's us," Robin said. "Besides my venue for the wedding I have in a month getting yanked. Duke will be home to help Mandie move, and then he'll go back to Alaska for a couple of weeks, and then he and Steve will come home."

She said nothing of Jamie, though Alice knew the fifteen-year-old wasn't easy for Robin to handle alone. She knew she missed Duke far more than she'd ever even told Alice. She knew Robin was strong, capable, and powerful, but that she also wanted her husband to take care of her, protect her, and make her coffee in the morning.

"That's about it for me, too," Alice said. "Oh, wait. Ginny is dating someone new, and he goes to Harvard. Frank says she's been up in Boston a lot lately, and he thinks they might be getting serious already."

"Wow, Harvard," Kelli said. "You and El's alma mater."

Alice exchanged a glance with El. "Yeah, he's starting his first year of law school there."

"That's great," El said. "I think my brownstone will be available at the end of the school year, so if he needs somewhere to live, let me know."

"Thank you, El." Alice's heart warmed at the kindness of her friend.

"I'll give him a good deal," she said. "I just want it taken care of."

"I haven't met him, obviously," Alice said. "He could be a total slob."

"Not if Ginny likes him," Kelli said. "She's such a great girl."

"She is," Alice said. She forked up another bite of seafood salad. "I feel a little abandoned by my children, which I wasn't expecting. Of course I want them to have amazing lives of their own. I just guess I wasn't expecting both of them to find a partner quite so quickly."

She kept her eyes down, because she hadn't told anyone that besides Arthur. Not even Robin.

"Alice," Kelli said.

"They'll always need you," Robin said, and Alice looked up and over to her. "Even after they're married. Children always need their parents."

She nodded and looked over to Kelli. "Someone else give us the news."

"I'm not sure I have any," Kelli said. "Julian is mostly moved, and Parker is going to go to Jersey for a week before school starts. Daphne is an amazing baby. Shad and I are happy."

"I think I'm about like Kelli," AJ said. "Asher is the best baby ever most of the time. You guys will come to his birthday party next weekend, right?"

"I've got it on the calendar," Robin said, and everyone else nodded.

"Jean is making the cake," AJ said. "Lisa is here to help decorate and throw the party. Matt is taking a whole Sunday afternoon off."

"Wow," Alice said with a smile.

"I think," AJ said, and she stayed quite serious. "I don't even want to say." She ducked her head over her lobster roll.

"Oh, you have to say," Robin said. "That's part of the Pact."

"It's not a Tell-All," AJ said, shooting her a fiery look.

"Fine," Robin said, and she dusted her hands of the sourdough crumbs from her three-cheese grilled cheese. "I call for a Tell-All." She fired challenge right back at AJ.

"Second," El said before Alice could.

"Come on, Ava," Kelli said. "It can't be that bad."

"I would've said it eventually," AJ said, rolling her eyes. "You didn't have to invoke the Tell-All."

"You never know with you," Robin said, and she wasn't wrong.

"I feel...bored," AJ said. "Stale. My life is everything I've ever wanted. I'm grateful for it. I have an amazing husband, and a little boy, and plenty of money and things and friends, and I'm..."

Alice waited for her to find the right word, her brain filling in several options. *Dissatisfied. Trying to be grateful. Selfishly wanting more. Craving my independence.*

"I know exactly how you feel," Alice said into the resulting silence. "I felt like this in The Hamptons."

Everyone looked at her, all of them with surprise and questions in their eyes.

"You have an amazing life," she said. "And you know it. You might even say it out loud to yourself, or to Matt, or just keep the words in your head. But they're there."

She looked away from her food and around to her

friends. "But you used to be important, and you don't feel important now. Or you feel guilty for wanting more when you have so much. So then you have this internal wrestle with what you really want—and if it's not the gorgeous husband, the money, the house, the baby, then what is it? And what kind of monster are you that you've gotten everything you've ever wanted, and you're still dissatisfied?"

AJ sniffled and wiped her eyes, and Alice knew she'd hit the nail on the head. Hard.

Alice leaned forward and reached past Kelli to AJ. She squeezed her knee and said, "You're important to me, AJ. You're everything to Matt and Asher. We all see you, and we all love you."

"I know," she said in a high-pitched, choked voice. "It's silly."

"It's not silly," Alice said firmly. "It's how you feel, and how you feel is valid."

"I think," El said, as she'd always been so smart and so mature. "How you feel is pretty normal for women our age in general, and you had to wait a long time to get your husband and kids—just like me."

Everyone watched her now, and Alice's heart filled with love over and over for Eloise.

"I say don't ignore it. Don't feel bad for feeling it. I'm trying to enjoy every moment and trying to reframe my thoughts to a place of abundance instead of narrowing in on that void inside my life."

"Yes," AJ said. "A void exists, and I don't know how to fill it." She looked at Alice, then Kelli. "You guys have jobs, businesses. You run an inn, El. Robin, everyone in the cove wants you to plan their wedding. I have...nothing like that. And you know what? I don't *want* a yoga studio or a busy business, but then I feel bad that I'm not using my skills and experience to—I don't know what. Do something?"

"The world needs good mothers," Robin said simply. Alice nodded, and she took another bite of her salad as AJ sniffled again.

"Thank you, Robin," she said. "That means so much to me. You have no idea."

She seemed done, and that only left El, though she'd said a few things already. Alice watched her look over to Robin, and the two of them most certainly had something only they knew.

"You four are my heart," Alice said. "You mean so much to me. I know we have other friends, and I know not every person can make every lunch, or go on every walk, or get to every event. It's not because you're not wanted there. Everyone is always, always invited." She pressed her fist to her heart. "Okay? We have to be united the way we have been in the past. It's us, you guys. It's always been about us." Alice wasn't usually the one saying such things, but that was how she really felt.

"I agree," Kelli said. "When we're strong, our families will be better. The other friendships will be strong too. It *is* about us."

"I love us," Robin said.

"So do I," El added.

"We are the best." AJ wiped her eyes and smiled at everyone. "Thanks for making us do this, Alice."

"Every summer," Alice said, still watching El. "I think Eloise has something more to say." She lifted her eyebrows at the other woman, who swallowed though she had no food in her mouth.

"Yeah." The breeze kicked up, ruffling the umbrellas, and Alice dug her toes into the hot sand, warming one part of her body while her bare arms and shoulders chilled slightly.

"Aaron's—well, Mandie found some recipes and letters at the library this summer."

"You have got to be kidding me," Kelli said. "Letters?" Her voice held plenty of disbelief, but also plenty of disgust. "I hope she burned them."

Robin grinned and shook her head. "She didn't. She found them romantic, which they are. They just also happened to be between my grandmother and Aaron's grandfather."

"They're related," El said. "Robin and Aaron. Half-cousins. Or something. His grandfather had an affair with her grandmother. His dad is their baby."

Alice didn't know what to say. Her ears rang and then white noise flowed through them. AJ and Kelli expressed a few words of awe, and Alice finally said, "I'm surprised this is the first we're hearing of this."

She raised her eyebrows at Robin, who she thought told her everything.

"We told El and Aaron," Robin said. "To see if it

mattered to them. Aaron took a DNA test, and I didn't know until a few seconds ago that we were related." She looked at El. "When did he find out? I expected him to call."

"Last week," Eloise said. "We had a lot going on with the girls, and he's had cops quitting as the end of the summer nears."

Alice's phone chimed, and she picked up her device as everyone else's did too. "Must be a group text," she said.

And it was, this one from Kristen, who said she'd like to host the next Wednesday luncheon at the clubhouse in her condo complex, and she really wanted everyone to come.

*We can change the day,* she said. *Sunday afternoon? Whatever. I want everyone there in September, once school is back in session, and life in the cove has calmed a little.*

Alice looked up at the others. "A weekend would be better, right?"

"Sunday afternoon is always better for us," El said.

"I'll suggest Sunday afternoon," Robin said, her fingers flying. She looked up when she finished, and Alice nodded at her.

"We're the best," Robin said, and she moved to the middle of the rainbow and gathered everyone into her. They all leaned in, a group hug forming easily and quickly.

"I love you guys," Alice said, and the best part of this year's Summer Sand Pact was that everyone said it back.

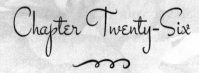

# Chapter Twenty-Six

AJ pulled up to the appointed house, and both she and Kelli leaned forward. "Looks normal," she said.

A minivan sat in the driveway, but the back looked raised in a way AJ didn't see very often. She wasn't sure about that, but she knew it had taken almost six weeks for Kate Forrest to allow her and Kelli to come steal her away for lunch. She hadn't said why too much, only that she couldn't. She had "something" on this day or "too much going on" on that day.

But today, she'd finally agreed, and as AJ watched, the front door opened and Kate emerged. She wore a white pair of shorts and a blue, green, and white flowered top that said summer perfection without a word.

She came down the steps in white sandals and an over-sized denim bag over her forearm. Her strawberry blonde hair had been pulled up and then curled, and she looked the ideal picture of stay-at-home-mom as she smiled and came toward the car.

"Is that her?" Kelli asked, and AJ was wondering the same thing.

"It's her." She got out of the SUV and moved toward Kate too. "Hey," she said brightly. "You look fantastic."

She took Kate into a light hug, and as she did, her eyes moved to the minivan. She once again saw the two carseats, as well as the room for the wheelchair. Then Kate started to pull away, and AJ put a smile on her face. "Ready?"

Kate returned her smile. "Yep."

"Who did you get to watch the kids?" AJ asked. "Is your husband back in town?"

Kate had said that her husband traveled a lot for work, then had a home office when he was in the cove, but AJ didn't know what he did for work. She didn't even know what his name was.

As Kate opened the back door, AJ realized she didn't know her very well at all. Still, she got behind the wheel, glancing over to Kelli as she and Kate exchanged hellos.

"To Porterhouse?" AJ asked brightly.

"I love their clam chowder," Kelli said as she faced the front. "Have you been there, Kate?"

"No," the woman said. "It's hard for me to take the kids out alone, and my husband is—" Her voice stopped completely, reminding AJ of what happened in a movie when the Internet connection got dropped. Like, the picture just froze, and everything went silent.

AJ pulled out of Kate's driveway, not realizing she'd

started to hold her breath. She coached herself to push it out and take another breath before Kate said, "I'm just going to tell you guys. I'm honestly surprised you don't know. It feels like the whole cove does."

"I live on Bell," Kelli said. "I don't hear hardly any gossip, unless it's political." She flashed Kate a smile. "My husband works at City Hall."

"My husband does real estate investing," she said. "He travels all over, looking for up-and-coming properties that he thinks will be worth big money soon."

"What brought you to the cove?" Kelli asked, voicing AJ's question too.

"He bought up a huge parcel of land on Rocky Ridge," she said almost absently. "He thinks it'll be the next hot spot on the East Coast."

"How long have you lived here?" AJ asked, realizing she'd just tag-teamed Kate.

"About a year," Kate said. "Ryan's been in the cove for maybe a month of that."

AJ looked over to Kelli, sensing so much to that story.

"I'm sorry," she said, because it felt like the right thing to say.

"We're getting divorced," Kate said. "He can't handle Holden, and he's too big of a coward to say it."

AJ swallowed, because she knew Holden was her oldest. Kelli said nothing, her jaw tight. "He's your oldest, right?" AJ asked.

"Yes," Kate said. "He's wheelchair-bound. He requires

constant care. He can't speak, or move, or do much of anything by himself."

"Oh, no," Kelli said. "Kate, I'm sorry."

"My sister has moved in with me for now," Kate said. "But she wants me to go live with her in Harrisburg. In all honesty, I should."

"You have younger boys too, right?" Kelli asked, now twisted all the way around to see Kate. AJ glanced at her in the rear-view mirror and found her facing out the side window. Everything about her sat very, very still, almost like she had to exist somewhere outside her body to say all the things she'd said.

"Yes," she said. "Jake and Logan. They're fraternal twins and full of energy and life." Her voice had lightened considerably. "But they're three, and I simply can't handle all of them myself. So we don't go out to eat often, and I really should move closer to Naomi."

"You keep saying 'should,'" Kelli said. "You don't want to?"

"Ryan's moved us every year or so," she said. "The kids are just getting settled, and so am I. It's hard to want to uproot them again."

"Does real estate investing require moving often?" Kelli asked.

"No." Kate cleared her throat, and AJ moved her gaze to her in the mirror again. "We'd move every time I found him cheating on me. The only way he said he could stop seeing whoever she was was to move. So we've lived in Sacramento, Boise, Phoenix, Oklahoma City, Boston, and now here."

AJ counted quickly and came up with five moves. Five separate instances of her husband cheating on her? AJ couldn't imagine that, and she gripped the steering wheel as Kelli sighed with frustration.

"That sounds awful," Kelli said. "You must really love your husband."

"I did," Kate said. "We—*I* tried very hard, but since being here, I've realized how much my kids are missing by having their dad gone. The older they get, the more I want them to have him around. And he doesn't really like any of us, not even the little boys."

She sniffled then, and AJ's heart cracked and bled for her. She pulled into the parking lot and parked. AJ twisted to look at Kate too, who finally turned to face her and Kelli, tears rolling down her lovely face.

"Oh." AJ got out of the car quickly and opened the back door. She slid into Kate, who moved over to the middle of the bench seat. She wrapped her arms around her new friend and held on tight.

"I'm so sorry."

"It's okay," Kate whispered. "I just don't tell many people. We're not divorced yet, and my neighbors think Ryan's just off doing what he's always done."

She straightened and took Kelli's offered hand. "Which he is, I suppose. Cheating on me; making excuses for why he can't do something or come home; avoiding questions about the kids and me."

"But he filed for divorce?" AJ asked. "Or you did?"

"I did,: Kate said. "Which is another reason I just need

to stay here for a bit. I've got hearings and whatnot, and I need this door to be all the way closed before I even consider packing up everything I own and moving to Pennsylvania."

More tears spilled from her eyes. "The thought of that..." She shook her head, and AJ just wanted to protect her from anything more that could hurt her. One look at Kelli told her that Kelli wanted the same thing, and as they'd both been through similar, hard things, even if it wasn't an absent husband or a handicapped child, their hearts had been wounded in similar ways.

"Just stay with us," AJ said. "We'll help you with whatever you need."

"Yes," Kelli said. "We'll take care of you."

AJ closed her eyes and hugged Kate, everything maternal inside her wanting to protect this dear woman.

"I'm okay," Kate finally said. "Let's go eat." She sat up, and AJ looked at her. "Really. I'm starving too, and I put makeup on for the first time in months." Kate exhaled out a smile and a laugh. She wiped her eyes. "Of course, then I cried it all off, but still."

"You should come to our group luncheon," AJ said, not sure where the invitation had come from. "It's not for a few more weeks, but you'd love it. Then you can meet the rest of our friends."

She looked at Kelli, who surprisingly nodded. "Yes," she said. "You'll love them, and so many of them live here on Diamond."

"I hate taking charity," Kate said. "But it's something God had been teaching me since we had Holden. I simply can't do everything myself. So yes. If I can bring him, I'll come. I can get someone to watch the twins, but Holden is much harder to care for."

"Kristen's place has all the accessibility implementations," Kelli said. "It won't be a problem at all."

"It's on a Sunday afternoon," AJ said. "I think some of us might have our kids." She'd already arranged for Matt to tend to Asher. He'd already scheduled dinner at his parents' house, and she didn't think anyone else would have their children with them.

But it didn't matter. Kate would be welcomed with open arms, because that was what the women here in Five Island Cove did.

They welcomed anyone and everyone who needed them, and Kate needed them—just like AJ did.

And that wasn't weakness or a flaw. It simply meant that when AJ knit herself together with others who loved her and whom she loved, all of them were stronger.

But she'd text everyone to make sure they knew about Kate and her sons, and that they'd be coming to the luncheon, so the web of support could start to be built ahead of time.

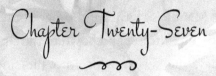

# Chapter Twenty-Seven

R obin rolled over in bed, feeling the chill of the air conditioning beyond the warmth of her comforter. She snuggled in deeper, expecting to pull the pillow to her chest. Instead, her pillow—which she'd been using as a replacement for her husband—wasn't there.

Duke was.

He moaned as he rolled toward her too, tucking her against his chest in a way that made Robin wake further with a joyful smile on her face. She didn't open her eyes as she gained even more awareness, because today was going to be a long, hard day.

"My back hurts," Duke murmured. "This bed is hard."

She didn't say anything, because Duke slept on a variety of surfaces. His bed on his fishing boat. Their bed at home. The bed in the oceanside cabin where he lived in Alaska. The couch.

And apparently, this hard bed in a hotel in New York City.

She heard the soft breathing of someone in the other queen bed in this room—either Mandie or Jamie. They'd packed all of Mandie's clothes and other household belongings into three big suitcases and flown to the city yesterday.

And today, she was moving into the single bedroom apartment. Off campus. With her best friend and her boyfriend.

Since they were college students, they didn't have a whole lot. But moving anywhere off-island required a lot of planning, especially if there was furniture involved. It wasn't like they could check a loveseat with the airline and pick it up on a baggage carousel later.

Their apartment had come partially furnished, and when Ginny sent pictures of what the three of them had to work with, Robin had gotten busy planning and organizing the things the three of them needed in the off-campus apartment.

The six-hundred-square-foot apartment came with a single couch, with a pull-out bed. That was where Ginny would sleep night after night, and Robin had insisted there would be enough room for a loveseat too.

They had a half-moon dining room table that butted up against the wall, with three chairs. Two barstools stood along the bar, and they had a TV cabinet with no TV to sit on it. That had gone on her list, and then Robin had focused on the bedroom.

Ginny needed somewhere to keep her clothes, so Robin

had found a dresser that looked a lot like a credenza that could be out in the living room. She, Mandie, and Charlie had agreed Ginny could use the coat closet in the short, narrow hallway as her bedroom closet, and the bathroom came with a shower rod—no curtain.

That had gone on Robin's list, as had a bed for the single bedroom. Mandie and Charlie would sleep in there, and the room came with a dresser and a desk and nothing else. The three of them had decided to get rid of the desk and use the table or lap desks for their schoolwork, and that left room in the bedroom for a chaise chair.

Robin had told Mandie she might want somewhere away from everyone—even Charlie, and having somewhere to sit in her bedroom would be nice.

So that meant another purchase. Another big item to figure out how to get up to the third floor in a ten-story building with an elevator barely big enough to hold six people.

Robin snuggled deeper into her husband's side. "I think we're ready," she whispered.

"Baby, you have a clipboard with multiple checklists on it. I'm sure we're ready."

Robin smiled against his chest. "We have the best friends on the planet."

"Do we?"

"Yes." Robin stretched up and kissed him. "Kristen found out about the furniture needs we had, and she immediately messaged Clara. She and Scott were redoing that inn last year, remember?"

"Oh, I remember," Duke murmured. He kissed Robin again, and she didn't mind the distraction or the interruption.

When he slid his lips to her neck, she added, "Clara had quite a few things in storage, and we got their bed and a loveseat for free."

"Shipping to the city isn't free," Duke murmured.

"Laurel started a moving fund for them," Robin said, as Duke had only been home for two days, and Robin hadn't been able to fill him in on everything yet. "Jean sewed curtains for all the windows. Kelli and AJ gave them a gift card to a nursery in the city so they can get some potted plants."

"Mandie can't keep plants alive," Duke said with a chuckle.

"Ginny can." She tilted her head back and let the pleasurable sensation of her husband's kiss along her neck slowly burn through her. She put the talking on hold while Duke kissed her, and as his hands drifted over her body and down her side, she pulled in a breath as quietly as she could.

"Duke, the girls are here," she whispered.

"Let's go shower then," he murmured, his lips against her belly.

Robin wanted to make love to him, but now wasn't the time or place. They'd be back in this room tonight, this time with only Jamie with them. Perhaps Mandie would let her stay at the apartment for an hour or Alice would take everyone to dinner tonight, and Robin could have her alone-time with Duke.

But for right now, she slipped away from him, gave him a smile, and went to shower alone. He got in after her, and they ended up waking up the girls with exclamations of, "It's moving day! Get up! You get to move into your new apartment today!"

Mandie grinned from ear to ear, because she did like having her autonomy. She'd made friends in her apartment last year, but the situation was totally different this year. Robin told herself not to worry about what she perceived as Mandie's limited opportunities. Her daughter didn't want to meet a different young man. She didn't need friends if she had Charlie and Ginny.

Neither girl showered, and since they didn't need to pack up and leave the hotel, they simply left the room and headed downstairs to catch a cab over to Mandie's new apartment. None of them said a whole lot, and Robin took Duke's hand in hers and squeezed.

He was her anchor, the one place she could voice all of her fears and worries to, and he'd validate her, calm her down, and give his advice, usually in that order.

Today, however, Duke squeezed her hand back with as much force as she'd had, and she knew this day was not going to be easy for either of them.

---

GINNY KELTON JUMPED TO HER FEET WHEN HER phone rang and showed her twin's name on the screen. Charlie and Mandie were moving into the apartment today, while Ginny had been here alone for a couple of nights now.

Her father and her boyfriend had helped her move in, and today, she'd help her brother and her best friend.

"They're here," she said to herself, so many nerves cascading over one another and through her body. One, she wasn't exactly sure how things would go living with a couple, even if it was with Charlie and Mandie. It might be weird, and Ginny simply didn't know.

Not only that, but her mom and Arthur would be with Charlie, and that meant Ginny would see her mom in person for the first time in a few months. And Bob was in town, and Ginny was introducing him to everyone today.

So her stomach swooped and it felt like she'd swallowed a couple of very hungry rats. They gnawed at her insides as she unlocked and opened the door to the apartment. It was a great place, and Ginny did feel blessed to have found it and gotten it. They sat at the end of the hall, so they wouldn't have everyone and their dog walking by their apartment. There wouldn't be the constant chiming of the elevator. They had extra windows in the living room and kitchen.

She peered out the doorway and found the hallway empty. She hadn't left in the past couple of days, because she didn't like living alone in the city. She hadn't met any neighbors. She was young and nervous still, and she only went out with friends, or Bob, or her father.

So relief filled Ginny when she saw Charlie turn the corner and head toward her, a suitcase getting tugged along behind him. When he saw her, his face lit up with a smile, and he laughed as he closed the last few steps to her.

"Charlie." Ginny breathed in the scent of her brother, a person as familiar to her as herself.

"I've missed you," he said as he hugged her. "We've never really lived apart before." He was right, though they'd had separate apartments last year. They'd still lived in the same building, and Ginny had gone to his apartment many times when she'd needed to feel utterly at home.

"Come see," she said as Mandie approached. She grinned as she went into the apartment and made room for Charlie to follow her with his suitcase. Mandie came inside too, and Ginny grabbed onto her. "This is going to be so fun."

"I hope so," Mandie said. "I'm so nervous about it."

Ginny pulled back and looked at her openly. "You are?"

Mandie wore her worry right on her face as she nodded. "Yeah. I just...I want this to be a good thing for all of us." She gripped Ginny's shoulder and added, "You'll tell me if you're not okay with any of it, right?"

"Yes," Ginny said, and while she was nervous too, she didn't know about what. So she couldn't tell Mandie what she wasn't okay with right now. "I think it's going to be fine."

"We won't know until it's not," Mandie said as Charlie returned to them, now suitcase-less. "We have to be honest with each other." She looked at Ginny and then Charlie. "So my mom has this Summer Sand Pact with her friends. They go up to the black sand beach on Rocky Ridge, and I don't even know."

Mandie ran her hands through her hair and sighed. "But I know they're honest with each other. Even with hard things. And I want us to be like that. If something's not right, or something makes us mad—no matter what it is— we get to say. Okay? We all live here, and it's a small space, so we get to say if something irritates us or bothers us or we're not okay with something."

Charlie nodded, and Ginny found herself doing the same. "Okay," she said. "Yes. I want to be able to say if something bugs me."

"You don't have your own room," Mandie said, her eyes wide. "Are you sure you can live like that?"

"Come see what I've done." Ginny turned away from the open door and walked along the back of the long, full-sized couch. "My bed is inside that. It only takes me a minute to get it out. I left room for the loveseat against that wall, and since your mom had the credenza delivered already, I lined it up with the TV cabinet."

She gestured to the living room, which was pretty full of things already. "That's my dresser. I put my jeans and sweaters and underwear and socks in there, and it's not even full yet." She went by the tiny corner kitchen and pointed to the fridge.

"I brought some magnets, so we can hang up take-out menus and our perfect essays and everything." She grinned, because while the kitchen was small, all the appliances worked. The hallway started, and Ginny pulled open the closet door, which stood right across from the bathroom door.

"My dresses and tee's are in here, and I put my shoes on a rack there. I left some room for you guys."

Mandie peered in with her, her head resting against Ginny's shoulder. "This is great."

"This must be it," Ginny's mother said, and her heart pounced through her body. For a reason she couldn't name, tears came to Ginny's eyes as she stepped away from Charlie and Mandie and the closet and rounded the corner to greet her mom.

"Mom." The word choked in her throat, and Ginny ran to her mom, who wrapped her up tightly.

"This looks like a New York City apartment," Mom whispered. "It's going to be perfect, Ginny-girl."

Ginny couldn't talk, so she simply held onto her mom while Arthur entered the apartment, and then Mandie's sister and parents, all of them with suitcases too. They went past her and her mother and down the hall to the bedroom, and Ginny still couldn't step out of her mom's arms.

When she finally did, her mom smiled softly at her and brushed her hair back. "Your hair is longer," she said. "You look so grown-up, Ginny."

She wiped her eyes. "I couldn't leave the apartment alone after I moved in," she admitted. "Bob helped me get groceries, and yeah. I've just been hanging out here, watching movies on my computer."

"Well, the television will be here today," her mom said. "So you'll be able to watch movies on the TV instead of your computer." She smiled and looked past Ginny. "Now, give me a tour of this place."

"We've got a loveseat here," a man said. "For a Robin Grover?"

Ginny's mom turned that way, and she went to sign for the furniture delivery. "Looks like against that wall there for that," she said. "You have anything else?"

"No, ma'am," the delivery man drawled, and he and his partner got the loveseat in place in less than a minute.

Ginny gave Arthur and her mom a tour of the apartment just as she had Charlie and Mandie, and when they crowded into the doorway of the bedroom, they found Mandie and her family unpacking her clothes. A stack of dishes and towels sat on the dresser, and Charlie picked them up with, "I'll go put these in the kitchen and bathroom."

He turned to face them, and Ginny saw his nerves plainly on his face. "She's just getting unpacked." He met their mother's eyes. "She says the delivery of the bed and chaise should happen before noon."

"Great," Mom said. "Robin, I signed for the loveseat."

Robin looked up, and she blinked a couple of times. "Oh, perfect. Let me see it." She stepped away from the partially empty suitcases and followed Charlie out of the bedroom.

"We've got dishes and towels too," Mom said. "Let's help Charlie get those out, Ginny."

"Yeah, sure." Ginny did that, filling the bathroom with their toiletries and other necessities. Then she moved into the kitchen and helped her mom hang the curtains Jean had sewn for them.

"I love them," Ginny said as she stood back and looked

at the blue and yellow ruffles. "They make this place feel more like real people live here."

"Kelli and AJ have this gift card for you to get some plants." Mom gave her an envelope, and Ginny looked at it.

"Really?"

"Really." Mom smiled at her and said, "Maybe you can leave the apartment with Charlie and Mandie to pick them out."

Ginny smiled, though her mom was teasing her, and then they all needed to move as the chaise arrived. The box springs and mattress followed, and Ginny decided to simply stay out of the bedroom while everyone else got things put together for Charlie and Mandie.

She sat on the new loveseat and pulled out her phone. To Bob, she sent: *Moving in is going great. Are you sure you're ready to meet my mom and step-dad?*

*Your twin too,* he sent back. *And yes, sweetheart, I'm ready to meet them all.*

Ginny sighed, because while she'd only known Bob for a couple of months now, she'd already started falling in love with him. She hadn't told him that yet, and he hadn't said those three little words either.

She hadn't met his family, as they lived in Wisconsin, and their dinner tonight felt like such a huge moment for Ginny. She trusted her mom's opinion, and her mom wasn't one to be able to disguise much, so Ginny would know how she felt the moment she introduced Bob to everyone.

*A few more hours now,* she told herself, and then she got

herself off the couch to help Arthur find a place for Charlie's mug collection.

# Chapter Twenty-Eight

A lice entered the New York City restaurant, something she'd done countless times before. It felt like all of those times in glittering, sequined dresses and late-start dinner dates with her husband had happened to another woman. She felt so different than who she'd been then. Changed completely by going home to a small town and rekindling her high school friendships.

The restaurants in the city hadn't changed, though. They were still tiny, cramped, and longer than they were wide. They all seemed to be on strike against the light bulb companies, and Alice blinked, wondering if she was going blind or if it really was simply that dark in here.

"Bobby," Ginny squealed, and she hurried past Alice and into the arms of a man seven or eight inches taller than her. He wore a bright, wide smile full of straight, white teeth, and Alice could admit that her heart softened at the way her daughter got held by her boyfriend.

Ginny turned to face them, and Alice put a smile on her face. How they'd all eat in this restaurant, Alice wasn't sure. There'd be nine of them, as Robin and her family had come with them.

"This is my mom," Ginny said, her face beaming with starlight. "Alice. Her husband and my step-dad, Arthur. My twin, Charlie." Ginny looked up at Bob, who had sandy blond hair and bright, sizzling eyes that Alice assumed would be blue. But in this lighting...

"Hello," she said as she stepped forward to shake his hand. "It's great to meet you. Ginny says so many wonderful things about you."

Ginny grinned and grinned, and Bob shook hands with Arthur, and then Charlie. Alice indicated Mandie, Robin, Duke, and Jamie "These are some amazing friends of ours." She named them all, and Bob took all of it in stride.

He then reseated his hand in Ginny's and looked at her. "I told them there would be nine of us, and they've got a table in the back."

"Great," she said, and then Bob led them all through the restaurant.

"They've got a table in the back," Robin whispered in Alice's ear while the young adults went first. "He's great, don't you think?"

"You've said hello to him," Alice muttered, though her first impression of Bob in a pair of black slacks and a blue long-sleeved shirt that had been buttoned all the way up was good. He dressed well, and he sure seemed smart and polite. No tie, but it looked like he'd had one on earlier. For what,

Alice wasn't sure, as he was a law student who lived in Boston.

The table was set and ready, but it also sat only a few inches from the one next to it, as per some sort of city restaurant code. In that moment, Alice did not miss living in or near the city. She sometimes needed reminders like this, and she took her seat across from Ginny and Bob so she would have the best opportunity to chat with both of them.

"So," Bob said. "Did everyone get moved in today?" He flapped his napkin and settled it over his lap, his demeanor friendly and kind and charming. No wonder Ginny liked him.

"Yeah," Charlie said. "It's been a beast of a day, but we did it."

"Now, you two are dating, right?" Bob gestured to Charlie and Mandie, who sat beside him.

"Yeah," Charlie said again, his smile appearing now.

Bob nodded but didn't comment further. He looked at Alice, who smiled at him just as the waitress arrived. "Drinks, anyone?"

"I'd love a glass of wine," Robin said, and that alerted Alice to her current mood. She didn't normally drink much, but they'd both been anxious and awaiting the day when their children would move in together.

That day had been today, and Alice picked up the drink menu too. "I'll take a Paloma," she said without really reading much on it. Arthur ordered a beer, and Duke passed on anything alcoholic. The kids ordered sodas, even Bob, and Alice told herself not to think of him as a child.

He wasn't a child. He held a degree from NYU, and he'd been accepted into Harvard's School of Law.

"So, Bob," she said. "How's Boston and Harvard?" She cut a look over to Ginny. "Ginny says you've moved up there."

"A few weeks ago," he said. "I had to start my job." He lifted his glass of water to his lips. "She says you went to law school there."

"I certainly did," Alice said. "Ginny's father did as well."

"I hope I survive it," Bob said good-naturedly. "I'm a little older than the other first-year students, and I've got my own apartment, so I shouldn't have too many distractions."

"Wow, your own apartment in Boston?" Alice asked. "What does your family do?"

"Oh, they're in the cheese business in Wisconsin." He gave a light laugh, and a rush of foolishness raced through Alice. She'd assumed he came from East Coast money, and she shouldn't have done that.

"I worked for a couple of years before I started college," he said. "To save for law school." He set down his glass. "I work during the school year too."

"During law school?" Alice asked. "How do you have time to do anything?" She looked at Ginny. "Like come to New York to see Ginny?"

"Mom." Ginny flashed Bob a look and then met Alice's eyes again. But Alice knew what it took to get through Harvard Law, and she didn't want to find out later that Bob took drugs to stay awake, stay alert, keep up with everything.

Her motherly worry rose up, and Arthur put his hand

on hers in her lap. She glanced over to him too, but everyone at the table seemed to be waiting for Bob to say he wasn't a drug addict.

"I've made enough this summer selling security systems to live on for the year," Bob said. "I work in a law firm as a legal secretary and assistant to get experience in the business." He looked down to Arthur, then Robin, then Duke. "I'm on a full scholarship at Harvard, ma'am. I'll study on the trains when I come see Ginny, because I sure do like your daughter." He ducked his head, as if he was somehow lesser than Alice.

Properly chastised and impressed, she said, "That's amazing, Bob. I'm sorry if I insinuated anything differently."

"I know a lot of college students take pills to stay awake, studying or whatnot." He cleared his throat and looked at Ginny. Her eyes were bright and wide, and she nodded to him slightly. "I don't drink, smoke, or do drugs. I've seen first-hand how that can ruin a person's life. It almost killed me once, and I—" His voice cut out and he cleared his throat. "I won't do that."

Ginny snuggled into his side, her smile relaxing as she did. "Bob's dad was an alcoholic," she said. "Burned their house down while everyone was inside when Bobby was only ten."

Horror moved through Alice now, and she blinked at her daughter and then Bob. "I'm so sorry," she said. "I didn't know."

"How could you?" Bob waved his hand as if Alice hadn't

done anything wrong. He pressed a kiss to Ginny's forehead and looked at Charlie.

"Maybe you don't need to go into family law mode, Mom," Charlie said.

Alice's gaze moved to his. "That's my job as a mother, Charles," she said smoothly. She smiled at him, then reached across the table to take Ginny's hand in hers. "It's what we moms do."

"Right," Robin said, backing her up. "But we will try to get Alice to tone down her questions." She smiled at Alice, who experienced a sting of reproof in her ribcage.

"All right," she said as a couple of other people chuckled. "No more hard questions tonight." She gave Bob a smile as she pulled her hand back.

"I don't mind, Alice," he said. "Really. I get it. You want to get to know me, and you're worried about how things will progress with me and Ginny."

"Yes," she murmured as their drinks arrived. "But really." She reached for her Paloma, which came in the nicest copper goblet. "No more hard stuff tonight. Tell me what branch of law you're doing at Harvard."

"Mom." Ginny groaned.

"What?" She looked at her daughter. "That's a totally normal topic. There are like fifty different branches of law."

"She's not wrong," Bob said, and that alone made Alice like him more. "I'm doing Science and Technology, Alice. You did Family?"

"It's under Social Change," Alice said. "But yes. I practice Family Law in Five Island Cove."

"Yes, tell me about the cove," Bob said next, getting a bit more animated. "Ginny speaks of it with such fondness." They exchanged a glance, and Alice saw everything in that moment. She didn't know when or how fast things would happen, but she saw the two of them together for a very long time.

She looked over to Charlie, who'd leaned toward Mandie as she said something in his ear, because again, the music in this restaurant had been turned up far too loud for normal conversation.

They were a handsome couple too, and Alice knew Charlie would do anything in the world to make Mandie happy. When she looked at Bob and Ginny again, she saw that same quality in him too, and while he was five years older than Ginny and certainly had more life and dating experience, Alice couldn't find a reason not to like him.

She really just wanted her children to be happy, and she should be happy that they'd found someone who wanted that same thing for them. So, while she hadn't anticipated them growing up quite so fast, Alice decided then and there to do everything in her power to support them. In their schooling, their lives, and their relationships.

Alice leaned into Arthur, who pressed a kiss right above her ear. "He's great," he whispered. "You okay?"

Alice nodded, her emotions surging upward and then pitching back down, the way a roller coaster did on a fun park track. She let everything go; just released her fisted fingers and let her children flow away from her and into their own lives.

She'd always be their mother, and she'd be there when-ever and wherever they needed her. But she didn't have to carry them anymore.

"What'll you have, ma'am?" the waitress asked.

Alice hadn't even looked at the menu, but as she looked up, she asked, "Do you still have the blue crab sandwich?"

"Blue crab sandwich," the woman repeated. "Fries or salad?"

"You know what?" Alice grinned at her, feeling lighter now that she only had to focus on loving and supporting her children. She'd taught them what they needed—for now—and she wanted to be in their lives as much as they'd let her. "I'll take the fries."

Arthur chuckled and muttered, "Oh, boy. You're really letting loose tonight."

Yes, she was, and she leaned into his chest as the waitress moved on. Alice watched Ginny study her menu, and then order before Bob, and everything he did seemed easy, unrushed, and smooth—including the way he pulled Ginny closer and kissed her sweetly.

Down the table, a round of laughter erupted, and Alice turned her attention that way. She didn't have to know how all of her feelings lined up right now. She had time to work through them, iron them flat, and discuss them with her friends.

Yes, she had friends in the cove who could definitely help her reason through these new changes in her life—and she'd rely on them to do exactly that.

# Chapter Twenty-Nine

~

K risten arrived at the clubhouse in her condo complex ahead of Robin, who'd volunteered to come help her set up the tables and chairs for that day's luncheon. She carried the enormous bowl of cookie monster salad over to the built-in counter top in the kitchen area, then sighed out her breath as she turned to face the rest of the space.

Everyone had RSVP'ed in the positive for today's event, and Kristen's eyes filled with tears at that notion, because there had been so many emotions running through the cove in the past year. Political issues that not everyone saw eye-to-eye on; smaller friendship groups that had formed; the expansion of their group.

Kristen still saw all of those things, but her Seafaring Girls from thirty-five years ago seemed stronger than ever, and they led the larger group whether they knew it or not.

"Hey, there." Robin entered the clubhouse. "Oh, good. You haven't started setting up yet." Her husband followed her, and Robin beamed back at him. "I brought some muscle to help."

"Duke." Kristen had seen him a couple of times since he'd returned to the cove from his summer fishing expeditions. She still hurried toward him and hugged him tightly. "Thank you for coming to help."

She didn't start to help with the tables, because they were a bit too heavy for her. She could unfold folding chairs, though, so she did that. She and Robin had no sooner placed the last chair at the long column of tables when the door opened again.

"They're here," Alice said over her shoulder. She carried the slow cooker from Kristen's condo, and when Kelli entered, she had one platter of cookies while AJ brought in the other.

"There's more there," Kristen said.

"You've been cooking for days." Alice gave her a side-eyed look and went to put the slow cooker on the separate table, which had obviously been set up precisely for holding the food.

Kristen didn't deny how much cooking she'd been doing. She'd arranged this luncheon, and she'd put off everyone who'd asked what they could bring. She'd made lobster bisque as an appetizer, plenty of cookies for before the event and after as dessert—and for the ladies to take home to their loved ones—and a main dish of cod cakes and a chicken, walnut, and cranberry salad. The cookie monster salad was another dessert, this time with green apples, striped cookies, and Jello, and Kristen had told everyone to BYOD.

Bring Your Own Drink.

She didn't have to make another trip back to her condo, because with every person who arrived in the clubhouse, another item to carry out the luncheon came with them. All the food, the dishware, and the prizes and presents she'd put together.

"What are those for?" Robin asked when she saw the gift bags come through the door. Laurel took them over to another table, and Kristen simply smiled at them.

"You'll find out," she said. She'd been sick and couldn't attend Asher's birthday, and she still had his presents. She'd wrapped those, and then the more she thought about it, the more she wanted to give everyone there a little something. Just something to remind them of who they were and how integral they were in her life and in each other's lives.

Kristen looked around, almost like a kindergarten teacher, and started counting the women who'd arrived. Before she even finished, the door opened again, and a pretty blonde women pushed a wheelchair in front of her as she entered.

"That must be Kate," she said, and she joined the swarm of people moving toward her.

"You guys." AJ held up both hands. "Do not converge. Stop it." She stood in front of Kate and her son, her eyes flashing. "I mean it. I told her we were nice, and that we wouldn't do exactly this."

AJ had texted everyone about Kate and her situation, her sons, and she'd said she really wanted to provide that hand-hold that Kate needed in her life. A cardinal, AJ had called it. Kristen loved that reference to the first book they'd read for the bicycle book club earlier this summer, and she'd been interested to meet Kate.

She tried to put herself in that situation, and she wouldn't want a dozen women rushing at her either. So she hung back, noting that Laurel and Eloise came to her side pretty easily. "She's pretty," Laurel said, one hand resting on her belly while she nibbled on a cookie with the other. "She seems nice."

Kate wore a wide, genuine smile as she shook hands with Robin and then Alice, who leaned in and hugged her. They fell back quickly, and Maddy and Julia welcomed Kate. Kristen waited until AJ brought Kate and her son, Holden, to her, and then she took the woman by the shoulders and hugged her.

"You are so welcome here," she whispered.

Kate nodded and said, "Thank you," as she pulled away. She wore plenty of emotion in her expression, and part of it showed her complete overwhelm while another part shone with joy and happiness to be included.

"Everyone's here," Alice said as she arrived next to Kristen, and she looked over to her.

"Would you whistle then?"

Alice smiled, a gleam in her eye. She waited for Kate to finish saying hello to Laurel, and then she pursed her lips and let loose an ear-splitting whistle. It brought all the conversations to a halt, and Kristen raised one hand.

"We're ready to begin," she said. "First, I want to thank you all for sacrificing time from your families and loved ones to be here on a Sunday afternoon." She looked around at all these beautiful female personalities, her love for them blooming to life and growing over and over and over again.

She started toward the gift table. "I have put together a little something for each of you." She picked up the baby blue bag first. "AJ, this is Asher's present for his birthday. I feel awful I had to miss it."

"Kristen," AJ said. "It's fine."

"Nevertheless." She held up the bag, and it got passed to AJ. "And for you, dear, I found the perfect thing." She pulled open one of the two larger gift bags and found the one with AJ's name on it.

The print was red, green, and white plaid, like a Christmas bag. It fit what was inside, and Kristen lifted it up for all to see. "Come on up here, AvaJane."

She did, and Kristen smiled at her as she handed her the bag. "Open it, and I'll explain."

AJ pulled the white paper off the top, and lifted out a cute wooden cardinal, about six inches tall. She sucked in a breath. "Kristen." She lifted her eyes from the mantle piece to Kristen. "I love this."

"I know the idea of being a cardinal for someone has really touched your heart," Kristen said. "I know you're trying to be that good omen for those around you, and I thought you could put this somewhere to remind you of how you are a light to those around you. You are a cardinal to all of us."

Tears spilled out of AJ's eyes, and she flung herself at Kristen. "Thank you," she whispered while the others clapped.

Kristen stepped back and let AJ fade to the side as she reached into the bag for another gift. This one came out splashed with white flowers over a bright blue bag, and she said, "Alice."

She came up, and Kristen gave her a moment to open the gift. She held it up for everyone to see, her laughter curving up her lips into such an exuberant smile. "It's a picture block." She rotated it. "Where did you get some of these?" She looked at Kristen with awe and joy.

"I texted Mandie," Kristen said. "Who has direct access to Charlie and Ginny, and I got them to send me some of their favorite pictures of themselves or the three of you." She took a breath and continued. "I know you miss them terribly and think you might lose them earlier than you anticipated, so I thought this might remind you that they'll always be your children."

"Thank you." Alice hugged her, and Kristen indicated the bag.

"You pick the next one."

Alice reached in and pulled out a small pink bag. Kristen took it and held it up. "This one is for Maddy."

"You did not have to get me something," Maddy said as she came up. She took the bag, which was small enough to fit in the palm of her hand, and took out a pair of earrings. "They're dragonflies."

"You manage a busy restaurant and a new marriage and your children with such grace and flexibility." Kristen smiled at her. "The dragonfly is a symbol of adaptability, as it can fly in six different directions. I thought it represented you really well, and I'm so happy you're here in the cove and part of us."

"Part of us!" Robin started to chant, her smile huge. "Part of us! Part of us!"

Everyone joined in; Maddy's face turned a healthy pink as she pulled out the next bag, and the chanting stopped as Kristen held up the next bag. "This one is for Eloise."

Eloise eyed her as she came closer, but she took the kraft-brown bag and pulled the pink tissue out of the top of it. She then lifted out a silver bracelet of interlocking circles.

Kristen smiled at it and said, "Eloise is the best friend to everyone in this room. We all feel like we can confide in you, and you'll listen, respect us, and keep things private if that's what we want. So this bracelet of interlocking circles represents your unwavering friendship and support, which is one of your superpowers."

"Wow," Eloise whispered. "Thank you so much." She hugged Kristen while the other ladies clapped, and then El wiped her eyes quickly and pulled out the next gift.

"Julia," Kristen said. She came up and extracted a canvas painting of the view from atop the cliffs on Rocky Ridge.

She pulled in a breath. "Kristen, I love this."

"I know you've been searching for a place to call home," Kristen said. "Whether that's on Sanctuary, or with Liam and Ian, or wherever." She wasn't sure how many of the other women knew all of this about Julia, so Kristen didn't want to give away too much. "But no matter what, Julia, I want you to know that no matter where you go, you will always belong with us. You are always home when you're with us."

"That is so beautiful," Julia said. "Thank you."

"When you hang art somewhere," Kristen said. "It becomes your home. That's why I got you the painting."

Julia gazed at it. "I love it. Thank you." She pointed out the next gift, and Kristen picked it up.

"Robin," she said, her voice cracking. Robin came forward, her bottom lip already quivering, and Kristen hugged her first. "I love you so much."

"I love you too," Robin whispered, and they separated. Kristen had known this would make her emotional. She'd wanted to bring them all together and let them know how amazing they all were. She wasn't sure how much longer she'd be here with them, and she'd been driven to do this.

Robin pulled out a beautiful, polished piece of jade, and her eyes widened. "I can't accept this."

"It's jade," Kristen said. "It's a stability stone, and it's meant to remind you that you're our grounding presence. It has protective properties, as do you. You do so much for everyone here, and to me, you're the foundation of us all."

"It will be beautiful on the shelf in my office," she said tearfully. Kristen nodded to the table, her feet starting to hurt a little. She still had at least half the presents to go, and she lifted the bag that Robin had selected.

"Tessa."

The dark-haired woman came forward, her face shining. She'd really come alive this summer, and while Kristen was still getting to know her, she loved her all the same. Kristen gave her the bag, and Tessa revealed a pair of dangly earrings that had been custom-made.

"This is *The Echoes of Avalon Park*," she said. She grinned out to everyone and showed them the mini books she could wear.

"You have done something amazing with the book club," Kristen said. "I found it fitting that you should be able to wear the first book that we did here in the cove, and here's to many, many more months of the bicycle book club."

The crowd cheered, and Tessa grinned and grinned while she chose the next present. Kristen called out, "Kate," and the blond woman glanced around as if there might be someone else there named Kate.

"Go on," AJ said, grinning and still clapping. Kate came forward, and Kristen just wanted to tuck her under her wing and protect her. She gave Kate the bag, which barely weighed anything.

She removed the single piece of tissue paper and then an envelope. "It's a massage," she said.

"No one can deny how much you're carrying, and we want to do anything we can to make your burden lighter. So

Kelli did a little investigative work, and she said you really miss getting a massage."

"I do," Kate whispered.

"This is a monthly membership for a year," Kristen said. "You can get a massage every month, and we'll come stay with the boys while you do."

"Thank you so much." Kate hugged her, and then headed back to her spot behind almost everyone—right next to Kelli. They definitely seemed cut from similar cloths, and Kristen truly believed that the right people came into her life and others' lives precisely when they were needed.

Kate hadn't chosen another bag, so Kristen picked up the one closest to her. "Clara."

Her daughter came forward, and while she hadn't had too much drama going on in her life recently, she bore a constant burden of work, maintaining and building her relationship with Lena, her daughter, and supporting her husband. Her bag was also very light and she pulled a postcard out of it.

Her eyes scanned left and right, and then she looked up. "It's a subscription to the Daily Delight Games."

"You love games," Kristen said. "They're how you escape after a long day of customer service and personal service to your friends and family. You've always been so willing to serve everyone, and these games are a way for you to escape and have something of your own that you love."

"Thank you," Clara said, and she pointed out the next bag.

"We're getting down to it," Kristen said. "This one is for

Jean, and the last two are Kelli and Laurel. All three of you come up here, please."

They started making their way toward her, and Kristen handed them each their bag when they arrived.

Jean pulled out a quilted square that had spools of thread stitched into it, along with the words "Stitched with love." Kristen smiled at it and then her. "It's a mouse pad," she said. "I didn't make it, but I commissioned it for you. It speaks to your love of sewing, but also to how you've stitched all of us together by simply being you. By making the cutest baby clothes for Heidi, Asher, and Daphne, and for volunteering your services for anyone who need it."

"Ginny and Mandie love their curtains," Alice said. "For example."

"Yes," Kristen said. "Great example." She nodded to Kelli, who opened her gift—one of the bigger ones. She lifted out a thick blanket and a basket of assorted teas. "You run your own business and manage a newborn, a teen, a husband, and all of us." Kristen put her arm around her. "And I know you like to snuggle in with something warm, so this tea and blanket are comfort items for you, as a way to remind you that you have always been such a comfort to all of us."

"Thank you, Kristen," she murmured in that strong, quiet way she had. In fact, all of the women standing with her possessed that same type of spirit, but all who remained was Laurel.

She opened her gift, but didn't hold it up. "I just have to say something." She swallowed and glanced at Kristen. "Can

I? I assumed there'd be an announcement time, but now I'm not sure."

"I wasn't planning formal announcements," Kristen said. "But if you have something to tell us, go ahead."

Laurel nodded and looked out to everyone. "Paul and I are expecting another baby." Her face broke into a big grin even as she ducked her head. "I'm due in February."

Congratulations and cheers went around, and Laurel's face pinked up. She held up her gift to get them to stop, and Kristen gazed at the tin dog figurine. "It's a dog," Laurel said. "Kristen, I love this."

It looked like it was made out of scrap metal, and Kristen had loved it on-sight too. "I got it for you, because you're one of the most loyal people I know. You're such a good companion no matter what we're doing, and everyone looks to you as a guide—something dogs can also be and do."

"It's amazing." Laurel tucked it back into her bag, and all three women retreated from the table.

Kristen looked at the gift table, which now sat empty. "Okay." She took a deep breath. "You are all so important to me, and I know you're important to each other. I think there's nothing better than a group of good women who support one another, love one another, and serve one another. That's you guys."

"No," Robin said. "That's *us*. It's all of us, including you, Kristen."

"It's us," Alice called out.

Kristen grinned and said, "It's us, and now, it's time to eat." She nodded like that was that, and now they could get to the important stuff—the food. But she didn't take more than three steps before her girls surrounded her, engulfing her in the middle of a group hug.

"You're the best," someone said.

"I love you all," another said.

"I'm so glad we're all friends," said a third.

Kristen just let herself stand in the midst of them, these powerful, strong, vulnerable, smart women, and love them unconditionally.

# Chapter Thirty

Tessa rode along with Dave after they'd gone to an early dinner. He'd said he had a surprise for her at his house before he'd drive her to the library for that evening's book club, and her son had texted.

Dave had said, "Take it. Talk to him," because Ryan certainly didn't message very often. Sometimes Tessa sent him texts he never responded to, and she had to take advantage of the conversations he was willing to have with her.

"He's met someone," Tessa said, her mother's heart warming. "I didn't think that would ever happen." She glanced over to Dave, who smiled at her.

"You sound like my mom," he said. "I didn't get married the first time until I was almost thirty."

"Ryan's getting up there," Tessa said of her twenty-seven-year-old son. "He's been working for a big construction firm that builds subdivisions up and down the East Coast."

"Sounds like he's busy."

"You know what? That's always been his reason for not dating." She laughed lightly to herself as she tapped out her next question for her son. *Where did you meet her?*

*Believe it or not, we met at a summer work party, but she doesn't work for Clayburn & Holt. She's one of my co-worker's nieces.*

Tessa smiled and smiled. *What does she do?*

*She's a graphic designer*, he said. *She works for a children's publisher in the city.*

*New York City?*

*Yes*, Ryan said.

Tessa refrained from lecturing him on having a long-distance relationship, or one where either party commuted and stayed somewhere else during the week. She knew not every relationship turned out the way hers had, and she really only wanted the very best for Ryan.

*Anyway, Mom, we want to know what you're doing for Thanksgiving. Charlotte has some pretty important family traditions around Christmastime, and she'd like to go up to her folks' house in December. So we're thinking of coming to the cove next month.*

Tessa's heart grew and grew, and she held out her phone as if she couldn't quite see it. "He wants to come for Thanksgiving," she said with awe. "Dave, this is big. I can't remember the last Thanksgiving I had with Ryan."

"That's great," Dave said as he pulled into his driveway. "We were going to do something with Julia and Liam and Maddy and Ben. Is that still going to happen?"

Tessa nibbled on her bottom lip. "Yes, we can still do that," she said. "It's two more people. I'll text Maddy right now."

She'd planned to host Thanksgiving dinner at her house, and she'd have both of her children and their significant others with her. Liam was bringing Ian. Tessa could certainly bring Ryan and Charlotte.

"I'll be right back," Dave said.

"I'm almost done texting, I swear." She didn't look up as he left the car and went inside. She fired off a couple of texts to Julia and Maddy, and they both came back with responses before Dave returned.

*Of course it's okay,* Julia said.

*How fun!* Maddy said. *Two more is no problem.*

Tessa relayed her plans to Ryan and told him how excited she was to meet Charlotte and have them and show them around the cove.

*Perfect,* Ryan said. *I'll be in touch with travel plans.*

Tessa sighed and sat back in her seat, her eyes not seeing much. Then Dave opened her door and said, "Come on, sweetheart."

She quickly unbuckled her seatbelt and stumbled after him. "What is this surprise?"

"You'll see." He took her hand and squeezed it. Bypassing the front door, he led her around the corner of the house and into his backyard.

"We don't have much time until we need to be headed over to the library," she said. The October book club book was a cozy mystery, and while Tessa didn't read a lot of fiction for fun, she'd enjoyed the light-hearted mystery. She'd even solved it only a moment before the sleuth, and she couldn't wait to talk about the red herrings in the book.

"It won't take long," he promised, and he reached for the latch on the fence. The gate swung in, and he took her into his backyard. It opened up to browning grass and trees with leaves that had started to turn orange and yellow.

The sun had been setting earlier and earlier, and Tessa sucked in a breath when she saw the flying spots of light flitting around a couple of shrubs that flanked his deck. "Fireflies," she breathed out. "David, you got fireflies."

"Took me a couple of months." He slid his arm around her waist and snuggled her against his side. "But I got the fireflies."

Tessa stood there and watched them buzz around, everything inside her vibrating in such a good way. "I love this," she said. "Thank you so much." She turned into Dave and matched her mouth to his.

They'd been dating for three months, and at her age, Tessa had been taking things slow. She hadn't told him that she'd started to fall in love with him, and he hadn't said anything either. But as he kissed her back, Tessa got reminded that actions spoke louder than words.

---

"WE NEED TO DO MORE FICTION," TESSA SAID FROM the doorway. She glanced over to Izzy, her new assistant since

Mandie had moved back to the city and her classes at NYU. "Look how many people are here."

This was their largest turn-out for the book club by far, and Tessa had already chosen next month's book, but she made a mental note to choose something Christmassy and fictional for December.

She already had the refreshments booked out for the next few months, and she could easily have the miniature Bundt cakes decorated to match the book in December. Tonight's cookies had been made in the shape of skull, as an illustration of one sat front and center on tonight's book club pick.

An alarm on Izzy's phone went off, and she silenced it. "It's time to start," she said.

"Yes." Tessa didn't push away from the doorjamb. "It's so nice to see them all chatting, isn't it?" She'd checked the list this month, their fourth month of the bicycle book club, to see how many repeat patrons they had coming.

Over sixty-five percent of the attendees had come more than once, with a full fifty percent of them having attended all four months. Tessa had pulled her friends' names out of the pot, and Robin, Alice, Kelli, AJ, and Eloise were part of the fifty percent.

So were Maddy, Julia, Jean, Kristen, and Clara, and Tessa felt like she'd struck the friendship jackpot when she'd come to Five Island Cove for a fresh start.

Tears filled her eyes when a couple of ladies moved, revealing where Kristen stood with AJ and Kelli, patting baby Daphne's bottom as she tried to get the little girl to fall asleep. Kelli had texted to say her daughter had been teething lately and had been an absolute bear.

Jean had gone to Bell Island to help out, as had Kristen and AJ. Maddy had sent food from The Glass Dolphin. Everyone else, Tessa included, had sent condolences and home remedies to help the baby be less cranky.

No matter what, they'd rallied around one another. Just like they had to help Robin get the wedding venue she'd needed last month, and to help Alice and Robin's children have the furniture they needed in their new apartment in the city.

As Tessa watched, she knew all she'd have to do to get any amount of help at all, with whatever she needed, was send a single text. That felt so good, and she grinned as she straightened and entered the room.

The first time she'd done this, she'd been so nervous. Tonight, only a confident version of herself moved to the front of the chairs and said, "Ladies, it's time to begin." She reached for the microphone and switched it on. "Find a seat, please. We've got a lot of mystery-solving to do tonight."

She lowered the mic as everyone surged forward to do what she said. She nodded at Robin and Alice, who sat off to the side in the second row. They signed up and came to book club, but they read the books too.

AJ and Kelli sat beside them, and neither of them had yet to make a comment during book club. Tessa didn't mind. She wanted the club to be whatever each woman needed it to be. If that was a place to talk, great. If not, that was okay too.

She didn't care if they came without reading that month's title. Tessa smiled at Julia and Maddy as they sat in the first row, and she easily found Clara, Jean, Kristen, and Eloise take up spots near the back. That felt so much like them, and Tessa's heart felt cozy and warm, like someone had knitted the perfect sweater for it.

One where she'd never want for anything, never be cold again, never have to be alone through anything again.

Laurel sat with Kate and another woman named Anna who'd come to every book club too, and Tessa recognized and had gotten to know many more in the audience. She couldn't believe something as simple as a book club had fulfilled her so completely.

She scarcely believed that something so easy and so accessible—books and reading—had brought her such joy, introduced her to more people here in the cove, and made her feel so important.

"Thank you for coming tonight," she said. "I've been praying the rain would hold off until after our discussion, and it looks like it has so far." Not that there were any windows down in the basement of the library. But Tessa just knew it still had to be dry outside, if only because she wanted it to be that way.

"Our refreshments tonight came from a dear friend of mine, who owns a bakery on Nantucket. She's thinking of opening up a branch here in the cove, so let's be sure to tell Helen Ivy how much we love and appreciate her skull cookies later tonight."

Several ladies started clapping, and Tessa did the same,

smiling to the beautiful, white-haired Helen, who stood at the back table near her edible creations. She really was an amazing baker, and as Tessa had been getting donations for refreshments this summer, she'd called Helen first.

Selfishly, she wanted Helen to move to the cove, but she did have a bakery in Nantucket that had been in business for more than fifty years. Tessa pushed away the memories of the island she'd come from. She wasn't going back there, and she only wanted to be in the present and look forward to the future.

"Let's get started," she said. "With the character of Elaine St. James. What did you guys think of our amateur sleuth?"

She moved away from the mic then and became more of a facilitator. She loved how the talk happened easily and respectfully, and as Tessa enjoyed October's book club, she felt like the luckiest woman in the world.

Afterward, her friends swarmed her, all of them clamoring over how much they liked the book and the way she ran book club in such a way that let everyone have a voice. That was important to Tessa, as she had often felt completely overlooked in her life.

"These cookies," Kristen said. "Are incredible."

"And that means something coming from her." Jean smiled at her. "Kristen is an amazing baker."

"Thanks," Tessa said. "I mean, I didn't bake them, but Helen is a master."

The older woman looked over at the mention of her name, and Tessa gestured her over. She'd met everyone before, but Tessa still introduced her around. "My friends," she said as she sank into Julia's side.

While life wasn't perfect, and plenty of them still had troubles and uncertainties, and surely the rain would come, Tessa also knew so would the sunshine. She knew that life was far easier if she didn't have to face the trials, the troubles, and the tumultuous weather alone.

So while tonight was nearly perfect, first with the fireflies, then an amazing book club, and finally with delicious cookies, Tessa knew it wouldn't always be this way. But she knew she could weather anything with her friends at her side.

---

READ ON FOR THE FIRST 2 CHAPTERS OF **THE HAMPTON HOUSE**, a brand new women's fiction novel that follows Mandie Grover 5 years in the future as she works with a prestigious historical preservation and reconstruction firm that restores and conserves abandoned mansions up and down the Eastern Seaboard.

Learn more about it and preorder by scanning the QR code below:

# A Note from Jessie

~~∂~~

What an amazing time I've had with the women in Five Island Cove! I sincerely hope you've found a place to belong among Alice, Robin, Eloise, Kelli, and AJ. I definitely identified with each of them at different times over the past ten books.

I love Laurel and Jean too, with their quieter personalities. Kristen and Clara rounded out our Five Island Cove residents, and then I brought over my Nantucket Point ladies too. After the mysteries and events they'd been through, they all needed a fresh start, and there's no better place to do that than Five Island Cove.

I always feel like I'm visiting old friends when I come here.

So, while I have more ideas for this series, I've also been gnawing on the idea for another book. As I wrote this one, and realized so much of the focus was on Mandie Grover, that book came alive in my head.

She'll be a central figure in *The Hampton House*, the next book I'm going to release. It'll be set five or six years in the future, and you'll get to see her, Charlie, Ginny, Bobby, with some amazing cameos from the ladies in Five Island Cove.

I'm also not saying there won't ever be another Five Island Cove novel. I do have three more covers in this series, and as I've said, I have more ideas for the women here! But I'm going to take a short detour to The Hamptons, and I'll hope you'll come with me!

This new series will focus on Mandie and her team of preservationists who go into abandoned mansions and restore them, clean them up, and get them ready to go back on the market. With Alice's ties to the Hamptons, and Mandie's love of history—and those YouTube videos I'm obsessed with!—I'm super excited to bring you the beginning of a planned trilogy!

You can read more about *The Hampton House* and **preorder it by scanning the QR code below.**

Oh, and I've written the first two chapters for you and included them here! Keep reading to get a taste for this next sweet romantic women's fiction novel.

~Jessie

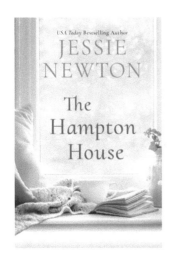

PS. Look at this BEAU-TIFUL COVER! I'm in love with it!

# Sneak Peek of The Hampton House, Chapter One:

~~~

Mandie Grover took a sip of her coffee, now lukewarm, and told herself to go dump it out and get some water. She'd been experiencing heartburn more often than not on days when she drank the entire cup of coffee she picked up on the way in to work.

She set the to-go cup further from her and reached for the next file in the pile. Part of her job involved looking through prospective properties, and she really enjoyed browsing through the "slush pile."

At tomorrow's meeting, she'd be expected to have her top three choices for the next clean-up project, appropriately labeled CUP in her department, and literal tally marks went up on the white board as the team reviewed their personal favorites.

Mandie had two files in her favorites folder already, but she told herself to have an open mind as she looked at the picture of the mansion on the first page in the new file. "Sixteen thousand square feet," she said. In all honesty, most mega-mansions approached ten thousand square feet, with multiple bedrooms, twice as many bathrooms, and ornate staircases.

Her heartbeat pumped out an extra beat, because she absolutely loved taking the abandoned and restoring it to full glory. That, and her phone had just sparkle-chimed with her husband's assigned ringtone.

Charlie had said, *I'm so going to pass this Pharmacology final*, with a smiley face emoji. *To celebrate, I'm stopping by Lin Chu's for dinner. You want those chickeny noodles?*

She grinned at his use of "chickeny noodles," abandoned the file, and reached for her phone to answer him. *You're finished with the final already?*

*Piece of cake*, he said, which was Charlie-code for *yes, I'm done and leaving campus.* He only had the one final today, and Charlie hated staying on campus when he could leave it. She'd find him in their one-bedroom apartment when she got home, and he'd most likely time dinner to arrive only a few moments before her.

She and Charlie had been married for almost five years now, and he took very, very good care of her. Mandie loved him with her whole heart, and they'd even started talking about starting a family.

Everything Mandie did required her to go through a minefield of thoughts, and she often felt like she'd made the wrong turn and gotten blown back to the beginning. She envied others who could made quick decisions with confidence, because that had never been Mandie's strong suit.

*See you at home*, she texted Charlie, and then she got back to the file in front of her. She had to have her choices done for tomorrow, and then she had some appointments to make with a restoration company for an apartment building here in the city that had sustained some flooding damage.

She loved her job at PastForward Restoration Company —PFRC—because they helped people who needed it while showing respect to the history of the dwellings and buildings on the East Coast. Some properties here were hundreds of years old, and Mandie felt a sense of reverence every time she got to go out on a field assignment.

The house in the file intrigued her, and Mandie leafed through the floor plan, read the story behind its abandonment, and embraced the growing excitement within her. She didn't often make her choices based on pictures, checklists, and facts. She relied on her feelings, and she reached for a green sticky note, which she attached to the front of this file.

It got placed in the yes-pile, and Mandie sat back. She loved learning about old things, and since she hadn't been on a field assignment yet this year, she muttered, "So you'll bring it up in your meeting tomorrow."

Part of her yearned to get out of this office building, though she'd once been tickled and thrilled to be riding the subway from Brooklyn, where she and Charlie lived, to the Flat Iron building every day.

She still was, but she definitely felt like some of the glitter that had first coated her job had started to flake off. She stood and stretched her back, glancing across the partition that separated her desk from the one in front of her.

The man who worked there had various camera equipment littering his space, and Flint Rogers looked up. "Hey." He leaned back in his chair. "My eyes are starting to cross."

"Editing your latest film?"

"Final edits," he said. "It's due to production by tomorrow night, and it should air next month."

"That's awesome," Mandie said. By "air," he meant the complete walk-through of one of the abandoned mansions. He led a film crew on field assignments, and they documented everything from the first step the team took onto the property to the final walk-through when a place went up for sale.

If he was lucky, he could work on one project per year, as his post-production was far more detailed than Mandie's. She was involved in field assignments from the first step to the sale, and that was it. She didn't then have hundreds of hours of film to go through and edit into a ninety-minute documentary.

"I can't believe the Maryland Mansion is almost done," she said.

"Hopefully, there will be something new at tomorrow's meeting," Flint said. He wore a neatly trimmed ginger beard, with a full head of hair to match. He was what Mandie would call a "clean hipster," as he showered regularly and didn't wear his hair long. His emerald eyes always seemed to see more than Mandie could, and he wore loafers everywhere he went, even into dangerous, abandoned mansions.

He rolled his khakis at the ankle, always wore skinny

jeans and skin-tight tees—if he didn't have on a too-small polo like he did today.

"You think you'll get another assignment right away?" Mandie asked. She leaned against the chest-high divider and took in more of his mess. How he worked in those conditions, she didn't understand. He had yellow legal pads filled with notes and numbers in black pen she couldn't read. But Flint somehow knew what it all meant, and she supposed that was all that mattered.

"Jo Ann's quitting," Flint said. "Which means they'll have to promote up another film lead, and last time Candace needed to do that, it took four months for me to go through multiple interviews, present my portfolios, and get named to the position."

Mandie drew in a breath. "Jo Ann's quitting?"

Flint looked away. "I guess that isn't common knowledge." He looked at Mandie with puppy-dog eyes. "Don't say anything, okay?"

"Yeah, of course not," she said.

Flint stood and stretched his arms above his head, his tiny shirt pulling up over the waistband of his khakis. "You haven't been out in the field in a while."

"Tell me about it." Mandie rolled her eyes. "I think Candace thought I'd get pregnant, and she didn't want to assign me to anything."

"So you're not pregnant?" Flint grinned at her, and Mandie smiled and shook her head.

"Even if I was," she said. "That shouldn't exclude me from field work. It's pregnancy discrimination."

"Sometimes those old houses are full of mold."

"We have protective gear for that." Mandie folded her arms, becoming more and more determined to get an assignment tomorrow. She'd had enough of desk work, phone calls, and file browsing. She swatted at Flint's chest. "Plus, you tromp through those sites in shoes with barely any soles and no socks. It's a miracle you haven't contracted gangrene or something."

Flint bellowed out a laugh, and Mandie allowed herself to smile. As he quieted, she said, "All right, Flint. Tell me how to get assigned to something tomorrow."

"Step into my office," he said, and Mandie scrambled to go around the dividers and into his disorganization. If it would help her get a field assignment, she could sit among cameras, flash lights, and micro SD cards.

---

"So the final went well?" Mandie asked as she entered her apartment. She tapped the door with her foot to close it, then noticed the candles on the table. She froze. "What anniversary did I forget?"

Charlie turned from the back counter, a plate of orange chicken in his hand. "Final went amazing. There's no anniversary."

"There's something," Mandie said as she got moving again. She'd brought home her top three files so she could obsess over them while she and Charlie watched TV tonight. He sometimes had her quiz him, especially with anything math-related, but he'd already taken that final, so she antici-pated an evening filled with some sort of action-adventure movie, and she could easily keep up with the plot while she looked through her files again.

"There's me finishing another year of school," he said. "That's it."

"Only one more," Mandie said as she dropped her bag over the back of the couch and shrugged out of her jacket. Springtime in New York could still be chilly, and Mandie hated nothing more than being cold on the subway.

She wrapped her arms around Charlie once he'd set down the plate of chicken. "You're amazing, baby. One more year of pharmacy school." She kissed him, glad she got to spend her evenings with her best friend in the whole world.

"Tomorrow, they're making assignments for the next major field assignment, and I want it so badly." She whis-pered the last few words, almost afraid to speak her desires.

"You'll get it," Charlie said. "You haven't been out of the office in a while."

"For six months," she said. "And I know Candace just got a whole heap of new funding. She might even schedule two projects."

"Where are they?"

"My favorite one is in The Hamptons," Mandie said as he pulled out her chair and she sat down. "It would be a dream to work on it. It's close, so I wouldn't have to live on-site. My other two favorites are out of the city. One in South Carolina—a really old plantation that would be pretty cool—and one up in Cape Cod."

"Mm." Charlie sat down too. He dished up some of her chickeny noodles, and Mandie simply watched him.

"Did you hear about the internship?"

"Another interview next week," he said casually, but Mandie knew he hated the multiple interview process. *Honestly*, he'd said. *If they don't know by now, I don't know what else to do to win them over.*

She smiled at him. "So we'll both have amazing news by this time next week."

"You'll have yours tomorrow." He grinned at her and took orange chicken and ham fried rice for himself.

"What if I don't get it?" Mandie let her vulnerability show. Only for him, and Charlie heard her and looked right at her. "She's been passing me over for some reason, and I just—what if I've gotten my hopes up and I don't get it?"

"You're going to get it."

She sighed, because frustration frothed through her. "Thank you, baby." She did like his confidence in her, but they'd been together long enough to see that sometimes confidence didn't always equate to getting what they wanted.

He hadn't gotten into the Pharm.D. program at Rutgers, for example. He'd had to settle for his second choice of St. John's, and while he loved his program there now, Charlie had definitely been disappointed.

"And if you don't," he said. "I'll have mint chocolate chip ice cream here tomorrow night, and we'll go away for the weekend. Go see your mom and dad in the cove." He raised his eyebrows. "Okay? It won't be the end of the world."

"It'll just feel like it," she said miserably.

"Hey, let's be positive," he said. "You've got a strong case for getting assigned, and they've picked your top choice the last four times."

"Yeah." Mandie twirled up some noodles and stuck them in her mouth. Salty, savory deliciousness moved through her. "Mm."

Charlie grinned at her, and suddenly everything was okay.

"And hey," she said. "If I do get it, I know I won't have to work with The Bulldozer."

Charlie choked on his chicken as he started to laugh. Mandie smiled too, though she truly didn't like working with Suzette Paxman. She'd been nicknamed The Bulldozer by everyone in the office, because she rammed through old houses like one. She held a degree in Anthropology, and she acted like she was the only human being alive who did.

In some cases, working with her meant Mandie didn't have to get her hands and feet as dirty, as Suzie wasn't afraid of anything. She'd go into any room, any broken-down pool house, over any surface, to get the footage and information they needed.

Every team had a bulldozer, actually, but none of the other employees at PastForward carried the nickname the way Suzie did.

She giggled with Charlie, because suddenly everything felt lighter. "I'm going to get it," she said, mustering up all the optimism she could. "And I'm going to have the best team ever, and it'll be the house in The Hamptons, and when we go home to Five Island Cove this weekend, it'll be to celebrate my new field assignment."

"There you go." Her husband beamed at her, and Mandie reached over and covered his hand with hers.

"Should I really get us tickets for the Steamer?" she asked.

He nodded. "Yeah, my mom would like it too. She'll take us to lunch to celebrate another semester done."

"Free food," Mandie mused. "I see how you are."

"Hey, I never say no to free food." Charlie grinned, and Mandie did too. She suddenly had so much to look forward to in the next few days, and her stomach flipped over tomorrow morning's meeting.

She just had to get a field assignment. She simply had to.

# Sneak Peek of The Hampton House, Chapter Two:

~~~

A licia Halverson stepped onto the elevator ahead of Mandie, and when she turned, she gave the other woman a look that spoke volumes. Thankfully, Mandie could understand looks where words weren't spoken, and she edged behind a tall African American man to position herself closer to Alicia.

"What have you got?" she whispered on the third floor, when half the people in the elevator exited. "Lish, don't hold out on me. I'm here an hour early to go over files I have memorized."

"Please." Alicia half-scoffed and half-laughed. "You're here early so you can pace in the bathroom and pitch yourself to your reflection."

Mandie's shoulder shivered back and forth, her way of conceding to Alicia without words. Alicia laughed, because she knew Mandie so well. She reminded her of her younger sister, and a powerful wave of missing rolled through Alicia completely unbidden.

"My thumbs are aching from how much I texted last night," Alicia said as the elevator struggled to get moving again.

"It better have been with Michael." Mandie sighed, and Alicia felt her frustration. She hadn't been assigned a field trip in months either, and once Mandie had texted last night, Alicia had taken it upon herself to figure out how to get the two of them assigned to whatever went up on the board today at PastForward.

"Michael, I wish." Alicia rolled her neck, and the day hadn't even started yet.

"He's going to ask you out. You just need to keep stopping by for those chocolate croissants."

"Yeah, and then I have to run fifty miles on the treadmill." Alicia shook her head now, the ends of her long, dark hair brushing against her elbows. She'd braided into pigtails today in an attempt to make herself look younger. Candace seemed to discriminate on any grounds she could, and only she knew what those were.

Alicia and Mandie had brainstormed that they changed all the time too, and it could be because Alicia left her food in the microwave too long or that she'd just turned thirty-five. No one really knew, and she wished there was a system for how people got selected for field assignments.

"Rory says there's no way Suzie will get picked," Alicia said once they'd passed the seventh floor. "She's still finishing up with the New Hampshire mansion."

"So we'll need another bulldozer," Mandie said, her eyes glued to the numbers above the doors. They were nearing ten now, and had five more to go. "Who?"

"Rory says the two of us would make a killer research and checklist team, with Flint behind the camera."

Mandie only hummed, but that said so much. Alicia knew she wanted this field assignment more than anything, and she'd known before Mandie had texted last night. She knew, because Alicia needed this assignment like she needed oxygen.

"You love Flint."

"Flint's the best," Mandie agreed. "So John as the third?"

"Could be." Alicia nodded as the elevator made another stop and then continued up. "Maybe Chevy. He hasn't been out since that Baltimore fiasco."

She and Mandie got off on the fifteenth floor and went past the ritzy real estate firm to their private historical restoration and reconstruction firm.

They both worked in the Preservation and Conservation Department, but they both also handled local clients who needed help getting natural disasters cleaned up when they weren't working on historical cases.

"I'm so bored," Alicia whispered as she opened the glass door and held it for Mandie.

"I might scream if I don't get assigned today," she whispered back. "Just right out loud, in the middle of the meeting."

Alicia laughed lightly. "I doubt it. Assignments always come at the *end* of the meeting."

Mandie scoffed and veered off into her desk area while Alicia continued down another two rows to hers. She quickly put her purse in her bottom desk drawer, grabbed her files, and went back to Mandie's desk.

"Top three. We have to be in perfect alignment."

Mandie already had her folders out too. She loved sticky notes and color-coding, which was why she'd be perfect for any field crew. The woman literally never missed a detail, and she had three folders, one each labeled with a green note, a yellow one, and a pink one.

"Is pink above green or below?"

"Pink is the prize, my friend." Mandie smiled as she slipped the marked folder to the top.

*Please let it be the Hampton House*, Alicia prayed as Mandie seemed to fall into slow motion. Alicia really couldn't leave her children for an off-site field assignment, and she wondered if Candace had somehow found out about her recent divorce.

She commuted from Queens, from the tiny two-bedroom house where her son slept in the second bedroom while her daughter shared her room with her. She and her ex had been living there for a few years now, so that hadn't changed. It would simply be difficult to be on-site for any amount of time, and she'd chosen the Hampton House as her top pick simply in the hopes that it would be chosen, and she could get the field assignment.

She earned more when on assignment, as they received a per diem for food for every day worked out at the site. Plus, the house held a magic to it that leapt off the printed page and permeated the air.

"I knew you'd like the Hampton place too." Alicia grinned widely when she saw the pillared mansion on the front page inside the pink-sticky-note-marked folder.

"It's the best property," Mandie said. "Though I did like that one in the Appalachians."

"The Mountain Mansion?" Alicia fake-swooned. "Isn't it amazing? Even full of someone else's stuff and those ghastly all-terrain vehicles. I can't even imagine the views." Alicia could admit she was somewhat of a romantic, but the images of her eight-year-old's and her five-year-old's faces grounded her. Brought her back to reality, and that meant she couldn't run off to Virginia even for an amazing mountain mansion.

"I didn't put it in my top three," Mandie said. "I don't really want to travel for the field assignment." She tucked her honey-blonde hair behind her ear as she bent over the Hampton House. "I'm worried that if it comes up a lot, Candace will choose it even if it doesn't have the most votes."

"She is so unpredictable," Alicia complained. "That's what I dislike the most. If I knew how things could go, if I could predict it, I wouldn't be so nervous." She flapped her hands a couple of times, then told herself to stop it.

She got to her feet. "Look, you're the natural choice for the researcher. I'm the perfect fit for the financial advisor. All we need is a bulldozer and a film crew, and this is going to be the best summer and fall of our lives."

Mandie clapped her hands together. "Yes! This is the kind of pep talk we need."

No one else had come into the office this early, and Alicia had psyched herself up appropriately. "Okay," she said, pacing to get out some of her extra energy. "We are going to pitch ourselves today. I *want* this assignment."

"I *need* it," Mandie said. "I'm tired of assisting on research and then staying here while the team goes out."

"This is ours."

"What's yours?" someone asked, and Alicia's gaze flew past Mandie to another blonde, this one with plenty of strawberry in her hair and so not someone she wanted to talk to this early in the morning. Or ever, really.

"Hey, Suzie," she chirped in a falsely bright voice. "You're here early."

"I've got to get this last form filed for the West Hills Monster."

Mandie got to her feet, her irritation like a scent on the air. Suzie barely looked at her, as if Mandie didn't hold any importance at all. Alicia reached out and grabbed onto her forearm, and that stopped Mandie. Thankfully.

"Leave it," she hissed as Suzie went by them. "We'll play our cards in the meeting."

Several seconds passed while they both waited for the blonde bulldozer to get out of earshot, and then both she and Mandie sat down in Mandie's desk area. "She thinks she's going to get another assignment," Mandie said. "Unbelievable."

"She's not going to get it," Alicia said. "There are so many deserving people—like us."

"Like us," Mandie agreed with a nod. "Okay, more people are starting to come in. We can't be seen conspiring, or Candace will for-sure give the assignment to someone else."

"Right." Alicia squeezed her friend's hands, then stood, and made her way over to her desk. The office started to fill, and before she knew it, Candace had stepped out of the conference room, the silver bell in her hand.

"Let's go, people," she called as she started to ding the bell over and over and over. *Ding! Ding! Ding!*

Everyone got to their feet like dogs, like the bell had triggered something Pavlovian inside them. Alicia joined them, her three folders and her notebook in her hands. She deliberately didn't allow herself to migrate to Mandie's side. Candace didn't like it when friends tried to get on the same teams, and Alicia panicked that her friendship with Mandie—which was well-known around PastForward—would suddenly hinder her.

Fourteen people crowded into the room, and Candace indicated the three trays in the middle of the oblong table. "First, second, third," she said, indicating a tray with each one. "Folders in."

Someone swore, and Jackson—another accountant with a degree in construction management—jumped to his feet. "I forgot my folders."

"Door's closing in ten seconds," Candace called after him, and though he was one of Alicia's main competitors for this field assignment, she hated seeing him humiliated. Candace had locked people out of meetings before, so her ten-second rule was not an empty threat.

Ten seconds later, Jackson sprinted into the room just as Candace said, "Doors, please."

He practically threw his folders into the trays. Candace glared at him as she pulled the first tray toward her. "Paula, please tally."

Another woman scrambled to her feet, and Alicia wondered why they all kept showing up here, day after day, to be ordered around and treated subserviently. Paula uncapped a blue white board marker, and Candace flipped open the first folder.

"Hamptons," she said, and Alicia shot a look over to Mandie. She sat very still, her gaze trained on Candace. "Cape Cod." Another folder. "Hamptons." She continued on until all the folders in the first pile had been read, and it was obvious that the majority of people in the office wanted to work on the Hampton House next.

Candace turned and looked at the tally marks. "Nine, wow." She smiled as she turned back and picked up the second stack of folders. She read through those, and the Cape Cod Complex came in second.

Their boss didn't even turn to get the remaining pile of folders. She steepled her fingers and considered the board. "I'm a bit surprised more of you didn't pick the Appalachian Jewel." She simply let the words hang there, and Alicia had learned not to justify anything.

If Candace asked her a direct question, she'd answer.

Otherwise, she wouldn't. If she didn't get an assignment today, Alicia wasn't sure what she'd do. Screaming, like Mandie had suggested, sounded about right.

She looked down the table to her friend again, and this time, Mandie's eyes darted to hers too. Then Candace spun, and Alicia jerked her attention back to her. The tension in the conference room pressed against the ceiling, against all the walls and windows, straining to get out. Alicia could barely get a decent breath, and she wondered if anyone else felt that.

"We might as well go over what's third." Candace started reading through those, and Paula dutifully tallied them all up. Candace, in all her bleach-blonde-bunned glory, turned to face the board again.

She never went out in the field, except to check-in once, maybe twice, during a project. She demanded detailed reports which she religiously read, and she'd email questions or call private meetings with teams. Alicia had never seen her wear anything but skirts that fell precisely to her knees, heels, and fluttery blouses.

Today's was pale blue, with a navy skirt and navy heels, and perfectly matching robin's egg blue earrings in the shape of dragonflies.

"Ah, there's my Appalachian Jewel." She grinned at the board, then swiveled back to the group at-large. "Thank you, Paula. Please take your seat."

Paula did just that, and Alicia looked down at her notebook, almost afraid to make eye contact with Candace. She forced herself to look up, because she couldn't show her boss any weakness.

"We have enough funding for two teams to get started," she said. "I'm going to send some of you to Virginia and this mountain mansion. I think it's the best in the bunch, and I'm honestly surprised it's not number one."

No one said anything, because it sounded like Candace had just started a lecture. Alicia gazed at her, and Candace looked her way.

"Let's start down there." Candace looked down at some notes in front of her. "Jackson." Alicia's heart started to pound through her whole body. If Jackson got the Jewel, she'd be the most logical choice for the Hampton House. "You'll manage the finances."

"Yes," he said, his smile spreading across his whole face. It only made Alicia want to squirm.

"Vanessa, I need you on point," Candace said.

"Yes, ma'am," Vanessa said.

"Chevy." Candace glanced over to him, and he was a bulldozer like Suzie.

"You got it, Candy," he said, and he was the only one who'd ever called Candace such a thing. A thread of horror moved through Alicia, but Candace only laughed.

"And on film..." She paused and sighed. "I'm going to pause on that for a minute. I want you guys to clear your afternoon on Monday. We'll meet to go over everything then."

Murmurs of assent moved through the group, and the tension in the room skyrocketed. Alicia shifted in her seat, and Candace looked at her. Her eyebrows went up, and Alicia's did too. That was about as big of a challenge as she could lay down, and she hoped the message had gotten across.

"The Hampton House," Candace said, consulting her notebook again. A few seconds went by, then a few more.

"Ma'am?"

Every eye flew to Mandie. She'd half-raised her hand, and she'd gone pale, like she might throw up. Candace looked at her, blinking rapidly a few times.

"I'm in love with this house," Mandie said. "I'd love to take point on it. I've already sketched out a few things to get started."

"You have?" Candace folded her arms and considered Mandie, her gaze sharp and hooked. Alicia's mouth had gone dry, and she had no idea how Mandie had the nerve to speak up in a meeting where people didn't do such things.

"Yes, ma'am," Mandie said. "And I'm completely available to meet with you and whoever else you appoint to the team anytime."

"Anytime." Candace nodded, though something cold definitely emanated from her. She leaned back in her chair and appraised Mandie for several long seconds. Then a couple more. Right when Alicia thought the air would snap, she said, "All right, Miss Kelton. Oops, I mean *Mrs.* Kelton. You can have point."

"Thank you, ma'am."

Alicia couldn't speak up now, but she wasn't a bulldozer, nor on film. If she didn't get named next, she wouldn't have an assignment. A voice started shrieking in her head, an internal monologue that left her feeling desperate, irritated, and hopeless all at the same time.

She had to get out of this room.

Now.

*Get out. Get out. Get out!*

She stayed right where she was, and Candace looked at her notes and then right at her. "Alicia, can you keep *Mrs.* Kelton within budget?"

"Yes, ma'am," she said, her voice grating like rusty nails against cement. "Absolutely, I can."

Candace nodded and looked around. Alicia's heartbeat now bobbed somewhere outside her body, but she still had enough wherewithal to pray, *Not Suzie. Please, not Suzie.*

"Brandt," she said. "You'll be on bulldozer, and Flint, I know you're just barely finishing up the Maryland Mansion, but I need you in The Hamptons."

"Sure thing," Flint said.

"Apparently, *Mrs.* Kelton has some notes already for us," Candace said dryly, and Alicia thought Mandie might blow her top. She'd turned bright red now, and since Alicia sat on the same side of the table as her, she could see her fisted hands.

"Mandie's the best," Flint said. "I'm sure she and Lish can get started without me and Brandt. We're more of the on-site crew." Flint threw Alicia a smile, and that settled some of the acid boiling in her stomach.

"I want the Hampton House team in my office first thing Monday morning." She got to her feet. "I'll have my own notes to go over." She gave Mandie a pointed look. "All right. Back to work."

She started stacking the folders, and Alicia filed out of the conference room along with everyone else...except Mandie. Alicia met her eyes and gestured for her to *come on! Don't stay in here with the Big Bad Wolf!*

Mandie shook her head slightly, her jaw set and her eyes filled with pure determination. Alicia moved out of the way, wondering if she needed to stay and back-up whatever Mandie said.

But Mandie asked, "Miss Ewing? Can I speak to you privately for just five minutes?" and Alicia ducked out of the room. She'd hear all about this five-minute meeting soon enough, and she didn't want to step on her friend's toes.

She closed the door behind her and practically rammed into Flint.

"What's she doing?" he murmured.

"It's suicide," Alicia said, turning to face the conference room. All of the blinds were open, but Mandie stood with her back to the office.

"So we'll be going to lunch today," Flint said easily. "If she's still alive, we'll hear all about it." He nudged Alicia with his elbow. "And hey, you guys got Brandt."

Relief filled her again and then again, and she finally felt like she could breathe properly. "Yeah," she said. "We got Brandt." Her gaze went back to the conference room. "And if Mandie doesn't get fired, we pretty much have the dream team for the Hampton House."

Then she turned and walked back to her desk, praying for her friend in a constant internal stream of words.

---

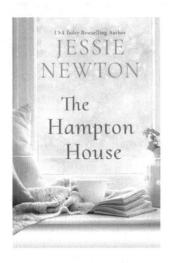

I AM SO EXCITED ABOUT this book already! I've had this idea in my head for almost a year, and I can't wait to bring an abandoned mansion — and the women who work on it — back to life in THE HAMPTON HOUSE.

**Preorder it on your favorite retailer by scanning the QR code below:**

# Books in the Five Island Cove series

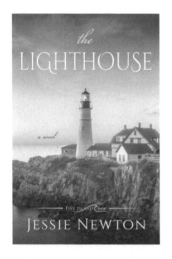

**The Lighthouse, Book 1:** As these 5 best friends work together to find the truth, they learn to let go of what doesn't matter and cling to what does: faith, family, and most of all, friendship.

Secrets, safety, and sisterhood...it all happens at the lighthouse on Five Island Cove.

**The Summer Sand Pact, Book 2:** These five best friends made a Summer Sand Pact as teens and have only kept it once or twice—until they reunite decades later and renew their agreement to meet in Five Island Cove every summer.

# Books in the Five Island Cove series

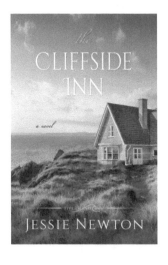

**The Cliffside Inn, Book 3:** Spend another month in Five Island Cove and experience an amazing adventure between five best friends, the challenges they face, the secrets threatening to come between them, and their undying support of each other.

**Christmas at the Cove, Book 4:** Secrets are never discovered during the holidays, right? That's what these five best friends are banking on as they gather once again to Five Island Cove for what they hope will be a Christmas to remember.

# Books in the Five Island Cove series

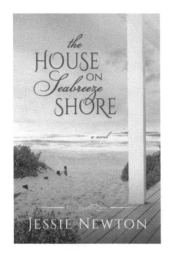

**The House on Seabreeze Shore, Book 5:** Your next trip to Five Island Cove...this time to face a fresh future and leave all the secrets and fears in the past. Join best friends, old and new, as they learn about themselves, strengthen their bonds of friendship, and learn what it truly means to thrive.

**Four Weddings and a Baby, Book 6:**

When disaster strikes, whose wedding will be postponed? Whose dreams will be underwater?

And there's a baby coming too... Best friends, old and new, must learn to work together to clean up after a natural disaster that leaves bouquets and altars, bassinets and baby blankets, in a soggy heap.

# Books in the Five Island Cove series

**The Seafaring Girls, Book 7:**
Journey to Five Island Cove for a roaring good time with friends old and new, their sons and daughters, and all their new husbands as they navigate the heartaches and celebrations of life and love.

But when someone returns to the Cove that no one ever expected to see again, old wounds open just as they'd started to heal. This group of women will be tested again, both on land and at sea, just as they once were as teens.

**Rebuilding Friendship Inn, Book 8:**
Clara Tanner has lost it all. Her husband is accused in one of the biggest heists on the East Coast, and she relocates her family to Five Island Cove–the hometown she hates.

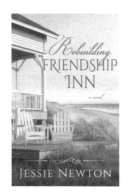

Clara needs all of their help and support in order to rebuild Friendship Inn, and as all the women pitch in, there's so much more getting fixed up, put in place, and restored.

Then a single phone call changes everything.

**Will these women in Five Island Cove rally around one**

another as they've been doing? Or will this finally be the thing that breaks them?

# Books in the Five Island Cove series

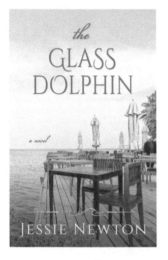

**The Glass Dolphin, Book 9:** With new friends in Five Island Cove, has the group grown too big? Is there room for all the different personalities, their problems, and their expanding population?

**The Bicycle Book Club, Book 10:** Summer is upon Five Island Cove, and that means beach days with friends and family, an explosion of tourism, and summer reading programs! When Tessa decides to look into the past to help shape the future, what she finds in the Five Island Cove library archives could bring them closer together...or splinter them forever.

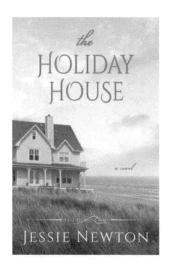

# Books in the Nantucket Point series

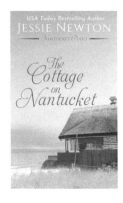

**The Cottage on Nantucket, Book 1:**
When two sisters arrive at the cottage on Nantucket after their mother's death, they begin down a road filled with the ghosts of their past. And when Tessa finds a final letter addressed only to her in a locked desk drawer, the two sisters will uncover secret after secret that exposes them to danger at their Nantucket cottage.

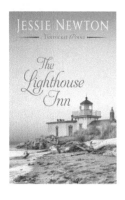

**The Lighthouse Inn, Book 2:** The Nantucket Historical Society pairs two women together to begin running a defunct inn, not knowing that they're bitter enemies. When they come face-to-face, Julia and Madelynne are horrified and dumbstruck—and bound together by their future commitment and their obstacles in their pasts...

# Books in the Nantucket Point series

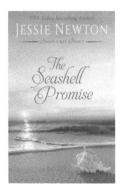

**The Seashell Promise, Book 3:** When two sisters arrive at the cottage on Nantucket after their mother's death, they begin down a road filled with the ghosts of their past. And when Tessa finds a final letter addressed only to her in a locked desk drawer, the two sisters will uncover secret after secret that exposes them to danger at their Nantucket cottage.

# Books in The Hamptons series

**The Hampton House, Book 1:** Mandie Kelton, Alicia Halverson, and Suzette Paxman are drawn together by the allure of forgotten elegance and the shadows of the past. They'll have to learn to get along if they have any hope of keeping their jobs, and as they restore an abandoned mansion in The Hamptons, they'll also discover the lost and hidden parts of themselves that make them into the women they're meant to be.

# About Jessie

Jessie Newton is a saleswoman during the day and escapes into romance and women's fiction in the evening, usually with a cat and a cup of tea nearby. She is a Top 30 KU All-Star Author and a USA Today Bestselling Author. She also writes as Elana Johnson and Liz Isaacson as well, with almost 200 books to all of her names. Find out more at www.feelgoodfictionbooks.com.

Made in United States
Troutdale, OR
07/07/2024

21074210R00249